SISTERS

of the

PENTACLE

Paul Taylor-McCartney

Book I
The Broken Pentacle Series

CORNWALL

First published in Great Britain 2022

1

by Hermitage Press Limited, Cornwall

hermitagepress.org

Hardback edition: ISBN 9781739856809

Paperback edition: ISBN 9781739856816

E-book edition: ISBN 9781739856823

Printed and bound by

TJ Books, Padstow, Cornwall

For Harvey

Chapters

'I conjure thee, O Circle of Power, that thou beest a meeting-place of love and joy and truth …'
~ Invocation of the Craft ~

The Genius of Mary Harries

Tenby, Wales, 1650

A t first light, the winding streets of Tenby resemble a graveyard, eerily silent and etched in grey tones. Beyond the high stone walls that mark the town's perimeter, villagers gather in their dozens. They shuffle forward in silence. Some crave news, others bear food parcels and all are desperate to let loved ones know they're never far from their thoughts, for the town is in the grip of a terrible plague. Even the guards have their visors down to keep the contagion spreading any further than the boundary lines set out by Cromwell when he stormed the castle just two years ago and claimed it for England.

On the cobbled path that stops short of the town's main gate, a twelve-year-old girl appears from nowhere. Grimy ankles and feet protrude from the dark cloak she hopes will hide her from prying eyes on the lookout for someone – anyone – to blame for the town's current problems. She focuses on the guards, who know her well by now, confident they will merely wave her through so she can carry out her important work.

'Look!' one villager says, pointing directly at the girl and drawing the attention of others nearby. 'It's Mary – Old Nancy's granddaughter. She's a witch, I tell you! May the Lord strike me down if I'm telling a lie!'

Aggression soon ripples through the crowd like an incoming wave, taking everyone with it. Mary instinctively raises a hand to her face as the first of the missiles – a pebble from the nearby beach, she guesses – finds its mark and meets the edge of her palm, making her cry out in pain. As a Knowing One, she's blessed with the gift of foresight, which she uses now to navigate a path out of harm's way. She wants to defend herself, tell them that witches didn't create the plague. Instead, she remains silent, slipping away from the crowd and into the town itself.

A cold wind whistles and moans, as if to herald a grim angel lifting knockers on doors and climbing down chimneys in search of more victims. Mary is carried along on one such gust, pausing now and then to slip into gaps between houses as a door creaks open, or a window slides upwards. Not so long ago, a witch could walk these streets with an easy mind. To some, they were even considered a force for good that could help a person in their hour of need. How times have changed for witchkind.

Mary soon arrives at the town square. All around her stand volunteers who've come to make themselves useful. Some are talking in small groups, others are stood away from people, preferring to work alone. Mary's first task of the day is not for the faint-hearted but one she's carried out many times before. She has to count the bodies of victims who have died overnight and been added to the pile, from a distance appearing like a jumble of unwanted clothes.

Wedged between one dead body and the next, she checks the children first. She hovers over each frozen figure like a guardian spirit. Occasionally, she stands aside so an adult can smooth their eyelids closed, something Mary finds she's unable to do herself without crying.

Looking up, she sees Owen Stevens, a local farmer and one of her only friends. Mary watches in silence as he patiently moves corpses from the road and onto the back of his cart. He speaks seldom but when he does it's always with authority. 'Pastor says there's no space left in the churchyard for new graves, so we're moving these to Caldey Island, Mary. You can tag along if you like?'

To this point, the outbreak has claimed the lives of over three hundred locals. Among that number had been Mary's very own mother and father, taken suddenly one night. The memory of discovering them is suddenly with her. She'd woken early to prepare them a special breakfast of eggs and bacon – their absolute favourite. She'd called out to them a few times and thought nothing of the peculiar hush coming from their room until she went to try to rouse them herself. But as she opened the door, she was confronted with the blackened, scorched skin of each lifeless body, their bedclothes twisted into knots and covered in a rancid liquid, as if her parents had been melted down as they both slept. *Just like wax candles*, Mary had thought at the time.

'What're you thinking about now?' asks Stevens, snapping the young girl back to the present.

Mary lifts a wriggling baby from its dead mother's breast and places it in the farmer's hands, saying warmly, 'They must have cast him out with his mother and now he has no one to take care of him.'

Stevens takes the baby from Mary and hands it to another volunteer, a woman whose maternal instincts and gentle smile seem to fool the baby into thinking it's been reunited with its parent.

A short time later, Mary falls in behind Stevens' cart. She thinks for a second she sees her parents among the pyramid of inert bodies, opaque eyes rolled back into each skull as if calling out to her. Water forms at the edges of her eyes, welling up from a place deep within her. Within seconds, she regains control, finally shaking free of the memory and raising her lamp high in the air. Against the silence, she calls out, 'Bring out your dead! Bring out your dead!'

Mary looks up at one window to spot a boy laughing to himself. Her right eye is already stinging with a ball of salty spit.

'There you go, witch! I brung something out for you!'

Mary merely raises her right hand, using one edge of her cloak to remove traces of the boy's hatred from her vision.

'And there's more where that came from!' crows the boy. But, with a flick of her wrist, Mary uses magic to have a second bout of phlegm halt mid-air, about turn and land in the boy's gaping mouth, making him tumble backwards into the inky darkness of the room beyond. With another flick of her wrist, Mary has two wooden shutters swing shut, thereby preventing the boy from causing any more mischief.

Before long, farmer and girl arrive at Tenby harbour, where various boats quietly bob up and down on the morning tide. Stevens goes on ahead and talks to a few fishermen, leaving Mary alone to wander away from the cart and close to the shoreline. Her bare feet slip noiselessly into the lapping waves, icy tendrils quickly curling around her toes and reaching as far as her ankles.

'A few have agreed to lend a hand,' says Stevens, back at Mary's side and staring out to sea. 'One even offered to loan us his boat for the day.'

Caldey Island lies less than a mile off the Pembrokeshire coast. In recent times it's become home to hundreds of witches that have been forced to flee the mainland, many disguised as dolphins, seals or birds. Mary's grandmother bravely chose to remain on the mainland so she could continue selling healing potions to those who had money enough to buy them. In contrast, these Caldey Island outcasts meet each night to carry out sacred rituals, issuing curses intended to create havoc in a world now distant and dangerous to them. But as the veiled morning sun casts its light onto the island's strip of deserted beach, Mary can't see any creatures – magical or otherwise – except a flock of carrion birds, quietly roosting in some nearby trees.

'We'll try and keep family members together,' says Stevens, wiping his forehead with a handkerchief. 'That's as good as can be managed in the circumstances.'

Mary nods before hoisting the boat's iron anchor overboard and following it into the waves. She is descended from a long line of powerful witches and suspects that the volunteers, Stevens included, keep her around precisely because they consider her a sort of lucky familiar, something to keep the deadly plague at bay. But they help Mary in their own way, too. When she's with them, she's out from under the wing of her over-protective grandmother. She can even pretend she's a grown-up and – dare she think it out loud – *a mere mortal.*

'We're being watched, you know,' says Stevens in an aside to Mary. 'There … a flock of ravens. Do you see them, sitting in the branches of those trees to the west of us?'

Mary squints, suddenly paying the birds more attention. Something about the way they're grooming their tail feathers with sharp, iron-grey beaks suggests to her they're not to be trusted.

'I'm sure they're harmless,' says the farmer, 'but we'll need to go back for a second load before we can cover the grave and I'm worried about leaving so many ... you know ... with the likes of them around.'

Mary knows immediately what it is Stevens requires of her, and they turn their attention to the boat and its sad cargo.

The group spend the rest of the morning working as one to create a large open grave, positioned not far from the stretch of beach. Mary helps by pouring everyone drinks from a small flask given to her by Stevens. *Brandy or rum*, she thinks, *judging from the fumes*. It improves the men's moods and the work is soon completed.

'We'll not be long,' says Stevens once the last of the bodies has been lowered into the makeshift grave. 'Are you sure you'll be okay by yourself, Mary?'

'The sooner you go ...' she begins, already occupied with locating a suitable wand from the trees surrounding the beach.

Stevens thanks her again before hastily joining the others, looking over his shoulder one final time to check on her as he boards the boat for Tenby.

Alone at last, Mary uses the sturdy holly twig she has found to mark the outline of a great circle. She knows her magic has the power to protect her from all kinds of sinister forces, so she's careful to include the grave and its grisly contents within the boundary of the shape.

'She, in the dust of whose feet are the hosts of heaven and whose body encircles the universe, I call upon thee …' begins Mary.

'… and hear ye the words of the sacred goddess!' someone or *something* suddenly shouts from behind her, making the hairs on her arms stand to attention.

Turning, Mary takes in the dark figure of a boy. He's statue-still. About his neck hangs a ruff of dark, silky feathers, while his feet are lined with claws where toes would normally be arranged. A nightmarish creature.

Suddenly, he leans forward and presses against the magic circle, his tone mocking. 'She, in the dust of whose feet are the hosts of heaven and whose body encircles the universe!'

Mary has the misfortune to blink and on opening her eyes notices the boy has been joined by seven more, similar, creatures. Each one appears to have been caught mid-transformation between bird and human, which also takes her by surprise.

'I'm a skilled witch –'

'Who happens to be trespassing on our land!' the boy snaps back at her, stretching his great wings. A grim shadow grows until it swallows both girl and the nearby pit of dead bodies.

Shocked, Mary takes a step back from the line in the sand and wonders if her white magic is a match for the dark, threatening sorcery that now confronts her.

'Where are your parents?' she asks.

The boy leads the group in a bout of menacing laughter, before he proceeds to peck at the invisible circle.

Fighting the wave of panic rising inside her, Mary shouts, 'I don't think you have it in you to harm a fellow witch!'

As one, the other ravens join their leader in jabbing at the magic shield. This increased power forces Mary to tumble backwards into the pit of dead bodies, the smell of decaying matter quickly filling her nostrils and making her want to retch. She senses a series of faint cracks appearing across her circle's invisible structure, meaning she has no choice but to reach for the necklace about her throat.

Concentrating, she manages to recite one of her favourite spells, possessing both power and skill to summon the magical creature locked within the pendant's sapphire crystal and created to protect its keeper in times of extreme peril.

'O thou blessed Genius,
My angel guardian,
Vouchsafe to descend with thy holy influence
And presence into this spotless crystal,
That I may behold thy glory.'

It takes a great deal of courage to face a Genius of the Harries variety. Their familiars usually assume the most fearsome of creatures: long-toothed crocodiles, raging bulls, deadly tigers, wild boars and venomous adders – in fact, the very species of snake that now leaps out the gemstone about Mary's neck and grows to three times her height. Rising above the open grave, it unsheathes its fangs and hisses at the young witch's tormentors, throwing them off guard.

Mary doesn't want to leave the safety of the circle but her Genius has distracted the raven children enough to provide her with an escape route. So, she takes her chance, leaving her human form behind and leaping out of the grave as a spirited hare.

The world becomes a series of dips and rises, each one taking Mary by surprise as she scrambles over heather and bracken, a blinding streak of grey and white fur. But she barely has time to plan the next stage of her escape before the air is knocked from her lungs.

Up she goes, higher and higher.

Quite dazed, all Mary can see is the rolling landscape directly beneath her as it retreats from view. And deep in her armpits, she feels the stinging grip of talons, forcing her to look up into the plumage of the great bird that has plucked her from the ground: pale-brown feathers flecked with narrow slits of sooty black. *A buzzard then, or an eagle,* she thinks, *is taking me to its nest to feed me to its young!*

In no time at all, Mary is passing over the narrow strip of water that separates Tenby from Caldey, soon in sight of the town's shoreline – beach, harbour and all – her hind paws almost hitting a chimney stack as the raptor rises high into the morning air, finally clear of the town.

A short time later, the bird lowers Mary onto an expanse of bristling grass. In fact, the terrain feels very familiar beneath the young girl's feet as she returns to human form.

'There you are, child! I've been worried sick!'

Even back in her own skin and clothes, the young witch feels a cold shiver travel through her body. She looks up in time to receive a woollen blanket, handed to Mary by her grandmother, the powerful witch, Nancy of Narbeth. Beyond the old lady, Mary is able to just make out the bright, whitewashed stonework of Rowan Cottage.

'Your Genius rescued me, Grandma!'

'It's been a long time since my Genius has seen the light of day,' says the old lady, drawing Mary to her as if she would never again let her out of her sight.

Confused, Mary looks up into the sky, which has turned the palest of blues, and notes the silhouette of a large bird. It circles above before banking away from Tenby and in the direction of Caldey Island.

'Who was it who helped me, then?' asks Mary, before giving in to exhaustion. Lost for words, the blanket about her body seems to limit her ability to speak further on the subject.

Nancy's voice is soothing as she says, 'We'll get you indoors and sat by the fire. A little heat and one of my special breakfasts will put you right again, girl, you'll see.'

Her grandma is right; the shock of Mary's adventure is soon soothed away by heat from an open fire, a cup of tea and a plate of delicious fried sausages, eggs and bacon. Eager flames caress the underside of a mighty cauldron and the cottage is transformed in an instant from prison to safe house. Mary had always despised its low, crooked ceilings; its small, cobwebbed windows; its threadbare carpets, thick with soil and cat hair; its lamps, pining for fresh candles; and its doors, creaking in the middle of the night to stir her from her sleep. But all now seems quaint and comforting to Mary. Her brush with real danger has helped her to see the cottage is very much her home, after all.

'What were you doing on Caldey, anyway?' asks Nancy, finally sitting down in her rocking chair. As the wooden seat squeaks, a black cat appears from nowhere and leaps up onto the old woman's lap.

'Helping Farmer Stevens.'

Her grandmother's smile quickly fades.

'Rounding up the dead, eh? Gruesome and dangerous work. And as for Stevens, you want to stay away from him, my girl. There's talk of him being a witchfinder. Some, not far from here and much younger than you, are being put on trial and either dunked or burnt alive before their families so much as notice 'em missing.'

'Nonsense,' says Mary. 'Stevens is a good man. Unlike whatever lives out on Caldey, which is possessed of a dark magic.'

Mary is unsure if she should proceed with a topic centred on the black arts but is still looking for answers to questions that have been on her mind since coming to live with her grandmother.

'Caldey, you say? For the love of the Mother Goddess, what have you been up to, child! And you shouldn't be so quick to condemn other witches, by the way. Not in such troubling times. Remember that a witch's magic is neither one sort nor another,' the old woman says rather sternly. 'It's a *grey* area, girl. You'll come to appreciate the truth of this in time, especially now you're passing beyond childhood. Out on Caldey today, you witnessed the grey area of our Craft, that's all.'

Mary, only half-listening to her grandmother, decides to broach the subject that has been bothering her.

'There's talk,' she says boldly, 'the plague is actually a misfired curse coming from this very cottage, Gran - that it was actually meant for Oliver Cromwell when he visited Tenby. Rumours like that could explain why most people have turned on us. A complete stranger spat at me today – and I was helping out at the time!'

Nancy gives a little shudder and the cat half-rouses under her hands.

'So, you trust the word of gossipers over your own gran, eh girl? Who puts these ridiculous notions in that head of yours, anyway? Stevens, I bet.'

'I know one thing,' says Mary, staring down into the dregs of her teacup. 'That if there is any truth to the rumour I'll leave this cottage at once and deny any connection with you – or any other Harries for that matter!'

Nancy is taken aback at the girl's words. In her long lifetime she has never met anyone who has successfully left a coven. Once a witch, always a witch – or so the old woman believed until now, faced with this outburst, and from a girl who had proven time and again she was naturally skilled in the ways of the Craft.

'I'll not hear of it,' says Nancy. 'Anyway, I'm the only family you've got now! I lost your poor mother before her time, and I'll not let the same happen to you.'

At this, Mary hands Nancy her teacup, which contains a distinctive pattern of leaves. In the design, a circle of some kind and, at its centre, what appears to be the face of young girl. She is similar to Mary in lots of ways, but also subtly different.

'Read them,' she demands of her grandmother, 'and tell me what you see!'

'What's this madness, Mary? You're over-tired, that's all. You need some rest after your adventure.'

'Read them!' the young witch insists. 'You're said to be skilled in divination, so prove it. Tell me my fortune!'

Mary's green eyes shine in the half-light of the kitchen and her blonde hair turns a rusty orange, reflecting the warm hues of the flames warming the cauldron. But she remains angry and will not be calmed until her grandmother takes the cup – which Nancy eventually does, holding it to a nearby candle to provide her with a little light.

'What did *you* see, child?'

'I saw nothing.'

'You're a Harries, so naturally skilled in divination, like me. I know this to be the truth, because all I can see is leaves! This cup has already revealed its secrets to someone and there's only the two of us here, last time I looked.'

Mary closes her eyes as they begin to prickle with tears of frustration. Kneading her hands in her lap and pressing her lips together, she tries to compose herself. This final confrontation is proving too much for her, especially after such a horrible day.

'I saw a circle,' she admits after some time.

'A circle?'

'Yes, a bright, glowing circle, Gran.'

'Anything else?'

'Inside the circle … I saw the face of a young girl.'

'Older or younger than you?'

'About my age. But different … One of *them*, you know … A mortal.'

Nancy squints. 'Go on.'

'Well, something about the girl's expression told me she was dead, I think, but I can't be sure.'

At this, Nancy throws the cup to the floor, smashing it into a dozen fragments.

'Gran!'

'It's true then, as set out in the prophecy!' cries the old woman. 'I was once told that the Last of the

Knowing Ones was to come from the Harries coven.
Not only that, but that they would sacrifice themselves,
for the sake of our Mother Goddess, when the time
came! They must have been referring to you, Mary. Oh
my, this is most dreadful!'

Mary reaches out, desperate to bridge the gap
between the two of them, although the old lady's hands
are ice cold to the touch, notes the young witch.

Nancy will not be calmed. 'Well, I won't let them take
you! I'll keep you here, under lock and key.'

'You can't do that!' cries Mary, frantically rubbing the
backs of the old witch's hands. 'I promise I'll be more
careful from now on. I'll stay home, keep away from
Stevens and the others, if needs be.'

Nancy shakes her head and says defiantly, 'You can't
be trusted, my girl. Helping others and leaving me each
day is playing right into the hands of the prophets.'

Mary waits until her gran is calmer, before asking,
'What prophets? Who do you speak of, Gran?'

Nancy is soon at the kitchen window, looking
beyond it towards a place out of view, but firmly fixed
in her mind's eye. 'The fairies of Harrowing Point, of
course,' she tells Mary. 'Like the witches out on Caldey,
they meet at midnight. When it's clear, you can see them
from the harbour, dancing about like stars that just fell
down from the night sky.'

In a flash, Nancy turns and casts a spell whose magic
is so swift and powerful that, in the instant she senses
her grandmother's intent, young Mary is bound fast
within the limits of a very different circle. Through the

skin of the bubble, the young witch watches Nancy utter another incantation, this new spell lifting Mary clean out of her chair until she is suspended between the cottage's ceiling and the cold tiles of its floor. The resident black cat senses trouble and quickly disappears back behind the nearest curtain.

'Gran! Please, let me down!' pleads Mary, punching at the bubble and trying a few spells of her own to make it pop.

'It's for the best, my girl,' Nancy cries, tears streaming down her face and, with one final push from her outstretched hands, forces the bubble to levitate across the kitchen and into Mary's bedroom. The sturdy door slams shut behind the young witch once she's safely inside.

Mary's pleas to be released are met with silence of the worst kind. The young witch even tries kicking at the dense wooden door, stubbing her big toe in the process and making her cry out. *So, I'm to be punished for telling the truth*, she thinks. *For telling what the leaves revealed to me and me alone.*

Hours later, following a long, unbroken sleep, Mary flings back her bedroom curtains and is greeted by a moonlit night. The trees that border the edge of the magically protected space around Rowan Cottage seem to send a message of ill-will as she looks beyond them to the coastal bay, which she knows will be rustling with the to and fro of tidal waters. And there, less than a mile from the cottage, stands Harrowing Point, just visible through the evening mist. The headland of rock rises high from the seabed, with a summit occupied by seabirds alone. Mary trembles as she recalls her grandmother's words: *the fairies of Harrowing Point … they meet at midnight*. She knows what she must do.

Turning to her bed, Mary surveys a set of Craft tools laid out in a neat arrangement across the blanket. Many of them have been handed down through countless generations of the Harries family. First, Mary studies the magical athame: a short dagger whose blade has been blunted to stress it is a tool of ritual, rather than of violence. A number of strange symbols are picked out in the moonlight, standing out against the dark backdrop of the weapon's hilt.

Mary has never paid them much attention until this evening; only now does she desire to fathom their meaning. With her mother's guidance, she is schooled in how to recognise some fairly ancient languages, including a number of long-forgotten alphabets. But the confounding symbols on the athame have always proven too difficult for either of them to translate.

With the time fast approaching midnight, Mary has to move quickly. She decides to take with her some of the objects that have come to define her as witch: the athame, the cords of charm, her father's sacred pentacle and her mother's cherished black mirror, whose ink-dark surface is so dense it's believed it can swallow light itself. The broomstick she'll leave behind, along with an ornate chalice that rejects all liquids save for water. She folds these remaining objects into a square of blue cloth and pushes them back beneath her bed, abandoning them to the realm of mice and spiders.

Once she's safely on the other side of the bedroom window and some distance from Rowan Cottage, she looks back one final time. By the light of the full moon, the thatched roof and chalk-white stonework stand out and Mary acknowledges a nagging ache in her heart. She senses that she may not return to Rowan Cottage for some time. Intuitively her eyes linger on the little kitchen window; it still glows with an amber light but, like old Nancy's heart, will eventually succumb to the encroaching dark.

○

The prospect of tackling the Point fills poor Mary with dread. Bent double, she carries the contents of her witch's bag over one shoulder. She has to pass through Tenby to reach her destination, so she's mindful not to be seen or heard, pausing only for a moment at the public tavern. She peers in through a window and sees Stevens idling against the bar, seemingly in a drunken stupor. It dawns on her she's never seen him in the company of family or friends; he's a mysterious man and very much a loner. The job of tending to the sick and dying had kept them both busy but also meant Mary had never properly got to know him. *Perhaps Grandma's right about him being a witchfinder*, thinks Mary, then banishes such thoughts from her mind.

As Stevens drains the last dregs from his tankard, he looks towards the half-open window, thinking he's being watched, but sees only vacant space. The young witch has already moved on, indistinguishable from the dense shadows.

Finally standing before the Point, Mary thinks the outcrop of rock resembles a group of creatures from the underworld. The air is damp and clings to her skin like a heady incantation, or the breath of a conjured spirit. As her climb commences, she reaches forward and makes a foothold of one crevice, but the scrub beneath her seems to twist and turn in several directions, threatening to send her to the lapping waters far below. She takes a breath to settle her nerves, sets her intention and – one foothold, one handhold at a time – she pushes upwards.

Once at the summit and quite exhausted, Mary peers into the wall of night and makes out the figure of a boy. He's a little older than her but there's something about his clothes – the tans and creams of the stable-hand's outfit – Mary recognises in a shot.

'Not all witches are blessed with the gift of flight,' she smiles, now recovered from her climb.

'Abe Aderyn,' he says as he steps forward. 'Pleased to meet you – in human form, that is …'

'Mary Harries.'

'I made sure you were safe,' he explains, 'before flying back home.'

The young witch feels a lump form in her throat as she mouths her next words. 'Thank you … for saving my life, I mean.'

Abe shrugs, 'That's okay. Come on, the fairies are about to appear.'

Abe grabs Mary's hand and the spark of energy she feels in his grasp takes her a little by surprise, until she realises his intention is simply to move her away from the edge of the cliff. As her eyes adjust to the darkness of the summit, with only starlight to guide them, she's able to make out curls of auburn hair framing the boy's jawline and a beak-like nose with two yellow eyes that seem to stare right through her. Mary wonders if Abe has abused his transformation power and become fixed somewhere along the line between human and animal, as has clearly happened to the raven children out on Caldey Island.

Suddenly, a single shaft of light begins to rise from the ground immediately to their left, drawing two sets of eyes in its direction.

'The fairies!' shouts Abe, gripping Mary's hand and drawing them both away to a spot considered safe by the boy but still in plain view of the spectacle that now engulfs the whole of Harrowing Point.

In a matter of seconds, the entire area has been consumed by a dazzling light show. It's impressive, but something about the display raises suspicions in Mary's mind. As an infant, she had often been visited by fairies. They are naturally timid creatures when around adult humans but with the very young they like nothing more than to gambol in the air, pull at each other's wings and send each other flying into the undergrowth; anything to create a reaction from their human audience. No, the phenomenon presently unfolding across the summit of Harrowing Point displays none of the features of those visits made by fairy-folk.

'Abe,' whispers Mary. 'This is a different kind of magic.'

Their eyes then fix on a number of ghostly images that begin to take on more definite shapes: the pillar of lights breaking up and re-forming as a face … or the lower half of a person … a man … a woman … a boy … a girl … Sometimes just a hand … at other times a single foot. Each of the images lasts only a few seconds, as if created by dragging a single stick of charcoal across paper and then rubbing each mark out using the edge of one's hand.

'What are they?' asks Mary.

Abe shrugs. 'I'm not sure. I only know they change each night.'

Mary's voice proves as shadowy as the figures forming and dissolving in the deep pools of her retinas. 'Do you think they can see us?'

Abe shakes his head and places a trembling hand on her arm, perhaps to steady his own nerves. 'I've gone close to the edge of the circle and they've never harmed me –'

Mary leaps to her feet, depositing her velvet bag of belongings on the grass, without waiting for him to finish. 'A circle, you say?'

Her premonition is suddenly at the forefront of her mind, bringing with it an odd taste to her mouth: that of ash, or cindered coals, perhaps.

'Where're you going?' asks Abe, but he can do little more than plant his feet in the hollowed-out prints of his new friend.

Mary strides away, full of energy and cutting through the long grass to get to where the spectral figures are dancing about within the circle of white light.

'I'm sure they're just ghosts,' she calls over her shoulder.

'Possibly,' says Abe, raising his voice to reach her. 'And shall remain happy ones, unless we go meddling with them!'

Mary knows Abe is talking sense, but this doesn't stop her from edging closer to all manner of phantoms that now fill the midnight air with their mimed laughter … and tantrums … and dancing … and dressing for dinner … and romantic kisses … some depicting private moments of sadness, others showing unsettling moments of fear and despair.

Without thinking, Mary takes a step towards the edge of the circle, its column of light suddenly brightening the very tips of her toes.

'Mary!' warns Abe. 'Remember this morning out on Caldey Island; you drew your own circle, and for safety. Be mindful of *all* magic, until you know its intent!'

Mary nods to appease him but her eyes continue to search the sea of images, as if hoping to identify one in particular.

'Your sacred circle was marked out to keep evil at bay,' adds Abe, now desperate. 'And your Genius was summoned to help you maintain the borders of your circle. Mary, be careful!'

But just as Abe reaches the conclusion of his warning, Mary has been drawn over the boundary separating her world from an altogether different one.

'There!' shouts Mary, her final words to Abe, 'I see her!'

So it comes to pass that the young witch Mary Harries, guardian of the diseased, the dying and the dead, steps into the swirling column of half-formed faces and limbs. The smallest molecules of her physical form begin to yield to a much more powerful brand of magic, one engineered in a laboratory many hundreds of years into the future but occupying the very same spot of land. Her whole body vibrates as though she is becoming one with the light orbs that pass back and forth before her eyes.

'Abe!' she screams, changing her mind about the whole adventure but unable to prevent herself from transforming from girl to hare a second time, so pronounced is her fear.

Abe stares into an unforgiving night that holds no record of what just happened. There's also no sign of the young witch who so recently set his soul alight and made him feel … *what, exactly? At peace, somehow,* he thinks. Indeed, the entire experience has left a black hole of grief in his chest, the like of which he's never felt before. Abe falls to the grass as he begins to register the full scope of his loss. Then his eyes alight upon an object: Mary's bag, lying just a few feet from him, in it the tools that are the trademark of a hereditary witch. She'd be back for them, surely, for without them she was powerless, with little to set her apart from other girls her age.

.

Miss Harriet Gordon, I Presume?

Tenby, Wales, 1900

Someone is knocking at the door that separates Harriet's room from the rest of St Catherine's Fort, home of the Gordon family. *It's not one of my brothers*, she guesses, *for they'd never think to knock*. They were always dreaming up ways to exclude or ridicule her – mixing the oils on her artist's palette, reading her private journal or making the worst mischief with her porcelain dolls – and she hated them for it.

'Harriet, are you in there?'

Her mother's high-pitched voice never fails to annoy, and this time it prompts Harriet to respond, 'In body – though perhaps not in spirit, mother.'

The door swings wide and into the room walks a woman who some say is small, but whose steely character is just about kept in check by the bones of her corset.

'One's s*pirit* is easily found, child,' says Mrs Gordon. 'If only you left the confines of your room once in a while.'

Harriet turns her easel a full ninety degrees towards the window, saying, 'I'm busy painting, Mother.'

'What's that, you say?' her mother asks, releasing a pin from her ebony hair and pressing it between her lips.

Soon at her daughter's side, Mrs Gordon turns the easel to face her. Worry lines grace the woman's brow and her mouth curls down at its edges. 'What *is it* exactly?'

Harriet's reply is more of a sigh. 'I'm not sure yet. But I think I'll call it … *Into the Light Ring.*'

The comment does nothing to reassure Harriet's mother that she had not, twelve years previously, given birth to an oddity. Of course, Mrs Gordon had tried and failed many times to have her daughter put her books to one side, to entice her to embroider something for the dining room, or for the family library, to do something worthwhile.

'Well, it's certainly original,' breathes Mrs Gordon. 'But I do wonder if you could be doing something more productive with your time.'

Harriet stares into the oil painting she recreated from memory alone: the swirls of whites, greys and creams, the black borders pricked with starlight and the face of a young girl at the centre of the canvas.

'Anyway,' declares Mrs Gordon, moving on, 'your father and I are entertaining this evening from seven o'clock onwards. A pair of distinguished guests will be joining us and our usual crowd.'

'What, in Tenby?' asks Harriet.

Mrs Gordon flutters from her daughter's side to a nearby window. As far as the eye can see, the blue-green waters of the seaside resort's much-loved bay shine and sparkle. But, despite its beauty, Harriet thinks the little town resembles a graveyard.

'Must you always adopt a tone that suggests Tenby *is not* and *never will be* London, child?'

With her mother's back fully turned, Harriet asks, 'Will I have heard of *any* of your *distinguished* guests, mother?'

Elizabeth Gordon smiles, neatly sidestepping her daughter's attempt at sarcasm. 'Why, none other than Mr Winston Churchill and the author HG Wells. It is simply too thrilling!'

Harriet thinks for a second the evening might not be so bad, after all.

'Seven o'clock – sharp,' Mrs Gordon repeats as she prepares to leave. 'And please avoid the colour black, Harriet, when choosing something to wear. Some days you look like some accursed creature that lives out in the woods.'

'You mean a witch, Mother?' asks Harriet, her eyes turning brighter for a second.

But it is too late to hear a reply, for Mrs Gordon is already on the other side of the bedroom door and off down the corridor.

○

A short time later, Harriet slips into the garden to enjoy a beautiful summer's day. She has a sketchpad tucked under one arm and a pencil safely lodged above her right ear. The house she leaves behind is a hive of activity, as her mother's large team of staff busy themselves with various tasks. Harriet passes among them without issuing so much as a polite, 'Hello,' or, 'Good afternoon to you, Jenkins; all well?' She even tiptoes past her governess's room, where Miss Arkwright can be seen arched over her desk, gluing entries into a fresh scrapbook.

With the fort behind her, the rest of the tidal island of St Catherine's Point stretches out before Harriet as if the giant chunk of prehistory were slowly dissolving into the sea below. It's a clear day after weeks of wind and rain, meaning Harriet's view of Tenby town is an unbroken one. Her eye follows the horizon of buildings from east to west, noting the town's haphazard roofscapes of lead and slate. The painted facades of the grand houses and hotels, lining both north and south promenades, give the impression Harriet is looking down into her own box of paints or up at a rainbow.

Alone, she considers it safe to dispose of her shoes – bare feet soon engaging with wet grass and forging a connection with some ancient part of her nature. She knows it is behaviour a girl of her age and station should be quick to condemn, rather than encourage.

Approaching the edge of the cliff, she shields her eyes with a hand to better discern light from shadow and makes out the figures of Charles, Peter and Rupert splashing about in the shallow waters far beneath her. It won't be long before they're forced to return home, for at high tide the sixty or so steps that are the Point's only means of access, will be cut off from the beach. Harriet likes the fact the fort's daily timetable has to be planned around the gravitational pull of the moon; more so that it inconveniences her parents and therefore irritates them beyond measure.

'*Harriet … Harriet Gordon …*' sings the wind as it sweeps across the headland. The young girl turns but sees nothing except the fort. In fact, the brutal lines of its sandstone structure are at odds with the bristling sea and sky beyond it. She'd stood on the same spot only yesterday when a similar event had unsettled her. Only then the voice had been accompanied by the image of a sparking circle of light, something she would later commit to one of her canvases.

'Who's there?' asks Harriet.

'On the stroke of twelve tomorrow evening I'll appear before you on this very patch of grass,' says the disembodied voice. 'My name is Indigo Carmichael and

I'm from the future. That is, I occupy a space in time far beyond your own!'

'Beyond 1900?' says Harriet, her whole body now trembling.

'Who are you speaking to, dear sister?'

Quite how Harriet's three brothers have managed to climb their way to the top of the Point to be with her, dried off and fully clothed, is a mystery to add to Harriet's growing collection of obscurities. She'd always assumed time ran in straight lines, reliable as the words of the great scientists she worshipped. But here she and her brothers now stood, clouds hassling the blue sky in places they'd not done a few seconds ago.

'Answer your brother,' demands Charles, the eldest of her tormentors and, at sixteen, already twice the size of his own mother.

'I was talking through an idea that had just come to mind,' lies Harriet.

'*An idea?*' asks Charles.

Harriet catches the eye of Rupert, twelve months her senior and the least intimidating of the gang. 'I'm working on an invention,' she continues, 'to rid the world of boys.'

Charles leads his brothers in a short bout of fake laughter, before bringing it to an abrupt end. 'Show her the object we purchased yesterday, brother.'

The most despicable of the herd, Peter – whose wild, untamed hair gives the impression he's recently crawled out of glacial mud – produces a short dagger from his waistcoat pocket.

'What are you doing with a knife?' asks Harriet, her eyes fixed on the object.

Charles smiles, 'Well, it's not strictly a knife, sister. It's a ceremonial blade, known as an athame.'

'Ah-*thay*-me,' Harriet repeats, slowly and deliberately, getting the feel of this new word. It seems, somehow, familiar to her.

'Now, watch closely,' Charles advises, 'as Peter makes ribbons of Father's wonderful lawn.'

Harriet watches on in amazement as Peter falls to his knees and sinks the athame's blade into the soft earth directly in front of her. He then proceeds to drag the weapon backwards and forwards, slicing and turning the turf as if preparing the ground for seeding, until he has formed a perfect circle about her feet.

'Pa will have a fit!' cries Harriet, although she knows the boys' collective word carries far more weight than hers when it comes to their father.

With the circle now complete, the remaining brothers issue various approvals. Peter even executes a little bow, basking in the glory of having carried out this mindless act.

Harriet's eyes catch sight of the little blade lying abandoned on the grass. She can't help but admire the run of symbols gracing the hilt of the weapon and feels, somehow, instinctively drawn to them.

Reaching a hand towards the artefact, she hears Charles saying, 'Proof she's a witch after all, eh, boys?'

Harriet ignores him and attempts to step out of the circle – only to find her body involuntarily springs back to its original position.

'And now,' Charles spits, 'the girl offers a dose of magic to stun and stupefy members of the audience!'

Harriet brushes strands of black hair away from her eyes as she asks, 'Where did you say you acquired the athame?'

Charles is now just a few feet from her.

'Antique dealer in town. The object is rightfully yours, anyway, for I had Rupert deduct a sum of coin from your private savings, which you thought were safely hidden!'

Charles reaches down and retrieves the blade from the ground, adding, 'Tell you what, we'll let you go if you can tell us the answers to three questions we've each made up in your absence!'

Harriet's heard quite enough but, when she tries to move, she finds she's still securely penned within the confines of the circle.

'Youngest to eldest,' says Charles, next handing the knife to Rupert.

The youngest of the boys turns the instrument onto a horizontal plane and puts it delicately to his lips, thereby preventing him from revealing his question, eyebrows knitted to show he's deep in thought. Harriet wonders why it is that no adult ever appears at the right time to bear witness to her brothers' cruelty.

Charles now circles his sister, as if he were a great bird whose outward beauty disguises the fact he's rotten to the core. To his consternation, despite his best efforts at intimidation, Harriet smiles.

'What's there to smile about?' demands Charles.

An image has popped into Harriet's mind that enables her to wrong-foot her brother.

'Rupert holds a flame for respectable Lillian Salford,' begins Harriet, 'but harbours thoughts of a far more unsavoury nature for Nanny Atkins!'

Harriet had merely hazarded a guess and only when the knife falls to the ground does she realise she's delivered a direct hit against one brother.

'How could she have known that?' shouts an exasperated Rupert, quite undone.

'You must have told Peter,' says Charles, 'and we all know how difficult *he* finds it to hold onto a secret!'

Peter says nothing as he lifts the blade from the grass and places it firmly between his teeth, a picture of malcontent and menace.

Harriet receives a second image, as clear as day, in her mind's eye. Her reaction to this one fills her with dread, rather than good humour.

'You burnt my Charles Darwin book? A *first edition*, too! Why would anyone even want to do that?'

She clenches her fists and finds she has to swallow more air to restore order to her heart and lungs.

Peter allows no crumb of surprise to grace his expression and, a mere second later, Charles nods to him. In a flash of metal the blade is safely in the hands of the eldest boy.

'Very good, sister,' smiles Charles. 'But your attempts at guessing are to be truly tested with one final question that must be met with a correct answer. That is, if you wish to be freed from your current –'

Before he can finish, Harriet answers, 'The plague struck Tenby in 1650 and claimed the lives of five hundred and seventy-one local people, many of them children. Although that was, technically speaking, two questions!'

Shortly before seven o'clock, the four Gordon children line up at the doorway that leads from the outside world and into the fort. No flicker of what had occurred earlier can be noted in their blank expressions but, beneath the surface, almighty shifts in power have taken place between Harriet and her brothers. She's currently unable to make sense of the supernatural forces that have been at work today, giving her full access to secrets locked within her brothers' minds. The intriguing athame blade, which she claimed as a prize, now lies coldly against her leg; bound with the blackest ribbon she could find, it is caught between her left calf muscle and stocking.

As expected, Harriet curtsies for each guest, hearing her father indicate for the group, 'Children, this is Mr Churchill. He recently fought in a number of important battles in Africa and is returned to us in one piece, no doubt with many engaging stories chronicling the courage and bravery of Her Majesty's troops!'

Harriet thinks the stout man with pudding-like features is probably a lot younger than her father would have them believe.

'Miss Harriet Gordon, I presume?'

'It's an honour to meet you, Mr Churchill,' smiles Harriet, detecting a discernible lisp in the man's speech.

'What a charming girl,' Churchill adds. 'She has a beguiling quality so rarely found in youth these days.'

Here, he throws a sidelong glance at the trio of giggling boys immediately to his left. *Yes*, thinks Harriet, *Mr Churchill did look back at me and wink, just the once.* In doing so, he has forged a bond of conspiracy with Harriet that warms her heart and makes her wish she were able to join the adults for dinner.

'And this is Mr Wells, children,' Christopher Gordon announces, indicating a plainly dressed young man with angular features and whose wire-framed spectacles sit perched at the end of his nose.

He peers over the rims of his lenses at the youngest of the children.

'Your father informs me you're a budding artist, Miss Gordon.'

'Yes, sir,' confirms Harriet. 'Although, I hope one day to be an inventor.'

Harriet has no idea why she's chosen this moment to reveal her life's ambition to a perfect stranger, and neither do her family, each of whom now look on in abject horror.

'*An inventor*, you say?' asks a delighted Wells. 'In that case, we shall have to dispense with the trappings of formal titles and, henceforward, I insist you address me by my forename ... Bert!'

The Gordon couple laugh off the author's remark and urge their next guests forward. This in turn forces the author towards Churchill, who is stationed in a world of his own, quietly smoking an enormous and pungent Cuban cigar.

○

After dinner, Harriet sits alone in her father's study, directly beneath a rather imposing grandfather clock. Her brothers have marched off in the direction of the roof terrace, leaving her with nothing more than the ice-cold blade that fails to admit any warmth to her skin. She can feel it now; its gentle sting somehow reminds her of the girl's eyes floating at the centre of her painting.

Eleven chimes of the clock later, Harriet wakes with a start. She had nodded off in her father's beloved armchair and remained undisturbed until the marking of time sounded its sequence of dings. Now she has the distinct impression she's no longer alone.

'Miss Harriet? It is I, Bert.'

As her eyes adjust to the semi-darkness, Harriet realises the author is positioned on the other side of the room from her, perched on the Chesterfield and to one side of a reading lamp. He has a book in his lap, his hands neatly folded and resting on its cover.

'I craved some time alone,' he smiles. 'I lack the desired amount of superstition to gain much enjoyment from a séance.'

'*Séance*?' asks Harriet. Alert now, she leans forward in the chair, eager to hear more.

'Your father managed to convince Churchill he should take part, hoping to establish contact with the late Lord Randolph Churchill, Winston's father.'

Harriet is intrigued and taps her foot rhythmically against the floorboards beneath her.

Wells adds for clarity, 'Randolph was said to be a stubborn, mean-spirited man who apparently meted out his frustrations on poor Winston.'

'Probably no less appalling than my three brothers,' says Harriet, reflecting on the afternoon's events.

'Your mother is convinced the spirit realm will speak *through* her,' says the author, emitting a playful smile.

Harriet is now rather unsure whether he'd just uttered an indirect insult aimed at the wife of his host. 'My mother – a spiritualist?'

'I get the sense there's more to your mother than meets the eye,' says Wells.

The young girl suspects there to be a great deal of unkindness and bitterness to her mother, besides hoarding chintz. *But an interest in the supernatural,* she thinks – *really*?

'By the way, I want you to have this,' says Wells, suddenly rising from his chair and moving across the room to Harriet. 'It's a short novel, about an inventor.'

'It will not surprise you to learn my parents are fans of certain penny dreadfuls.'

'Maybe to offset their appetite for pulp, then …'

Harriet looks at the leather-bound cover of the book and reads the title aloud.

'*The Time Machine*, by HG Wells.'

'Bert, for short,' he says, opening the cover for the young girl to see he has personalised this copy with, 'To Harriet, with esteemed regard, Bert.'

'Why, this is one of your books!' says Harriet, awed by the author's generosity.

'I consider it a meagre work of fiction. But it is now yours.'

Harriet wants to begin reading without further ado, but equally has been taught that, 'one must remain charming until company no longer requires one to be so.'

'I think I hear voices outside,' says Wells, getting up and looking at the door. 'I'm afraid I must return to the world of adults, Miss Gordon. It's been an absolute pleasure meeting you. Forgive me; I notice only now it must be long past your usual time to retire.'

Harriet waves his own novel at him as he readies to leave. 'Goodnight to you, Bert – and thank you for your wonderful gift.'

Sitting up in bed, with her gas lamp casting a warm circle of light through the night, Harriet reads *The Time*

Machine from cover to cover. The wonderful characters and vistas of her own planet, presented 800,000 years into the future, make her shiver with anticipation; perhaps Indigo is not a figment of her imagination, after all. Perhaps her painting, the strange dagger and the chance meeting with Bert Wells are somehow all connected.

As she drifts off to sleep, she hears the first twitters of a dawn chorus, forcing her to thrust her head beneath the covers and create a blackout into which she might momentarily dissolve.

Harriet takes breakfast much later than her family and guests, much to the annoyance of her mother, who announces she has asked the housekeeper to have all lamps and books removed from Harriet's room. Harriet's second punishment for presenting a picture of ill-discipline is to join her mother on a short trip into town, to acquire fresh lavender – and a new corset, of all things! It's approaching low tide, so they must be away immediately, Harriet is told.

The men of the house, including her despicable brothers, set off along North Beach away from St Catherine's Point, seemingly oblivious to the inclement weather, which appears to loop about the peninsula like a cloying, wet rope.

Mother and daughter enter the town in silence, save for the sound of Harriet's boots clattering over the cobbled ground. She wants to ask her mother about her skills as a clairvoyant, but she's still reeling at the thought she may not be able to read anything for the remainder of the holidays, so says nothing.

Entering the high street, the various smells of market day compete with one another, the fishmonger's pungent odours filling Harriet's nose and altering the taste in her mouth. It sums up her feelings about living on the coast; the smell of death lingers, and it sticks to everything. As they pass the stand, Harriet looks back over one shoulder at the mole-ridden face of the stallholder, a man who happily bags haddock and cod for little old ladies as if he had not an inkling or the imagination to do anything else.

Once outside the seamstresses' shop, Harriet expresses a desire to call in on the little bookshop she has made use of in previous summers, looking up at the clock embedded in the stonework of St Mary's Church and promising her mother she'll return within the hour.

'Make sure you stay out of mischief,' is all her mother can say.

Harriet races through town, realising she has further to go than the bookshop, which is actually second on her list of places to visit. First, she heads to the antiques shop, with time very much against her. Many locals shake their heads as she bumps into this or that shopper, even knocking one hapless woman to the gutter. She refuses to be helped back to the vertical by a red-cheeked Harriet but is assisted by two of her neighbours. Harriet imagines their censure as she rushes on her way.

'What a way for a young lady to behave!'

'What could be so important she'd risk the safety of good, honest people like us?'

'She has the devil at her heels, that one, but God will catch up with her!'

Then, as she bursts through the door to the antiques shop, 'Good day to you, Miss Gordon. How may I be of assistance?'

Thankfully, this final voice is not one that has been produced by Harriet's paranoia, so she nods and closes the door behind her, silencing the little bell. Only then does she wonder how the shopkeeper is able to recognise her.

'An odd occurrence, I must say! Your brothers were in here just yesterday.'

'Good morning, sir. But I don't believe we've been formally introduced.'

'I pay attention to all window shoppers, particularly those of your standing, Miss Gordon. The arrival of your family certainly has put our little town on the map.'

'I believe my brothers purchased this small knife,' says Harriet, removing the dagger from its sling of ribbon and placing it heavily on the glass counter.

The shopkeeper, whose fluffy white hair makes his head resemble a large ball of cotton wool, quivers with delight when he sees the athame has returned to him – and so soon after its departure.

'You'll forgive me for correcting you, miss, but this fine item is an athame, not a knife.'

Harriet says she knows little about antiquities, pointing out the confounding string of hieroglyphics on the hilt of the instrument.

'Yes, I saw those; quite astonishing!' says the shopkeeper. 'It was seeing these that urged me to write to a London friend who is far more knowledgeable than I when it comes to such matters. He surmised,' the dealer remarks with authority, 'the symbols were used by an ancient witchcraft cult. The oldest known examples date from around three thousand years ago.'

Harriet's mind reels from the news.

'That's very old. Witchcraft, you say?'

'Yes, miss.'

'But how did something so valuable end up here?' Harriet asks, and then checks herself. 'I meant to say, why is it not in a museum?'

The old man's hair appears to expand further as he takes the athame by the handle and holds it against a dusty window. 'Until recently, it was the centrepiece of an exhibition that toured a number of important galleries and museums in both London and New York.'

Here he pauses. For effect, thinks Harriet, more than anything else. She keeps her eyes firmly on the athame, the weave of its mystery slowly beginning to unravel.

'That was,' says the shopkeeper, 'until a number of people who regularly handled the artefact began falling ill with a mysterious infection whose symptoms resembled – dare I even say it in this town – the Black Death.'

A bolt of fear travels down Harriet's spine, rendering her silent.

'And yet, there you are, and here I am,' the old man adds. 'I've not yet been struck down with any manner of illness. Have you?'

Harriet's eyes narrow a little further.

The dealer continues, 'I lived on Caldey Island before I moved to Tenby, you know.'

'The island out in the bay? Is that where you found it?'

'Yes; I discovered it in my greenhouse, among some tomato and strawberry plants.'

'How unusual,' says Harriet. 'Who do you suppose hid it there?'

'Not it by itself, miss. For the item was paired with a second piece, more valuable in my opinion, believed to have been crafted by the same cult that forged the athame.'

Harriet hopes no one stumbles in off the street and interrupts their conversation, not now it has become so enthralling.

Turning, the shopkeeper removes a tray from a vast wall of identical metal trays behind him. He places it on the counter, where it fills the space between him and Harriet. 'This treasure I found in the same bag as the athame,' he says, smiling. Opening the small padlock with a key he produces from the back of his fob-watch, he eases back the box's lid, releasing dust into the air, which makes Harriet sneeze.

'Bless you, miss! Apologies, it's been a while since it's seen the light of day.'

Harriet's eyes widen as the old man removes the article from its velvet casing and sets it down before her.

'Pray tell, what is it?' she asks, her heart almost in her mouth.

'It's a fragment of a witch's sacred pentacle, miss.'

Harriet examines the object with an appetite to understand its every mark and blemish. The partial section is triangular in shape, made from a dull grey metal and contains a symbol made up of two crescent moons, back-to-back.

'A complete pentacle is a witch's main tool,' the shopkeeper breathes, 'allowing them to carry out rituals and witness the grace of the Mother Goddess in all her glory.'

Harriet glances up from the fragment and searches the eyes of the old man. 'If they were once so common, what made this particular pentacle so special, and therefore this fragment?'

The old man merely says, 'Well, this pentacle was said to be the most powerful one ever made. But, alas, a magical object that will only reveal its true power to the rightful owner. For the rest of us? Well, it remains a mere artefact from some forgotten age.'

He could not have been more direct in his confession that he was a witch himself and, in the way he's regarding the young girl handle both the athame and the fragment with great reverence for the witches that once fashioned them, clearly suspects Harriet to have a similar lineage.

'Where are the other fragments?' she asks, her voice barely a whisper.

'You may well ask, miss,' he says. 'And you may well go in search of them if you crave to see the pentacle whole again.'

It's nearly midnight as Harriet makes her way from her room to the fort's main staircase. She's shrouded in the darkest clothes her wardrobe could manage. About her neck hangs a band of black ribbon to match the one that is still wound tightly about the upper portion of her calf and holds the athame securely in place. The second length of fabric holds the chip of metal given to her so charitably by the shopkeeper that morning. Like the athame, its surface temperature never rises above an arctic-cool zero. Yet, with both talismans tightly bound to her young frame, she feels more powerful than she has at any point in her short, albeit fairly uneventful, life.

But it would seem, as happened in the library with the enigmatic Bert Wells, that her time beyond the fort walls is not to be spent entirely alone.

'Good evening, Miss Gordon.'

Harriet's cover is blown. On the steps leading out onto the lawn – still bearing its circle of upturned soil – stands Winston Churchill. He signals for her to join him, before tapping his cigar so that a pile of grey ash falls neatly within the lines of the athame-made circle.

'Good evening to you, sir.'

'For the life of me, I cannot guess to the kind of caper a girl your age might be up to, costumed like the good Queen herself, and at such an ungodly hour!'

Harriet decides to square with the guest who has already made such an impression on her family, particularly her younger brother, Charles.

'I'm afraid you would label me a fantasist, good sir, if I were to put it to you that the ground on which our home rests is capable of great magic.'

'*Magic*, you say?'

Churchill strikes a match to relight his cigar, chuckling quietly to himself as he leans against the stone wall that runs a short distance from the circle. The sudden flash of sulphur highlights for Harriet the level of Churchill's amusement and she regrets the decision to be quite so truthful with the most distinguished of her parents' guests.

'It was wrong of me to assume you would understand,' she adds. 'After all, until a few days ago, I believed there was little more to the world than men who ruled our great empire with gunpowder, violence and strategies designed to conquer the weak.'

Bemused, Churchill thinks for a moment or two, taking a few puffs of his cigar before committing to further passages of dialogue with the young girl.

'Sometimes, in the middle of a battlefield or a skirmish, I've caught myself thinking the exact same thought, Miss Gordon.'

Harriet says nothing to this, wondering if the man's cigar is to last much longer. *It must be very close to midnight by now*, she thinks.

'Well, I'm for my bed, Miss Gordon, with a recommendation to follow me back into your home and put to one side any interest in magic – at least until tomorrow.'

As he begins to turn away towards the fort, the landscape all about them starts to crackle and fizz with light, sparking through shades of blue, purple, red and yellow.

Churchill, perhaps confused and thinking the fort is under attack from enemy forces, tackles young Harriet to the ground, forming a protective barrier between himself and the riotous fireworks. Then, as quickly as they exploded into being, they settle as a column of brilliant white light containing flickering orbs.

'My circle!' Harriet beams, trying her hardest to wrestle free of her would-be saviour, but failing.

About her body, she feels the witch's tools finally begin to radiate warmth, so much so that, as she puts a hand to them, she wonders if the pentacle fragment will leave a triangular-shaped weal in her flesh.

Churchill is soon drawn to his feet when he judges the column of light to be no threat to their safety, becoming entranced with the images of ghostly figures moving within the orbs, each one ephemeral as powdered pastel.

'It's a miracle!' he says. 'What witchcraft or devilry do you suspect this to be, Miss Gordon?'

Harriet keeps to the shadows, waiting until such time when Indigo Carmichael, the girl featured in her painting, will reveal herself.

'Is that *me*?' Churchill asks incredulously, stepping towards the circle of light and using his cigar to indicate snatches of forgotten moments from his childhood: his father towering above him and then vanishing into thin air as a cane comes crashing down across the back of young Winston's head; scenes from boarding school showing Winston sat alone, or being mocked by prefects; the friends he dined with before watching them lose their lives on the battlefield – and under his command; even the walk he'd taken that very morning with the Gordons and Bert Wells!

Now the lights are presenting snapshots of a future Winston: this one far older and more serious, a heavy woollen jacket struggling to contain his bloated form and a black bowler hat sitting proudly on his head.

'Mr Churchill, look away!' begs Harriet, realising the orbs have somehow been persuaded to reveal their magic to an unwitting victim, in place of her.

Her eyes then follow a steady line of ash leading from the cigar, which Winston has by now dropped on the grass, to a pile of the same matter innocently tipped into the circle.

'And who's that?' he asks.

Harriet peers at the image of a stern-eyed gentleman that now fills the light ring, before confessing she has not the faintest clue who he could be. His upper lip sports a wedge of black hair and a band about his upper left arm features two diagonal lightning flashes, crossed where they meet. Churchill takes another step forward.

'He's shouting something!'

Harriet grabs her companion's arm, as though somehow she will be able to restrain a person twice her size, and says, 'I don't think he can see you, Mr Churchill. It appears his world is like an album of photographs being flicked through at tremendous speed.'

Harriet is shocked to see more footage spun for them by the orbs held inside the column of brilliant light: this time, strange ships cutting through a cloud-filled sky, each of them unloading fat barrels of gunpowder, which fall to the ground far below. At this point, she senses Churchill edging closer to the circle so she takes his hand, giving it a little squeeze. In response, he grips the young girl's hand ever more tightly.

Before them, a fresh reel of images appears and shows an even grimmer picture: children the same age as Harriet, dressed in striped uniforms, working the land or standing about in groups; pale, hollowed-out faces and ribs showing through paper-thin clothes; and then – *horror of all horrors* – whole families being marched onto trains that are pointed towards dark horizons of ... *What is that? Soot?* wonders Harriet.

'Sir,' she says with some urgency, trying to free her hand from his grip, 'You're getting closer to the circle and I do not think it made from altogether trustworthy magic.'

It's at this critical moment that Churchill, emotionally wrought from having witnessed such scenes of human degradation, passes out. He pitches towards the ground, taking Harriet with him ...

After a few seconds of blackout he comes to, shaking his head.

'Miss Gordon?' he calls, looking about him. But Harriet is nowhere to be seen. The lightshow has ended and there's no record of what just occurred atop St Catherine's Point. He stands for a moment, considering his next move. A girl is missing and the finger of suspicion will surely point at him if he admits any of what happened this evening.

Winston Churchill treads the remains of his cigar into the ground and simply retraces his steps back to the fort, dissolving back into the darkness whence he came. Not once does he look back over his shoulder in search of Harriet Gordon.

Indigo the Turnkey

Tenby, Wales, 2080

As the Carmichael complex is now home to some two-dozen species of mammal, reptile and insect, Indigo is reminded of the wooden ark mentioned in a book she discovered in her father's library, only yesterday. *The Illustrated Bible for Children* even has an inscription:

> 'To Harriet Gordon,
> One of God's more reliable emissaries.
> With love and fondness,
> Ma and Da,
> Christmas 1899.'

Indigo reflects again on the brief union she enjoyed with Harriet, captured in the screen of her father's broadcast portal. But on the very evening Indigo had planned for the crossover to occur – her father soundly asleep in his bed and unknowing of her plot – something had gone terribly wrong, meaning she'd lost contact with Harriet entirely.

Another chance to establish a link with Harriet had yet to present itself. So, in the vast underground complex of straw-filled cages and heated glass tanks, Indigo plays turnkey to everything from apes, lions, tigers, goats and snakes to tarantulas and even cockroaches. They've become her only friends, these pitiable creatures that know the four corners of their nominated spaces and little else.

'Good morning, Mary!'

The hare doesn't flinch, its shiny, button-flat eyes revealing nothing as the human girl edges closer to its cage.

'I know you're in there,' Indigo smiles, 'and I doubt you want to stay in that coat for very much longer!'

The hare twitches its round nose, a brown-edged lettuce leaf straying near to its mouth and quickly becoming a snack.

Due to her poor eyesight, Indigo sometimes uses a cane, especially in dark spaces. She now wields it to establish a clear spot in the cement floor, eventually registering it against her kneecaps as she lowers herself to animal level. She often does this with the more stubborn specimens in her care, as if she's able to reason with them. 'I can appreciate how you may think me selfish for tempting you from your home like I did, but I need your help.'

The hare hops towards the mesh, as if readying itself for transformation, only then to drink from the cage's water-dispenser. Once sated, it returns to its nest of hay.

Indigo is crestfallen. She'd hoped today to meet Mary Harries and make an ally of her. It was clearly a vain hope that the girl would set aside her anger and join Indigo in locating the five missing fragments of a sacred pentacle.

A short time later, Indigo steps out onto the uneven terrain of Forgotten Point, murky September sunshine much warmer than it should be for this time of year. Half a mile above the undersea Carmichael complex, the seasons come and go with their usual regularity, but the planet is in real turmoil and has been for a number of decades. Icecaps continue to melt at both poles, meaning that each year the tides around the Pembrokeshire peninsular rise higher, edging ever further inland.

Indigo comes here often, to watch the mighty waves, far below her, peak and collapse all about the thick outcrop of sandstone, as if attempting to swallow it – and Indigo – with each mouthful. Right now, though, it is still low tide and she gazes across the finger of exposed beach to Tenby. Most of the town has already succumbed to the elements, with many of its beachfront properties abandoned en masse when increasingly high tides pushed those living there further away from the coastline.

The gusting wind buffets Indigo, who braces herself against it. The feel of it lifts her spirit far above the limitations of her physical world and she wonders if she would be missed if it were to whisk her away to another place altogether, especially as her father makes very little time for her these days.

On giving birth to Indigo, her mother had quietly passed away, as if drifting off to sleep. Indigo's father had been there, holding onto his beloved wife's hand until nurses dragged him away into an adjoining room to begin his grieving. Indigo had been little more than a slip of mottled flesh in the hands of the midwife: cord snipped, bottom slapped, cleaned, weighed and deposited in a crib to one side of the lifeless woman who had carried her precious cargo for nine months.

Although Indigo has always had the notion this life is not her first, confirmation of her ability to re-incarnate only came to her fairly recently when, on her tenth birthday, she chanced upon one particular present among a mountain of others. It was neatly gift-wrapped but had an ancient heart lurking at its core. Even now, she can clearly remember her first glimpse of the book's title, *Handbook for Witches of the Broken Pentacle*, on the cover of plain black leather. Inside, the young girl read many revelations that made her question reality itself. It hinted at the possibility of past lives and of a future where witches would attempt to save mortal humans from self-destruction.

Alone on Forgotten Point, Indigo experiences a familiar stinging pain in her lungs. She won't be able to linger too long on open ground, for air pollution is now so rife and unstable that her lungs, already prone to asthma, quickly fill with harmful contaminants. With no birdsong filling the air – many species had become extinct decades ago – she can hear instead the great whirring filters of the complex as they purify the sea air and feed it through vast pipes into living quarters stationed many hundreds of metres below her.

Ready to go back indoors, a realisation suddenly dawns on her. She's standing on the same spot of land she's seen time and again in the large glass eye of her father's broadcast portal. A few years ago, Lance Carmichael had been keen to show her the magnificent screen that presents images of the past – fleeting moments that had been out of reach, until now. She recalls the moment he explained the science behind his time machine. She would have been about six years of age at the time …

'What are the lights, Daddy?'

'They're powerful lasers, darling. Thousands of them shoot out from four corners of a mighty corridor, meeting at a central point where they form a region of distorted space-time. It's something scientists call frame-dragging.'

Indigo watches as the screen fills with a halo of light so intense it forms tiny pockets of saltwater at the corners of her eyes.

'Why?'

'Well,' her father says, 'frame-dragging is a sort of magic trick that is helping scientists like me open doors between periods of time that have previously been kept apart from one another.'

'Doors, you say – with handles?'

'I suppose you could say I've found one handle,' he smiles, 'that has made possible the opening of lots of doors.'

'When will you go through your special door?'

Carmichael treasures these moments of frenzied inquiry led by his daughter; they're proof they already have so much in common.

He answers without hesitation, 'Not yet. But when I do, I'm hoping to find Mummy.'

'But I thought you said Mummy had gone to live with the angels?'

The brilliant mind of the six-year-old is suddenly thrown into confusion. Indigo knows she began life at the moment her poor mother had issued her last breath, so how could her father manage that level of magic? Would two versions of Indigo exist in the same period of time? Soon-to-be-born Indigo alongside an older version of the same girl?

'Daddy?'

'Yes, darling,' he says, now setting the young girl to the ground.

'How're you going to bring Mummy back, if she's already in heaven?'

He kneels down until he's level with her, their eyes a perfect match. He merely pinches Indigo by the narrow shelf of her shoulders and, with a tenderness he rarely shows, says, 'My clever machine will find a way. It's all I live for, to see her again, darling. Don't you want that, too?'

Following another dinner spent by herself, Indigo recovers the most sacred of texts from a little alcove located beneath floorboards in her bedroom. She has to kneel down low – not the easiest of feats for her – placing an ear to the grain of the wood, and feel in with her right hand made into a pincer of sorts. Eventually, she catches one edge of a book and pulls it free. Several works of fiction lie in waiting in this same hidey-hole, each one saved from execution at various points in the clearing out of the old fort's library.

Flicking through the stained pages of the handbook, Indigo has in mind a section, found mid-way through, that details the methods of transformation open to a witch. She soon locates it alongside a range of incantations and spells that could be cast to dispel the magic that may have, Indigo now suspects, rendered Mary Harries unable to return to human form.

'Ah, here it is,' she whispers to herself.

'And so, we come to the topick of animagus stasis, wherein a witche is imprisonede within a specifick animagus. It is required for the afflicted subjecte to seeke the helpe of a fellowe member of her coven to acquire the ingredients listed belowe, to then invoke an anti-animagus stasis spell suitable for the breede of mammal, fish, reptile or insect she has founde herself trapped within.'

So Mary might not be cross with her after all; she might not actually be able to turn herself back into human form!

There follows a set of cooking instructions, requiring a number of plants with herbal properties. Indigo guesses they'll have to be picked, purchased or stolen to cure Mary Harries of her current affliction.

'Methode of Infusione
Bringe a cauldron of pure springe water to the boil.
Adde to the bubbling liquid the following ingedientes, payinge close attention to the order in whiche they shulde be added:

1 four-leafe Clover, finely chopped
2 droplets of distilled essence of Beta vulgaris
Half a seasoned Burdocke roote
3 petals of blossomed Borage plante

Liquide should simmer gently until infusione is complete. Strain and coole before administering to the patiente.'

Indigo doesn't get as far as understanding the complement of spells included within the chapter, for the idea of not being able to trace one or all of the specified ingredients causes her to feel anxious.

Then comes a rat-tat-tat on her door.

'Just a second,' she calls, snapping the handbook shut and sliding it back beneath the floorboards.

'Indigo, it's me, your father.'

Luckily, she's on her feet and has straightened her dress by the time Carmichael enters the room, hastily followed by three men the young girl doesn't recognise and isn't aware had even landed at the Point.

The leader of the group, unfeasibly tall with a parting in his hair like a neat fold in velvet, wears horn-rimmed spectacles whose glass centres are more akin to two black mirrors that admit not even a fraction of light. About his mouth a goatee-beard hangs, threaded with minute grey hairs. Numbers two and three are identical twins, Indigo guesses. They match her in height and have shocking blonde fringes hanging low over their foreheads.

Her father seems uncharacteristically on edge.

'Indigo, my guests expressed a wish to meet you in person, and so here we are! This is Sir Rees-Repton and his sons, Maxwell and Anton.'

Rees-Repton stretches a single hand to meet Indigo's, but the young girl finds herself instead managing a badly executed curtsy.

'Pleased to meet you, sir.'

'Likewise,' the man breathes, mouth crinkling in contrived pleasure. 'We at Sentinel Technologies have been following your father's work with a great deal of interest.'

So, it is now possible to put a face to one of the key funders behind her father's experiments. Indigo is also mindful to acknowledge Maxwell and Anton now standing next to their father – two weak shadows framing a column of eerie light.

'My father's a genius,' says Indigo.

Rees-Repton smiles.

'The type of genius that runs in families, Miss Carmichael?'

'I think not, sir. A talent as substantial as my father's is rarely repeated in a single lifetime.'

Rees-Repton's gaze seems to penetrate the shield of his glasses, finally issuing a crisp, 'Good evening to you then, Miss Carmichael. I'm hopeful we'll get chance to talk again before we depart tomorrow.'

Once they're gone, Indigo collapses onto her bed. She begins to suspect her visits to the accelerator engine room have been monitored by technicians at Sentinel Technologies, if not directly by Rees-Repton himself. And if they know about the experiments she's conducted to date, how is she to re-engage with Harriet Gordon in past time and request that girl track down each of the ingredients needed for a healing infusion? And how is Harriet to forward said ingredients to present time via the engine, anyway, allowing Indigo to break the spell presently binding another of her subjects? The young witch closes her eyes to the sheer impossibility of it all and, only after some time, drifts off to sleep, her mind, body and spirit very much wearied.

The next day, Indigo is up early as she has a lot to do. Holding on to her shopping list, she's in the kitchen even before Cook has appeared to start preparing breakfast. As Indigo suspects, the task of finding the rare items mentioned in the handbook proves impossible. Foodstuffs presently lining the cupboards and freezers are the usual processed kind found in most homes these days. With the advent of industrialised 'farmanufacturing', fresh, hand-grown ingredients rapidly became a thing of the past. The world now has its regions of extreme heat, with traditional fertile regions falling victim to the planet's rising temperatures. In response, scientists have learnt to harness new technologies to create imitation crops, with flavours and colours attempting to simulate those of their fresher cousins, but entirely synthetic. Of course, Indigo's appetite knows no different, thinking the apple she sinks her teeth into as succulent as any appearing in past times.

All the same, the cupboards brimming with cloned produce look dreary and unappealing to the young girl as she registers the reality of what previous generations have done to her planet.

'Oh dear,' sighs Indigo, 'there really are no substitutes for the items on this list.'

'What list is that, then, Miss Carmichael?'

Behind Indigo looms the broad figure of their head cook, Mrs Dalrymple, whose indistinct facial features give the impression she was constructed from her own bread dough but left to prove over many decades, instead of hours.

'Mrs D, you gave me a fright!'

'And why exactly are you scurrying about in my stores?'

'I'm after ingredients for a healing potion. One of my animals is very sick and hasn't responded to any of the usual medicines or treatments.'

Mrs Dalrymple snatches the scrap of paper from the girl's fingertips, reading to herself in silence before declaring, 'It's been a good number of years since my eyes fell upon such exotic-sounding ingredients, miss.'

But, thinks Indigo, *Cook has heard of the ingredients, at least!*

'You'll not so easily lay your hands on these,' Mrs Dalrymple adds, swiping one hand into the fridge and retrieving three blue eggs. 'And I doubt your father would approve of any quest that has them as its treasure.'

Indigo is not so easily moved by Cook's threat. 'Father will not find out unless one of us tells him.'

Cook then crosses the kitchen with her usual bluster and, without taking her eyes off Indigo, she reaches for a large pan and sets it to heat on the enormous range.

'This was your father's home when he was a child. Did you know that?'

Indigo is staggered by the news.

'I see you did not,' says Mrs Dalrymple, cracking the three eggs into a large pan and responding to the hiss of burning fat with a shrill, '*Pah!*'

'I thought Father knew nothing of Tenby until his research brought him here?'

'There are a multitude of stories just out of sight, Miss Carmichael, each one waiting to be discovered!'

Indigo begins to speculate how her father might once have been a prisoner of the complex as she often considers herself to be. She'd always thought her grandparents were wealthy Londoners who'd shared a passion for the arts and sciences, whose lives bristled with the vibrancy of city life. She had no idea they were the ones who purchased the fort – and there's no record of their occupation in the building above ground. Indigo also wonders how the fort arrived at its present state of dereliction, simply marking the gateway to the much larger complex positioned beneath the seabed.

'I was here, then,' Mrs Dalrymple adds, 'a serving girl in the pay of your grandfather.'

'So, you remember my father *as a boy*?'

Indigo hoists herself up onto the long counter, just as she hears the voices of other kitchen staff newly arrived and milling about next door.

'He was considered a reclusive boy, was Master Carmichael. But he had about him a look of real mischief, even from a young age.'

'Did he have many friends?'

'None at all, save for me and … the voices in his head, of course.'

Indigo leans in until close to the old lady, marking the scent of lavender hanging in the air between them.

'Voices?'

'One mustn't be cruel, Miss Carmichael, but I'm in no doubt *they* told him to build those blasted machines he now works on day and night!'

The young girl doesn't flinch, taking the conversation in a different direction. 'Mrs D, do you know the gentlemen you've been asked to cook breakfast for this morning?'

The old woman shakes her head, pointedly moving away from Indigo and towards copper pans hanging above a long avenue of ovens.

Undeterred, Indigo presses on. 'Do you know at least *why* they've decided to visit my father?'

Cook thinks long and hard before deciding to share her thoughts with the young girl, aware she could lose her position for gossiping. 'I heard them talking last night,' the old woman whispers, 'about how your father has one week to prove himself a … erm … a witch worthy of their praise.'

Indigo's hands become mere strips of damp skin against the table-top's surface. '*Witch*, you say?'

'*Witch*,' Cook repeats, handing the scrap of paper back to Indigo and turning her attention to a group of cooks who have entered the kitchen and will need to be issued with a list of instructions if breakfast is to appear at all this morning.

An uneventful stretch of five days follows Mrs D's revelation, much of Indigo's time consumed by work she carries out in the animal compound. Some shift or change in the atmosphere has made many of the inmates restless. They nudge against their cages, with fur standing to attention, whenever Indigo comes near. Many of the more trusting, such as the monkeys and the goats, retreat to the backs of their cages as the young girl approaches with her trusty shovel, bags of food or arms laden with fresh bedding.

'Mary?'

Indigo peers through the mesh wall but cannot see the hare anywhere within its pen. She begins to panic and extends one hand to release the manual lock on the door.

'Mary Harries! Where are you?'

'What an unusual name for a pet.' Her father's voice comes from somewhere directly to Indigo's left. 'But equally curious is a mammal that wears about its neck jewellery of such striking quality.'

Indigo smiles as her father steps forward. She sees he currently has the creature by its ears, as if preparing it for the cooking pot.

'I came looking for you and found this peculiar specimen – that is, one *Mary Harries* – tearing around the yard like there's no tomorrow. How do you think she got out?'

'I've no idea, but you caught her!'

Carmichael's mood has lightened greatly since Indigo last set eyes on him. There's now an easiness to his manner, as if a great weight has been lifted from his shoulders.

'Well, does the necklace belong to you?' he asks, holding up Mary Harries' treasured sapphire pendant.

Indigo smiles.

'Yes, I found it washed up on the beach, only last week.'

'The beach, you say?'

'Don't worry, I only popped down for a few minutes when the tide was fully out and wore my oxymask the entire time, Father.'

He watches on as Indigo sets the hare in its unsoiled pen of straw. 'I'll try to help out more, down here,' he tells her. 'And maybe we could go for short walks together, that sort of thing?'

Indigo replaces the latch on the cage door and turns to face her father. She takes a step towards him, knowing her vision will sharpen the closer to an object she becomes. He places the pendant in her outstretched hand and she looks up, noting how his hair curls neatly about his face, but his skin remains washed-out, almost colourless.

'Has your research been successful then?' she asks.

'Its outcome I'll reveal to you when I consider it right to do so. For now, all I can say is that I intend to make your welfare my principal concern!'

Indigo looks down at Mary Harries, now without the necklace that had gone unnoticed by her turnkey, of all people.

'Such an exquisite jewel,' she whispers across the space between them, twisting the pendant until it catches the light issued by a nearby electric lamp.

A whole day and evening later, Indigo finds herself entering the familiar set of eight numbers into a square panel that grants her access to the accelerator engine room. Of course, Indigo, like other Knowing Ones, has a natural skill in reading the minds of those around her, so gaining the code from the vaults of her own father's memory had proven no difficult feat. All those weeks ago, when she'd first stood at the panel, she had simply willed the numbers into her mind. They appeared as pronounced digits in the full sphere of her vision:

3-2-7-4-9

Success at the panel this time means she passes over the familiar threshold and into the secret depths of her father's laboratory. As she follows the hum of powerful computers engineering long strings of complicated equations, Indigo imagines herself to be a tapeworm burrowing into the hidden recesses of her father's mind. The accelerator engine sits at the centre of the maze, symbolising the perfection of Lance Carmichael's dream to construct a machine that would allow him mastery over space-time itself.

Reaching the chamber that contains the all-important broadcast portal, Indigo looks about her for evidence that Sentinel Technologies could be spying on her. Then again, she knows micro-science could attach a camera to a single grain of salt if it needed to, so she wastes little time in trying to confirm their presence.

The blankness of the white room hits Indigo as she taps a switch and brings life to a series of terminals. Ranged before her are a chain of clear glass plates – five in total – all waist height to an adult. They're suspended from the ceiling by a line of perpendicular wires, each thread as fine as cotton but constructed from one of the strongest materials known to humankind: titanium. The first time she'd powered up the engine, Indigo had marvelled at the sheer elegance of the technology her father had worked so hard to create and refine. Each glass disc differs in size to the next one, from smallest to largest as one's eye moves from left to right. The first is no bigger than a saucer, the last the size of an antique dining table.

Something like instinct had made Indigo set her hand to the first of the plates and the great engine revealed itself to her on the other side of the room's glass partition. The machine itself had been constructed as an unassuming corridor, three metres wide by three metres in height, its internal walls painted black and mounted with thousands of miniature laser cannons. Once activated, intervals of solid wall that run along the length of the passage begin to rotate, resembling a vintage fairground attraction Indigo had once seen in a film, where paying customers stepped through the centre of the swirling structure.

Indigo soon discovered she could have the enormous engine do her bidding; she had only to set a hand to one of the discs and have it read the web of fine lines gracing her palm. She also noted the smallest of discs made the region of space between the laser lights spin at speeds that made her open mouth turn dry. At the other extreme, a hand to the largest of the plates sent alternate rows of lasers in opposite directions to one another, creating a portal of riotous colour, the likes of which engaged the young girl for long periods of time, as if she were being sucked into a different dimension. In each case, where lasers criss-crossed or met, and from her position at the end of the corridor, she could just make out a perfect O of white light that shone fiercely in the unprotected eye until she was forced to apply goggles, turn away, or power down the engine.

Tonight, with Mary's necklace safely about her person, Indigo places two perfectly composed hands on the edge of one glass plate. Its coldness is bracing, but Indigo knows that any fear she feels will subside once her thoughts are allowed to settle on the whereabouts of Harriet Gordon. She also knows well the incantation found within the pages of the handbook and recites it now, line for line, as she stands before the broadcast portal.

'I conjure thee, O Circle of Power,
That thou beest a meeting-place of love and joy and truth;
A shield against all wickedness and evil;
A boundary between the world of men and the realms of the Mighty Ones;
A rampart of protection that shall preserve and contain the power that I shall raise within thee.'

Slowly, the bleak square of corridor begins to spin, soundlessly at first and eventually settling on a high-pitched whistle, making Indigo want to cover her ears. The square of laser fire warps and bevels, until white heat highlights the circumference of a perfect circle.

But as Indigo pulls the protective goggles down over her eyes, a boy's face appears in the glass screen of the broadcast portal. His bird-like features leave a distinct impression in her retinas and the image soon reveals the boy to be at work in a dark room containing an open furnace. Indigo watches on as shapes come apart and re-form in a fresh tableau, this one showing the same boy plunging a large pair of iron tongs into a broiling bucket of liquid and producing a cloud of steam that makes him reel back in shock or displeasure.

Unwavering, Indigo moves her hand across the plate towards its centre and the tunnel duly responds, the lens this time settling on the object the young boy has recently cooled, which lies to one side on a small steeple of bricks.

'A pentacle,' whispers Indigo.

'A counterfeit to be proud of,' says the boy, Abe, as if engaging the unseen witch in conversation.

Indigo's hand suddenly slips from its position on the glass circle and the portal turns black.

'*Counterfeit?*' she asks. 'Meaning a fake pentacle? But why would the portal present me with an image unrelated to the whereabouts of the original sacred pentacle?'

It's only as Indigo moves to a larger glass disc stationed to her right, triggering the lasers into another frenzy of activity, that she manages to place the boy's face. He'd been there at Mary's side the night she stepped into the circle of light and crossed the many hundreds of years that separated the two of them.

But, thinks Indigo, *his work at the furnace was as forger; for some reason, he'd set himself the task of creating a second pentacle!* The young girl wishes she'd brought the handbook with her, for it contains important detail on how the sacred pentacle was shattered into five equal parts, sent to far-flung ends of the planet for protection, until the time was right for it to be reassembled.

It comes to Indigo quite suddenly: the handbook states that, when the time comes for the pentacle to be made whole again, order would be restored to a planet that was fast coming apart at its seams. The broadcast portal had actually chosen to show her the moment in time when one young boy, Abraham Aderyn, had realised unscrupulous authorities had set out to track down the artefact he was shortly to disassemble – or perhaps he had just done so. Indigo then begins to suspect that Sentinel Technologies was perhaps more than a few decades old, as was the Rees-Repton family. Then she hears a voice.

'Indigo, are you there?'

She responds, 'Harriet, *is that you*?'

A halo of coiled, ebony-black hair suddenly fills the portal, in direct contrast to the garish lights of the laboratory.

'Indigo, where have you been?'

Indigo shakes her head out of sympathy for the young witch's situation. 'Please accept my apologies, Harriet. This is the first chance I've had to re-establish contact with you. You have to believe me!'

'It's been truly dreadful. I shouldn't even be outdoors you know, for the year is 1943 and blackout means exactly that!'

'Blackout?'

Harriet's breathing is wild and uneven. 'The last time we were due to meet, something went wrong and I was transported to a different time in Tenby's history!'

'I suspected so,' Indigo says, her voice falling away to nothing.

'Don't be worried if I suddenly cut you off. The column of light that's allowing me to talk with you is drawing unwanted attention from sentry guards stationed at my brother's fort. You must think of a way to rescue me!'

With one hand still pressed to the glass disc, Indigo uses her free hand to rummage about in her pocket for the scrap of paper containing the healing potion recipe. With some speed, she instructs Harriet to acquire the list of ingredients and requests they meet again the following day.

'Make it early evening, though,' says Harriet.

'Let's say 7pm?'

'I'll do my best, but I make no promises. Rationing doesn't allow for luxuries such as – Harriet screws up her face, furrowing her brows – *distilled plant essences.*'

'Until our next meeting then,' concludes Indigo.

Harriet nods once before disappearing entirely from view, leaving Indigo to the sounds of a vast engine slowing to standstill.

'Who's there?'

With lightning speed, Indigo flicks the switch on the wall and executes a blackout of her own, mere seconds before Carmichael marches into the laboratory, hoping to surprise any trespassers.

Undetected, Indigo slips behind a metal cabinet to escape from view, closing her eyes and pressing Mary Harries' necklace to her chest.

When she next comes to, Indigo suspects the world has been magnified, easily outsizing her twenty to one. She has in fact transformed from human to animal, becoming a white-haired mouse no more than five centimetres in length and half that in width. The metal cabinet to her right now towers above her, stretching impossibly towards the distant atmosphere of the ceiling. The black-and-white exactness of her surroundings make her think of an old postcard she once found, with ornate handwriting recording that it was, *'1901 (Tenby, high summer)'*. The timeworn photograph showed people milling about on South Beach promenade, melting ice-creams stippling the ground and ladies' straw hats deflecting the rays of an unforgiving sun. Indigo could never see anything of her own Tenby in that tiny snapshot of its forgotten past.

Carmichael doesn't think to look down, so he doesn't discover the tiny mammal nestling against the run of skirting board. Instead, he gives the entire room the briefest of inspections before, shaking his head, he asks out loud, 'What in Einstein's name is going on?'

As he leaves the room, mindful to ensure the door behind him releases its deadlock, he doesn't mark the streak of white fur fall in behind him: a mouse on the move. But he pursues an unexpected route, moving through corridors of closed doorways in a sector of the building Indigo didn't even know existed until now.

She has to sprint to keep up with him, a flash of fur always a few feet behind her target and casting a small pocket of shadow about her four paws. The large enclosure they're navigating reminds the young girl of the zoo she maintains on the other side of the compound. Except here there's a cruel tone to the atmosphere that makes Indigo think her father acts as turnkey to prisoners of a very different sort. They arrive at the final cell at the end of a long corridor of chambers.

'*Uxor*,' Carmichael breathes into a voice recognition panel. Within seconds, he's entering the occupied cell, his daughter almost squashed beneath his left foot when she guesses incorrectly where it's going to land. Indigo knows to make for the immense shadow made by the room's sole item of furniture: a short, narrow bed, its grey blankets tucked neatly beneath a thin, ineffectual mattress.

Once safely hidden, Indigo twitches her whiskers and sniffs at the dank air. There are two people in the room: her father and someone else. She watches as two sets of ankles re-distribute their weights, before a conversation fills her large, satellite-dish ears.

'How are you this evening?'

The subject with narrow ankles seems upset.

'What exactly do you hope to gain by continuing with this charade, Professor?'

The mouse nears the edge of the shadow, for Indigo's father is addressing a woman and the young girl wants to put a face to the pair of elegant ankles.

'Hilary, I've already gained so much in seeing you each day. Your continued presence sustains me in ways you could never fully understand or appreciate.'

Indigo dares not blink – not until she admits to herself that her father is talking to her dead mother.

'I'd prefer it,' the woman says, 'that you didn't call me Hilary. My name's Helen.'

Indigo edges out into the open plains of light, her pink eyes arching skywards as she thinks, *So this is my mother, very much alive and being held captive!*

'Tomorrow I'd like you to meet our daughter,' says Carmichael. 'I think you'll like her. She has your tenacity and my intelligence.'

The woman puts her hands on her hips and tosses her head, flinging back the long fringe of red hair that, until now, has hidden one half of her face. 'I already have a daughter,' she snaps, 'and it makes me sick to think I may not see her again!'

Indigo is suddenly overcome with a great sadness, for the poor woman was indeed *a version* of Hilary Carmichael but, like the counterfeit pentacle Indigo had seen Abe forge in the blacksmith's workshop, was a mere copy of the smiling woman she had seen in her parents' wedding photographs.

'Tomorrow, you *will* meet our daughter,' Carmichael insists, pressing on with his own truth. 'And we'll take it from there – one step at a time, if needs be.'

Indigo next hears the clicking of a latch and realises her father has left the cell – his daughter in mouse form and now entirely alone with a woman he'd located using the science of his accelerator engine, someone he'd snatched from her own dimension to live alongside them.

At the door, Indigo puts her pink nose to the narrow gap that will not admit her bulk, only then realising her mother's doppelganger harbours an irrational fear of mice and is presently screaming her lungs out at the other end of the containment cell.

Blackout

Tenby, Wales, September 1943

Harriet regains consciousness with some difficulty. For one, there's a pounding headache she guesses was created by Churchill when he threw her forward into the circle of light, her head connecting with a small rock protruding from her father's lawn. It was the last item of experience presently to hand, for the fog of her journey through space-time has muddled her senses and left her feeling dazed and confused. This mental blurring of one's edges, as she aptly titles it, is also accompanied by an acute burning sensation, located somewhere along her left thigh.

Struggling to reach down, she discerns the athame caught awkwardly between her thigh muscle and the hard ground. She can smell iron in the air, too, and soon discovers blood seeping through the fabric of her dress, the blade – blunt though it is – having dug in and drawn beads of the precious liquid from her body.

'Oh dear,' she groans.

But Harriet Gordon is yet to learn that the circle of light has catapulted her – and her alone – through a gaping cleft in time and deposited her safely on the same spot of land, forty-three years into the future.

'Mr Churchill ... Sir?'

Only the wind can be heard howling its haunting song back at Harriet.

'Bert? Mr Wells – are you there? Can anyone hear me?'

With each unanswered question, the young witch's voice rises in pitch until, at last, she issues a drawn-out cry of genuine woe.

'Miss?' comes a voice, at the very point when Harriet has consorted with her own skeleton to have it stand upright.

'Who are you?' asks the young witch, without her customary regard for social protocols.

'One might ask the same of you,' the voice replies.

A young soldier slowly comes into focus: cropped hair and a khaki-coloured uniform.

'My name's Harriet Gordon.'

'A relative of Colonel Gordon, then?'

Quite where the young man has appeared from is anyone's guess, so Harriet provides him with clarification.

'You're addressing the only daughter of Christopher and Elizabeth Gordon – the present owners of St Catherine's Fort, which stands directly behind you.'

'Private Harold,' the young man offers. 'But I know not of any Christopher and Elizabeth Gordon. I'm guessing they must be related to Colonel Rupert Gordon?'

Harriet's eyes widen and the soldier wonders if he should not offer to escort the young girl towards the fort's entrance, at least. Once there he could have his commanding officer deal with the matter, for it all seemed quite beyond the young man's comprehension.

'Rupert Gordon is my brother; he's thirteen years of age and could not be trusted to keep up with his own shadow.'

'Shadow or not, your brother is no boy, I can assure you, miss. In fact, he's somewhat senior in years and a decorated war hero.'

'*War hero*? Don't be ridiculous! Anyway, what war do you speak of?'

'As I suspected, you're in the throes of a very nasty concussion,' Private Harold says, attaching himself to Harriet's elbow. 'You'd best come with me, so we can sort this little mess out.'

As Harriet walks along the corridor that leads from the front to the rear of the fort, the soldier by her side attempts to set the record straight. 'It's 1943 and Britain is at war with Germany for a second time, miss. Although you could say the Great War was a mere trailer for the main feature that is now playing to packed houses!'

Harriet struggles to take it all in, noting how the fort no longer rings with the sounds of a household conducting its usual business, as it had done only yesterday. Now there's a terrible silence that clings to an unfamiliar, arctic-cold atmosphere, as if all warmth and goodwill has been sucked entirely from it. This is the reality of time travel, Harriet wants to tell Bert Wells: landing in a future that only partly resembles one's past – but enough for it to make one take a second look, as if one had become a ghost in one's own skin, or home.

'I should like to see my room, please.'

The soldier declines Harriet's request.

'All in good time. First, I must register your presence with this station's commanding officer and, of course, the colonel.'

'Very well,' Harriet concedes, her eyes falling on the large oak door that leads to her father's study, a place that once admitted few visitors.

'Wait here, please,' says the soldier, tapping twice on the door before entering.

After what seems like an interminable wait, in which time Harriet argues for and against exploring the fort by herself, the door before her opens again, silently bleeding warm air into the chilly hallway.

Private Harold's cheeks are flushed as if he's been reprimanded, the slope of his shoulders a little narrower.

'You can go in now, but you might want to alter your story, miss. The very mention of your name sent the colonel into a temper unlike any I've seen in all my time here!'

'Is he alone?' asks Harriet, wondering if she's prepared to confront the boy who had, alongside his brothers, tormented her for years.

'Our commanding officer, Major Rees-Repton, is in attendance,' says Private Harold, holding out an arm to indicate she may proceed through the open doorway without him.

Before doing so, Harriet instinctively reaches for the pentacle fragment looped about her neck, then removes it and places it in her pinafore pocket. A soldier is holding the door open for her, partially blocking her view into the room beyond. He introduces himself.

'Pleased to make your acquaintance. Miss Harriet, is it? Major Rees-Repton, commanding officer of Pembroke's Fifth Division.'

'Good evening,' says Harriet politely, casting her eyes quickly around what she can see of the once-familiar room before bringing them back to rest on the soldier. Rees-Repton stands like a liquid shadow that grows and shrinks in size as it breathes. His eyes are little more than pinpricks of emerald-green light and his hair is neatly trimmed into a dagger shape on each side of his skull. He steps aside and motions her forward. Harriet's brother, advanced in years now but Rupert all the same, is lying sprawled, all temper spent, across her father's old writing desk.

'Drunk,' Rees-Repton explains.

Harriet is shocked.

'But he's a war hero!'

'Indeed,' Rees-Repton smiles. 'Please, take a seat.'

Harriet moves with caution, the pain in her thigh still smarting. Rees-Repton watches her, unblinking, as if he were recording her every move.

'So, you claim to be a relation of Colonel Gordon's?'

The young witch suddenly stumbles on an idea that will serve as a cover story to her real identity. After all, who would believe she was a time-traveller, newly arrived in war-torn Tenby? She would be in the care of asylum staff before the day was out.

'I don't know what Private Harold told you, sir,' she begins, 'but it's been a long day and my journey has proven a strenuous affair.'

'I see,' breathes Rees-Repton, his prey still firmly in his jaws. 'So, you're not a Gordon, after all?'

Harriet pauses, her mouth forming another mistruth.

'Oh yes, a Gordon, through and through, sir! My name is Elizabeth; I'm the surviving granddaughter of one Harriet Gordon, and named so after my great-grandmother, Elizabeth Gordon, who once resided here.'

Rupert looks up and across the expanse of blotting paper and fountain pens. When he speaks, his voice is paper-thin.

'Harriet ... is that you?'

The young witch improvises as best she can.

'He must think I'm his long-lost sister, newly returned to him! I'm said to resemble my grandmama, right down to the colour of my eyes.'

'Harriet, you've come home!'

Rees-Repton places a paternal hand on Rupert's shoulder and rubs gently, soothing the man's frayed nerves.

'There, there, sir. Don't work yourself into a state.'

'I want to sleep, Anthony, I *so* want to sleep.'

'Of course, we'll get you to bed,' intones Rees-Repton.

Harriet watches on as the colonel uses his elbow to clear the surface of dirty glasses and an empty bottle of whiskey, the whole lot falling into a waste-paper basket on one side of the table.

Harriet does her best to continue.

'My mother, Charlotte Grantham – the poor niece you never met – has passed to the other side, God rest her soul. I'm orphaned, Great-uncle Rupert, and I come to you penniless and destitute.'

'I'll have one of the men make up a room for you,' says Rees-Repton, Harriet's brother now being carried out of the door by two soldiers – one of them Private Harold.

'My grandma's old room will suffice,' Harriet smiles. 'That is, if one of your men could take me to it?'

For the next few hours, Harriet sits on her old bed contemplating her situation. It's as if she'd been catapulted a great distance, only to have landed in her old skin but greatly altered by a singular ordeal. Her room is little more than a museum piece, a shrine to the girl who left the family home one night, never to return. Throughout the torment of waiting for news – Churchill and Wells no doubt having cleared their names – the Gordon family must have gathered about the hearth, united in their disbelief that their darling Harriet would have hated any of them enough to leave home. In her mind, Harriet conjures up images of her brothers lined up, each one cross-examined by a series of solemn-looking police inspectors, the newsprint and local gossipers ignoring the real story of how she was bullied, day-in, day-out. *But where are they now?* she wonders. The realisation suddenly hits her, that a single day of her life contains decades of time, during which her parents would have aged enormously and that, almost certainly, they would both be dead by now.

At the room's little oval window stands the easel containing her unfinished painting, *Into the Light Ring*. But its oils now flake and come away at her fingertips, the white pigment of her picture contrasting with the warmer tones of her own skin.

'Oh dear,' she cries quietly to the painting, as if it were a dear friend. 'What am I to do here? What purpose can it possibly serve to enclose me within this grim chapter of history?'

Harriet wonders if Rees-Repton believes her story, or if her brother would ever be *compos mentis* enough to conduct an actual conversation with her. She has no hard, physical evidence to validate her story, other than the fragment of metal she'd hidden from view before meeting everyone.

'Tomorrow's another day,' she yawns to her old collection of porcelain dolls, many of them now girdled in grime and dust, as she nestles down amongst the bed clothes, feeling her eyelids begin to droop. 'And a witch can achieve much in a single day, providing she is sufficiently rested.'

The next morning, Harriet resolves to visit the little town of Tenby, a place she'd once famously termed, 'the dourness of dreariness'. At breakfast, she sits opposite an empty chair, having been informed her brother is rarely spotted before noon and only then to bestow the bitterest of moods on those around him. *In the intervening years, the number of house staff has been reduced*, notes Harriet, *so one is forced to endure a long wait for a bowl of cold oatmeal, charcoal-black toast and lukewarm tea.*

'With rationing, there's to be no bacon and eggs this week,' is all the fort's butler manages.

Not really an apology at all, thinks the young witch.

Harriet doubts there's anyone in the building who remembers her, the little girl who liked her eggs paraded before immaculately cut soldiers, with a thin film of marmalade gracing four triangles of toast. *Rationing?* thinks Harriet. *What has the war done to the middle classes?*

Leaving the fort with more confidence than when she'd entered it the previous evening, Harriet trips nimbly down the stone stairwell that connects it with South Beach and the town's main promenade, beyond. The tide is presently out, distant waves forming little smiles on the curved edges of her vision. Of course, to her it was only the day before yesterday she'd been taunted by Charles, Peter and Rupert on a spot of grass high above her on the Point.

Today, everyone in town stares at her and it's only now that Harriet begins to comprehend the enormity of her problem. She's truly out of place. Her clothes, her hair, even her gait as she walks. She just doesn't quite fit in here. And as for Tenby, things seem out of time, too. There are far more women than men comprising the local population, with soldiers zooming about the town's cobbled streets in vehicles that make Harriet's mind spin.

Eventually, she reaches her destination at the far end of the town square, only to discover a dispiriting sign on the shop door: Closed Until Further Notice. Peering in through the window, Harriet wonders if the man with the cotton wool hair might still be propped up behind his counter, awaiting her return. He'd trusted her with both the athame and pentacle fragment. From his confident display in her abilities, she'd suspected he was also a witch. *Was that really only the day before yesterday?*

'When will my luck turn?' she breathes, stamping her right foot out of sheer frustration.

But as she readies to depart, something catches her eye on the other side of the glass – a scrap of legible script, etched into the layer of dust coating the surface itself:

yedlaC mraF worraB

'Barrow … Farm … Caldey,' she surmises after a few seconds. 'He's left an address, knowing I might one day strive to track him down!'

Energised by her discovery, Harriet flutters over the cobbles of the little town like a happy phantom. At one point, she catches sight of her reflection in a run of shop windows: a series of broken images really, but nonetheless captivating. *Have I not grown an inch, or two, taller?* she wonders. *Maybe time has stretched me a little as I travelled through the portal?* Such questions occupy her mind as she makes for the island ferry in the little harbour, nestled in the corner of Tenby's southern-most shore and not so very far from the steps that lead back up to the fort.

'What business have you on Caldey, young lady?'

Harriet confronts the ship's mate with a flat, 'I live there, sir. Did you not see me disembark yesterday morning on my way into Tenby?'

'I didn't work yesterday.'

'Well, I came over to see a darling relative, a great aunt, in fact. And now it's time for me to return home,' she says, 'and I've certainly no intention of paying twice!'

'Well … Get on, then, before the tide turns and my good mood with it.'

The young witch, feeling pleased with her deception, affords the gentleman the briefest of smiles as she passes from land to vessel.

Harriet had never set foot on Caldey Island before today. She'd refused to accompany her family on day trips across the sound, enjoying the temporary serenity of a fort emptied of its irritating occupants. With family gone, Harriet had the entire run of the house, the servants bending to meet her every whim and desire, if only for an afternoon.

As she prepares to disembark it strikes her that she has no idea in which part of the island she will locate Barrow Farm. She couldn't ask the ferryman, for such an admission that she'd fabricated a mistruth would land her in even deeper water should their paths cross a second time. Harriet spots a fingerboard sign pointing to 'Caldey Abbey' and decides to throw herself on the charity of the monks. She sets off, through a morning mist which is bathing the whole island in an eerie light.

Quite alone with her thoughts, she feels the island far too quiet a place to ever be considered welcoming. Its mournful-looking trees sway haplessly against the wind, hinting at secrets they'll never willingly surrender. *No birds spoil the canvas of sky*, Harriet notes, *and nothing but the odour of peril is cast out from the heads of dying flora.*

'Can I help you, young lady?'

Harriet snaps free of her trance.

'Good day, sir.'

Standing in her way is a monk attired in rust-coloured garments and sporting strawberry blonde hair. He's evidently been gardening, for in one hand is a trowel, complete with clumps of damp soil and roots.

'Where are your parents?'

Harriet looks away briefly, giving herself time to think.

'Both deceased, sir, so I was forced to move to Tenby. I'm currently living with my uncle at St Catherine's Fort.'

The monk frowns. 'I thought Rupert was the last of the Gordons. Forgive me; I didn't think his sister was found alive, let alone a niece. God be praised!'

'Thank you, Brother …?'

'Jones,' the monk replies, before lowering his brow, his blue eyes edged with concern. 'Of course, I'm deeply sorry for your loss, but may I ask how old your dear ma was when she died?'

Harriet, who has never proven consistent when it comes to fibs, is quietly admonishing herself for having put herself in such a position. She quickly works out that, given she was twelve in 1900, if she hadn't time-travelled she would now be fifty-five. Too old, really, to have a 12-year-old daughter!

'Apologies, sir – Rupert is my *great-uncle*. Great-uncle Rupert and my grandmother, Harriet Gordon, were siblings, you see.'

'And might I inquire as to how your parents died, Miss …?'

'… Elizabeth,' she answers, thinking for a moment of the infantrymen in their vehicles and quickly adding, 'Car crash, fatal – both gone in an afternoon.'

She feels guilty for inventing such a horrid story, but she's eager to move on to Barrow Farm.

'Tragic family when all's told,' the monk sighs. 'Two brothers killed in action: Charles in the Great War, Peter only last year. Although I'm guessing from the changing colour of your complexion, you're only now discovering such?'

'Don't be silly,' Harriet says, forcing a bright smile, 'of course I know my own family history. Now, I really must be on my way!'

'Where exactly is it you're going?'

Harriet detects fresh tears swaying against the dams of her eyelids but manages to hold them back for a moment or two longer.

'Barrow Farm.'

'*Barrow Farm*?' repeats the monk. 'Why, no one has visited that place in years.'

'Well, my great-uncle has trusted me with a message to be delivered to its owner.'

Reluctantly, the monk uses his trowel to mark out a map of the path Harriet is to follow if she's to reach her destination, adding, 'Do be careful, Miss Elizabeth, the farm is said to be a place of ... *spiritual unrest*.'

'Stuff and nonsense,' she calls over her shoulder. 'Good day to you, Brother.'

◯

The news that she has lost two of her brothers in the opening and closing of a light ring presents Harriet with a mixture of feelings, so she puts them out of mind – for now. Instead, she focuses on locating the whereabouts of the mysterious shop owner, soon chancing upon a desolate courtyard, framed by half a dozen derelict buildings.

With care, she retrieves the pentacle fragment from her pinafore pocket and places it about her throat. Prepared as she is for unpleasant surprises, she decides to explore the most imposing of the buildings: a sandstone farmhouse whose windows are like a pair of eyes with both lids sewn shut.

'Hello?' Harriet calls, passing through from the warmth of the sunshine to the building's cool interior. 'It is I, the witch Gordon, and I have tracked you down, good sir!'

Harriet kicks up loose grit as she walks through what she suspects would once have been the farm's kitchen. In a small alcove off the main room, she inspects an old fire-grate and alights upon a cast-iron poker. It feels cold to the touch, but Harriet uses it to pick out objects amongst the dirt and dust.

'That's not yours, miss. Please, put it back!'

The ghostly voice seems to rise up from beneath the room's floorboards, so Harriet kneels down to inspect the run of wooden slats, asking, 'Why do you hide underground?'

She does her best to conceal any outward signs of worry, but she suspects a spirit might be able to identify such in her aura from a thousand yards, let alone a few feet.

'It's not safe to be seen above ground.'

'I promise I'll do my best to protect you,' says Harriet.

'All the same, it's probably best you come down here. Stand back,' the voice advises.

Harriet steps away from the boards in time to witness an oval-shaped trap door materialise in the floor's design. Just as quickly it dissolves, leaving behind a black hole some three feet in diameter.

Another magic circle! thinks Harriet.

A ghostly hand suddenly emerges from the darkness and stretches out towards her.

'Take it,' the voice urges. 'It'll draw you underground, where we can meet. But hurry! We haven't much time before the raven children conduct their daily tour of the farm, determined to track me down.'

Gripping the hand, Harriet is drawn from a world of substance to a place consisting entirely of fantastic forms. Like Lewis Carroll's Alice disappearing down the rabbit-hole – one of Harriet's all-time favourite stories – the young witch travels down a tunnel of indeterminate length, its muddy walls exuding an intense heat.

'You're safe now, miss. You can open your eyes.'

Harriet's vision takes a short time to adjust, gradually acknowledging the realm that lies before her, one bathed in rich, wondrous colours.

'How splendid!' she says, eyes fixed on a run of decorative chandeliers suspended from the ceiling of a great ballroom, each one heavily jewelled and emitting a beguiling light. All about the air a multitude of musical notes linger, each one contributing to a melancholy waltz. They briefly connect in pairs, before establishing a fresh communion with another complementary, or contrasting note. Harriet's ears ring with the delightful tune, but it somehow makes her mourn for the life of dinners and dances she was once so keen to leave behind.

'Come, sit with me,' the voice says, Harriet able now to see it belongs to a boy, roughly her age, with a mass of shabby hair. He's perched upon a throne of gold and quite lost to a mountain of velvet cushions.

Harriet remains bewitched.

'This place is remarkable!'

'My name's Victor Aderyn and I welcome you to my home. The great handbook prophesied your visit, of course. Although it didn't state the exact point in time you would appear!'

'It's September 1943,' Harriet says, a little too matter-of-factly.

'You must find Tenby a very different place to the town you left behind?'

Harriet nods, but hunger pains are suddenly with her and sound out as a rumble for her host to hear.

Victor claps his hands twice, declaring, 'I shall set out a great banquet for my guest – that is, if you would allow me to do so?'

A table suddenly appears before them, resplendent with dishes of every description: roast chicken, pies, venison, vegetables and all manner of cakes and desserts.

Harriet takes a small pork pie and makes light work of it. After dispensing with a second one, she asks, 'How is this possible?'

'More than *this* is possible, Harriet, with magic in your life!'

'The pentacle, you mean?'

Victor silently directs an invisible hand to lift a silver spoon and plunge it into a sundae glass full to the brim with ice cream. It scoops out an enormous spoonful and hovers, waiting for him to finish speaking before it can deposit the swiftly-melting dessert in his mouth.

'The pentacle, yes! Or rather, by unleashing ancient magic from the pentacle fragment you have about your person.'

Harriet flinches defensively, drawing a hand to her throat, the musical notes on both sides of the table abruptly falling into muted silence.

'You spoke of a handbook that foretold of my arrival. Please, tell me more about it.'

With the clicking of two fingers, Victor casts a magical spell. The food suddenly comes to life, as do the plates and cutlery – the table's entire contents, it seems. Even the musical notes and the magnificent chandeliers glisten for a second before shrinking in size until they're no taller than chess pieces. One after another the notes, plates, chandeliers and banquet items march into an opened book that now rests on Victor's palms, giving Harriet the impression that the mysterious item is in fact a gateway to a hidden world.

'Here; it's yours, anyway,' he says.

Harriet reads aloud the words that grace the book's worn cover: '*Handbook for Witches of the Broken Pentacle.*'

Victor nods, his monochrome skin turning a darker grey.

'You are one of three witches mentioned in the handbook and you have in your possession one of five pentacle fragments, each of them sent on very different paths in order to protect them.'

Harriet gazes at the cover of the book, her eyes narrowing as Victor continues, 'I'm a direct descendent of two powerful witches, Abraham Aderyn and Mary Harries. It was they who first engineered the idea of creating a handbook for future generations of witches.'

Harriet brushes the cover from one corner to another, tracing an invisible diagonal line across the volume's pock-marked skin.

'It's nearly four hundred years old,' Victor murmurs.

It's only now that Harriet realises she's actually positioned in a dark burrow of earth where tree roots masquerade as chandeliers and musical notes are nothing more than sounds made by droplets of water as they fall into pools of dank liquid, off to her left.

Victor continues, 'Mary Harries was the first of the chosen witches. You are the second. And the book speaks of a third.'

'I've spoken to her,' Harriet says. 'Her name's Indigo Carmichael.'

Victor laughs.

'Unusual … But I suppose that is as good a name as any!'

Harriet then asks, 'But how are we connected, us three?'

Victor replies, 'I worked it out some time ago. You and Indigo are re-incarnations of Mary. Different versions of a single witch but all daughters of the Sacred Mother.'

For once, Harriet is unable to find any words.

'You're stronger together, of course,' Victor adds for good measure.

'And who exactly are the raven children you mentioned on my arrival here?' Harriet's question makes the boy withdraw further back into the splay of velvet cushions.

'They appear again and again in the handbook: vile creatures who seek to undo the work of those appointed to protect the pentacle.'

'But why are they after *you* specifically?'

Victor looks directly into Harriet's eyes.

'Because I'm an Aderyn, and they seek vengeance for what my ancestor, Abraham of Tenby, did to one of their kind, centuries ago.'

'But you're a powerful witch,' Harriet assures the boy, placing a hand on his forearm. 'Look at the marvellous sights that greeted me today.'

'Visual trickery, nothing more, miss.'

'Well, now you've performed your task and given me the handbook, perhaps you should leave Caldey?'

'It wouldn't make any difference; I'll never know peace so long as they live. Well, goodbye, Lady Gordon, until our next meeting.'

'Goodbye, King Aderyn. Enjoy what remains of your banquet!'

As Harriet feels the gentle tug of the phantom hand pinch her left shoulder, she thinks she sees the crystal chandeliers restore light to the chamber, the walls suddenly draw away from the centre of the burrow and a thousand musical notes take to the air to commence with another wondrous dance.

As she boards the ferry back to Tenby, Harriet presses the handbook close to her chest, another piece of a complex puzzle falling snugly into position. And as the boat bobs up and down on the turquoise waves, she begins to devour the text that Victor claims is over four hundred years old.

She begins with the title page, where Mary Harries and Abraham Aderyn claim dual authorship. If she had looked up, if only for the briefest of moments, she would have registered a flock of dreadful black V shapes trailing behind her boat in search of the fort, for the raven children have left Barrow Farm for the first time in centuries.

For the next five days, up to the point when Harriet re-establishes contact with Indigo Carmichael, the young witch keeps to her own domain, appearing only at mealtimes when her brother Rupert sweeps into the dining room and regales her with tales of his heroic derring-do. He bores Harriet to tears, even insisting she whoop for joy in all the right places, as if she were a member of his own troupe of court players.

Only at the mention of Prime Minister Churchill does Harriet tune back in for a moment. She wishes to personally congratulate the gentleman on his rise to power, of course, but equally scold him for his error that night out on the Point, when he cast her forward into the future with no regard for her safety.

Then one evening, when Rupert leans more towards sobriety than inebriation, he presses her for proof of her identity. Her initial instinctive suspicions about Rees-Repton have strengthened over the intervening days; she can't quite put her finger on it but she senses he is not to be trusted. Now she suspects he has orchestrated the plot to foil her, so insists she and her brother be alone for the actual producing of evidence.

'But Anthony is to act as witness!' says Rupert, forcing Harriet's hand.

'Very well,' Harriet yields. 'But your commanding officer must promise not to be shocked by any revelations concerning the character of our family; I must be assured he'll act with discretion at all times.'

'*Discretion* was my nickname at boarding school,' Rees-Repton says with great solemnity once he is in the room. It's a rather comical line which unites Harriet and Rupert – albeit briefly – drawing a chuckle from them.

The young witch then proceeds to remove three objects from her leather satchel: the handbook, the pentacle fragment and, last of all, the magical athame. She places them on the desk before the two men, much to their joint amazement.

Harriet's mouth turns quite dry as she commences, 'These once belonged to my grandmother, Harriet Gordon, formerly of St Catherine's Fort.'

'They were bequeathed to you then, upon the death of your mother?'

Harriet trembles beneath Rees-Repton's glare.

'Yes, sir. They're a rare sort of inheritance.'

But one of the objects has the desired effect of re-connecting Rupert with a forgotten version of his character – a metaphorical length of rope cast out to bridge the gap between boy and man.

'The day before Harriet disappeared, we led my poor sister a merry dance, as was our way with her.'

Harriet scowls at her brother.

Rupert continues, 'We called her names, a dozen words for a single insult. She turned on us eventually, using dark magic to read our minds and prove that afternoon she was exactly the thing we accused her of being – a *witch*!'

Harriet knows Rees-Repton is regarding her closely, so she carefully retrieves the athame from the tips of her brother's fingers as he utters the word 'witch', returning it to the desk that divides them.

'Proof then,' she concludes. 'Now, please confirm that the athame set before you today is the same one that belonged to your sister, Harriet Gordon.'

'I confirm it!' Rupert announces, finishing his whiskey with a flourish. 'Do you hear me, Anthony? This is the athame that was once the property of my dearly departed sister – easily identified by the object's unusual markings, if nothing else.'

Of course, by the time Indigo manages to secure a communication link through which the two girls can converse with one another, Harriet has read the entire contents of the handbook twice through, although not entirely understanding its meaning in places. She's relished its haphazard attempts to compile facts on ancient Craft lore, acting more than anything as a kind of compilation of useful spells and invocations. Some pages have fared better than others, so some are very hard to read. Harriet notes how the spelling of simple words alters greatly over the course of many centuries. She also finds perplexing the legibility of the handwriting styles of the volume's many contributors. The final entries she assigns to the penmanship of Victor Aderyn, whom she'd met just a few days ago.

Indigo's words are suddenly with her.

'Please accept my apologies, Harriet. This is the first chance I've had to re-establish contact with you. You have to believe me!'

And Harriet's own response, 'It's been truly dreadful. I shouldn't even be outdoors, you know, for the year is 1943 and blackout means exactly that!'

Harriet decides not to reveal to Indigo that the discovery that most of her family are dead is proving harder on the young witch's mood than any war being fought between Britain and Germany. Blackout is something she is forced to do with her feelings most hours of the day since arriving here.

Their union broken, Harriet returns to the relative safety of her room and commits Indigo's message to paper – particularly the list of ingredients she is required to set within the perfect circle of light, to have them transported to future time.

And yet the contents contain some ring of familiarity, she thinks, retrieving the handbook from its alcove beneath floorboards adjacent to her bed.

'Just as I thought,' she says, at last. 'Here it is. The very same ingredients and in an identical order to those read out by Indigo!'

It dawns on Harriet that Indigo, her sister of the broken pentacle, must already have in her possession the self-same handbook, but some 140 years into the future. *I was obviously destined to retrieve it from Caldey and bestow it somewhere here in my brother's fort*, Harriet deduces, wondering next why it is that Indigo requires Harriet's assistance in acquiring the ingredients. *Are they scarce commodities in future Britain? And what is to become of me,* muses Harriet, *as already decreed by future time? Do I perish in this war, the next one or perhaps in childbirth?*

'And so, we come to the topick of animagus stasis,' reads Harriet from the handbook, 'wherein a witche is imprisonede within a specifick animagus.'

She's positive she's also read that word – animagus – in the opening pages of the handbook. And so it is her research continues into the early hours of the next day, her quite brilliant mind establishing subtle connections between names and concepts. She draws together the disparate clues that eventually lead her, at three in the morning, to Rowan Cottage and the first of the witches: Mary Harries.

Rowan Cottage may still exist, thinks Harriet, suddenly quite overcome with tiredness, *its garden overgrown with a witch's stock of herbs and flowers.* The sound of advancing waves can be heard beyond her little window, drawing blinds of skin over Harriet's tired eyes and nudging her towards a more comforting sort of blackout.

Harriet rises late – towards noon if her bedside clock is to be believed – and curses herself for a display of idleness when time was proving such a precious commodity. She dresses quickly, splashing her face with cold water and racing through the fort like her whole life depended on locating Rowan Cottage.

'Where are you off to in such a hurry?'

Her way to open territory beyond the building is presently barred by Rees-Repton, as if he already possesses knowledge of her plan.

Harriet stands her ground.

'I promised a friend I would help her shop for a hat.'

Rees-Repton bears down on her.

'*A friend*, is it? One made in a relatively short space of time and who turns a blind eye to the sacrifices most are making at this time.'

'I trust this war is not one that will suffer too greatly if a pair of girls spend a little money on a hat, or two, Colonel?'

'You're right. You go tend to your business, Miss Elizabeth,' he says. 'Savour your afternoon shopping for hats, with your newly acquired *friend*.'

But as Harriet disappears down the steps that connect fort and beach, Rees-Repton emits a thin whistle from his lips and a dozen ravens flock to him, hanging in the air above like manifestations of his downcast mood.

'Observe her from a distance, but no losing her!'

One by one, the birds ascend the bright September air, their collective *cronks* at odds with the serene setting.

According to an old map of Tenby, which Mary and Abe had thoughtfully included in the handbook, Rowan

Cottage is situated half a mile or so out of town, on what is now a main road carrying traffic in and out. At the point where Harriet is confident there is some relationship between what the map within the handbook details and the actual physical dimensions of the road set out before her, the young witch takes stock and observes her surroundings.

'*Tenby Cemetery?*' she ponders, disappointed she's not stumbled across a quaint tumbledown cottage lost among bracken, apple trees and rhododendrons.

With a heavy heart, Harriet pushes open the iron gate and enters the grounds, suspecting she's taken a wrong turn along her journey, or miscounted the number of steps from the centre of town to her current position.

Headstones present her with innumerable blank expressions, moving off in neat horizontal lines from a central walkway. She treads lightly among the remembered and the forgotten, checking various epitaphs and dedications. Her twelve years of spirited youth and vitality tempt the nodding harebells that grow along the path to lift their chins to the sky, each flowerhead registering her presence before bowing their heads again, as if in sorrow. On she walks, wondering if Rowan Cottage ever stood here, or if its wild garden has survived the evolution from natural habitat to community cemetery.

In a few minutes she stands before the largest and most ornate of headstones as it towers above its counterparts. Harriet admires the quality of the craftsmanship on display, but also the rather perplexing message at the object's centre:

Here where the Lance and Grail unite,
And feet and knees and breast and lip.
Darkness and tears are set aside
And the Sun shall come up early.

On the same stone, the names of those people presently sharing that portion of earth: Harriet's father and mother, as well as her deceased brothers, Charles and Peter. And there, too, is her full name sitting alongside the date she disappeared.

Fresh tears sting the edges of her vision like pins heated over an open fire and applied with some pressure to the exposed flesh. Reflexively, she falls to her knees and offers a short prayer for the passing of each family member. But at the point when she recites lines she'd once learnt as a young child in Sunday school, the most astounding floral scent enters and fills her nostrils.

It seems that all about the Gordon family headstone an array of weeds, flowers and herbs has miraculously appeared, clustered tightly together. Harriet recognises a few; many are as yet unfamiliar to her. *A veritable witch's garden,* thinks Harriet.

She knows burdock, and scrabbles with her hands to dig up a chunk of root, thrusting it into her satchel. The four-leaf clover she treats with great respect as she plucks it from the soft grass. Then, having no idea what beta vulgaris or borage might look like, she pulls up one of each of the other plants growing around the grave, adding them to the store in her leather bag.

'Lance and Grail,' Harriet says under her breath, after a few minutes of gathering her thoughts, as well as more plants and flowers. 'Father and Mother, I think. 'Feet' has to be Peter for he often rushed headlong into trouble; 'knees' must be Rupert for they knocked together when even so much as a doorbell rang. 'Breast' is the female among the number: me, the witch, Harriet Gordon and 'lip' has to be Charles, the most eloquent of our clan ...' And on she continues, muttering to herself, 'I'm positive the handbook mentions Lances and Grails, as if my parents left a coded message to be deciphered all these years later. Could it be they were practising witches, themselves?'

Harriet exits the cemetery that afternoon with confusion marking her every thought and action. While high above, the sky is dotted with ravens – each pair of eyes like lumps of coal whose fuel has just been ignited.

○

That evening, Harriet leaves the fort in a similar fashion to how she'd left it seven days ago. She's packed her satchel with raw ingredients and left the handbook hidden among the family's library of reference books, enclosed in a sheet of wrapping paper. Harriet is hopeful that it will one day find its way into the hands of Indigo Carmichael. The pentacle fragment and athame she keeps close, where she can reach them with relative ease. Harriet is optimistic the raw plants will suffice, suspecting someone of Indigo's talent would be able to convert them into whatever balm or salve she desires them to become. Secretly though, Harriet plans no recurrence of her last journey into the light ring. This time she'll step into the circle with greater surety and meet up with her sisters of the sacred pentacle, changing the course of future time because she would not – indeed, could not – resign herself to a life of rationing, air raids and blackouts.

Unfortunately, at the stroke of seven, no column of light emerges from the ether, as Indigo had promised. Of course, Harriet has no idea Indigo is presently occupying a cell with a doppelganger of her own mother.

'Where are you Indigo?' she calls again, with nothing but a screeching wind for company.

After a further ten minutes of observing rapidly diminishing daylight, Harriet has to avoid a pair of sentry guards patrolling the grounds and decides to take matters into her own hands.

She stands on the same spot as she did the previous day, when Indigo had issued her instructions. Inhaling, Harriet brings the blade of her magical athame down into the lawn, carving and then stepping into a rough-edged circle. As she does so, she recites an incantation she had committed to memory that afternoon, before leaving the handbook behind in the library.

'Open for me the secret way,
The pathway of intelligence,
Beyond the gates of night and day,
Beyond the bounds of time and sense,
Behold the mystery aright:
The five true points of fellowship.'

Almost instantly, Harriet feels the pentacle fragment drive its furnace-hot metal into her skin, making her cry out in agony. She tugs at the cord on which it hangs, until it appears before her, heavy as lead and swinging with a pendulous motion, back and forth, back and forth …

A single curved wall of unrelenting white light surrounds Harriet in her makeshift circle, blotting out the world beyond and the summit of St Catherine's Point and rising up, carving space into the very air above her. Her eyes catch this or that image on the blank wall of the column's interior … And there – small comfort at last – she sees Indigo, apparently at the other end of a long corridor and staring into the light ring, her hand outstretched. She is accompanied by a tall, angular man. *Possibly her father,* thinks Harriet, noting the family resemblance.

'You're safe inside our time machine!' shouts Indigo.

Harriet presses a hand to the wall of the circle, to connect with the mirror image of Indigo on the other side of the partition.

I think I'm being presented with an image of the future, guesses Harriet, her panic increasing and realising that the face she painted onto the canvas back in the fort – was it really only last week? – was possibly her own, not Indigo's.

'I'm the sacrifice; it's me!' Harriet screams across time itself.

Future Indigo merely shakes her head as if mocking her sister and draws her hand away from the wall of dazzling lights.

Urged on by instinct alone, Harriet bangs at the protective barrier that separates the two sisters, until finally sliding down the wall next to her, quite spent.

In despair, she watches the final images playing in the light ring. Bizarrely, Indigo decreases in height and her hair gets shorter, while her father's beard disappears into minute pores in his skin, before the pair leave the room, walking backwards away from Harriet, as if time had been put into reverse. Finally beaten, Harriet closes her mind to the impossibility of it all …

She's next awoken by the hushed tones of the man she'd last seen standing alongside Indigo in her unusual premonition.

'Hello. I'm Professor Carmichael. Welcome to the future, young lady.'

Harriet looks about her at the grey walls of the room, hoping to spot Indigo.

'And what do we have here?' he asks.

Half-girl, half-fox, Harriet scratches at Carmichael with sharp talons that have extended beyond the pads of her paws, reclaiming the pentacle fragment and satchel from the scientist in a flurry of skin and fur.

Meeting of the Rivers

Tenby, Wales, 2080

Only when the small white mouse reverts to its original shape – that of a four-foot-tall girl – does Helen Carmichael's panic eventually subside. She had raised a hand in self-defence and the forefinger on her right hand is still arched high above the young witch when, shocked rigid by the transformation she has just witnessed, she gasps, 'Imogen?'

'Indigo, actually,' says the young girl, straightening her hair and pressing a hand to her throat in search of Mary's magical necklace. Her stomach gives a lurch as she realises the precious artefact is missing, that it must have caught on something as she transformed, back in the laboratory, and that she will have to find some way to retrieve it. Then she realises she is being stared at by Helen Carmichael.

'Forgive me, you look so like my daughter.'

Indigo, unsure how to respond to this, says, 'Well, I've long suspected my father capable of unethical practice, but kidnapping people I'd always put beyond him.'

'The man who was in here a moment ago, that's your father, I take it?'

'Lance Carmichael, yes.'

'A scientist capable of … How did you phrase it – *unethical practice?*'

'Never done with any sort of malice, you understand,' Indigo says, patting the space next to her on the bed. 'But, yes, I'd say pretty unethical.'

Helen is keen to find out more.

'How exactly did he manage to bring me here?'

'What do you remember of the final moments before you were taken?'

Indigo watches the woman's mouth loosen as she relays her tale.

'Well, I was unrolling a blanket in preparation for a picnic. Me and my daughter were in the grounds of an old, ruined fort. We've loved Tenby for as long as I can remember, and we always holiday here at least once a year. Just me and Imogen.'

'*Fort*, you say?'

'Yes, St Valentine's Fort. It's been pretty much unoccupied since the close of the Third Age, if my schoolgirl history could be called reliable.'

'Interesting. Please, go on.'

'Then I saw Imogen getting very close to the edge of the cliff.'

Helen remembers then, with some clarity, the moment of her departure. Tiny tears flash here and there in her blue eyes.

'Suddenly, a brilliant column of light appeared at the edge of the blanket and rose up from the ground.'

'It sounds like Father has finally found a way to open doors between universes!'

'He continually makes the error of calling me Hilary, by the way. Is that your mother's name by any chance?'

Indigo peers beyond the small oval window in the cell door.

'*Was* … My mother's dead.'

Helen places a sympathetic hand on the young witch's shoulder.

'I'm genuinely sorry for upsetting you. You have a good soul. And I'm sorry about your mum … I hear others cry out, you know. Other women and men, as well as children.'

'Time-napped,' Indigo says. 'Yes, I suppose that's all any of you are to my father: displaced objects, plucked from other universes with no thought for what happens next.'

'If you're so against his work, you must help us escape,' Helen says at last. 'Try to help me and the rest of your father's prisoners get home.'

'Home … Yes,' agrees Indigo, turning her attention to the problem of the locked door and away from the prisoner, who is now smiling.

Harriet follows Lance Carmichael down a number of featureless corridors, as if she were working her way through the intestines of a giant serpent. Every so often, strip lighting appears above their heads to make shadows of them. She grasps her satchel ever more tightly and purposefully breathes in the clinical air of the building. She still hasn't quite understood how she managed to conjure the magical circle. *Or had such merely coincided with the scientist's plan to open up a portal between two worlds?* she wonders. Harriet has many more burning questions and, now her form once more resembles a human, she ventures to speak.

'Where are we going?'

'All in good time,' says the professor, without turning to face her.

Harriet decides not to mention Indigo, concerned it might indicate an established relationship between the two girls.

'Anyway, what year do you think it is, Miss Gordon?'

Harriet thinks carefully before replying for, strictly speaking, she does not belong to any particular time. She says, with a certain dose of ambiguity, 'I'm of my time, sir, neither predisposed to dwelling on the past, nor overly concerned with the future.'

'A radical then, living comfortably out of step with modern man's pre-occupation with time!'

Harriet registers the cold metal of the athame against her thigh and the pentacle fragment looped about her throat, its metal reflecting the pale glow of her skin.

'We're here,' says Carmichael after a minute or so, tapping a series of numbers into a keypad and making a heavy door swing out and away from them.

What, a prison? Harriet thinks as she moves over a line in the concrete floor and into a very different part of the building.

At first glance, it doesn't appear the room has about it the qualities of a jail, as people mill about the space rather peacefully, or are sat at small tables arranged in the centre of the room, many of them playing board games or cards. What is immediately obvious is that the room's occupants appear to be drawn from wildly different social strata; such a disparate collection of individuals would never intentionally spend time with one another. *Something, or someone, has forced them to live together*, she thinks.

'I notice none of your guests are smiling, Professor,'

'Well, I suspect many of them are inconsolable with grief.'

Harriet turns to him.

'Why should they be grieving?'

Carmichael chooses his words carefully.

'Unlike you, Miss Gordon, my *guests* here are certainly *of a particular time* – and long to be returned to loved ones.'

'What are they waiting for?'

'A miracle, I should imagine.'

One of the captives, an old man, stops a little way short of the pair. He stands no taller than Harriet's five feet in height and possesses a bald pate atop his head that slowly leads the eye down to tight white curls above both ears. Harriet thinks there's something familiar about the gentleman, particularly in his manner of dress, which is positively Victorian in her eyes; in many ways, he makes her pine for home.

Carmichael's tone is sharp when he says, 'What is it, Charles?'

'Professor, I was wondering if it would be possible to procure a fresh supply of notepaper?'

'I'm sure that can be arranged,' says Carmichael, tapping at his temple. 'Have made a mental note: *more stationery for Mr Darwin*. Now, on your way, old chap.'

Harriet's eyes become little saucers of surprise, as the old man ambles back to his chair.

'Darwin … as in *Charles Darwin*?'

'You've heard of him, perhaps?'

Harriet struggles to find the words, 'Heard of him? He's a hero of mine!'

'Well, a devotee of *the* Charles Darwin you shall remain, for that man is a pale imitation of the genius that occupies a special place in both our hearts.'

'Forgive me, I don't follow. You, yourself, addressed him as *Charles Darwin*.'

Carmichael coughs once, gently done and into a cupped hand as if clearing his throat of a deception.

'I think it's time you learnt more about my research, Miss Gordon. Over the last few years I've been busy experimenting with time machines.'

Harriet's mouth gapes open. She has privately longed to meet an inventor whose contribution to the scientific community had been the design and development of such a machine, as once detailed by Bert Wells in a mere fiction.

'Well,' Carmichael says with some modesty, waving his hand before the hall of weary-eyed occupants. 'One machine I created is capable of bending the fabric of space-time itself, opening little windows onto other universes. But, Miss Gordon, my invention has always been unable to locate intervals of experience along *a singular timeline*, as it were, only presenting me with versions of history *similar* to one another.'

For all her bravado, Harriet is quite lost for words, her Victorian mind struggling to make sense of the information.

'Imagine, if you can,' the professor says, 'a book with no start and no conclusion. It is laid open and face up. The *present*, per se, is an unmarked sheet of paper placed on top of the most recent leaf, refreshed with each second of time that elapses. Now, let's see if I can employ a metaphor to help represent my machine to someone with your ... *sensibilities*, I should say. Ah, yes: a letter knife. Imagine if you were able to insert a letter knife into such a tome. Yes?'

Harriet thinks of her athame, nodding once for Carmichael to continue.

'Now, Miss Gordon. My problem has always been that every time I insert my knife into the book – looking for a familiar page perhaps, or a character description one is fond of – I could only ever open the book to a random page. And should I use the knife to remove a page from the book, I found I was in an entirely different book altogether! Adding to my complications, each time I withdrew my knife it brought a page with it – *character description and all* – but subtly altered in some way, making it unique from all the other pages in unfathomable numbers of unseen books.'

'Gosh,' enthuses Harriet. 'Hence, why your Charles Darwin over there isn't the same genius we both respect and admire?'

Carmichael smiles. 'Exactly; nor could he ever be, Miss Gordon!'

'He's a version of the original but doomed to walk the earth as an inferior model. What a pity!'

Carmichael seeks to correct his young companion.

'No, *not inferior*, Miss Gordon. Less offensive than that: let's say *different*. Less prolific, yes, but potentially no less useful to his or her society.'

Harriet smiles. 'But what has all this got to do with me, Professor?'

Her question is blunt and throws Carmichael for a moment, before he recovers.

'Well, I consider it safe to say you are the first page to be extracted from a book that belongs to *my* timeline, Miss Gordon.'

Harriet's mind races and connects an assortment of facts and concepts. She is slowly able to fathom why Indigo had contacted her to secure the ingredients now contained within Harriet's satchel. It also dawns on Harriet she wasn't the first of the sisters to be removed from their original timelines, even if the professor believed such to be the case.

Harriet says eventually, 'But it could be said, sir, that it was I that found you.'

'That's surely a matter of perspective,' says Carmichael, guiding Harriet away from what she has now realised are prisoners, rather than guests, and towards the room's exit.

Deep in the bowels of the complex, a small hare reaches the summit of its patience, kicking its powerful hind legs against the wire front of its cage. Mary knows that as each minute crawls into the next, her human characteristics continue to dissolve before her twitching nose, her whole identity being replaced by that of a mammal whose daily routine requires her merely to hop about, munch on discarded vegetable matter and defecate into clumps of straw.

A forceful thump and thwack to the metal grid leaves her exhausted and in need of a rest but, drawing a fresh lungful of air, she returns to the task with a renewed determination to succeed.

'What's your problem then, eh missy?'

Mary turns and looks up at the zoo attendant, Michael Kilpenny, a short, ruddy-cheeked individual who enjoys abusing each of the specimens in his care when he's feeling ill-tempered. This, though, is always done when Indigo is absent, for fear of being exposed as a bully. Mary especially hates the way that, in the pelt of a lowly hare, she can't issue a suitable response, or a disarming spell. Instead, she backs into one corner of the tiny hutch and hopes her persecutor will move onto the next one.

'Trying to stir up trouble are you, eh missy?'

Kilpenny makes a visual check of the compound, undoubtedly looking for signs of human activity. Then, discovering he's alone, he pulls at the bunch of keys tied to his belt. The spill of metal rattles in his grip until he locates the correct key and opens her cage.

'You've had this coming for a long time, eh missy?'

It dawns on Mary that the attendant comically frames every one of his sentences as a question.

'You going to cause me trouble now, eh missy?'

But as Kilpenny reveals to her his weapon of choice – a short horsewhip that he uses on all manner of creatures, save for the horses – Mary darts between the legs of the attendant in a bid to secure her freedom, strewing bedding in her wake.

'Where do you think you're going then, eh missy?'

Kilpenny turns, comically slipping on the straw. 'Dare to escape from me, eh missy?'

Mary doesn't look back. Not once does she pause to guess at the distance she has already set between herself and the breathless, slipping and sliding attendant.

He knows he is in trouble, now he has let one of Indigo's favourite creatures escape.

'Trying your luck now, missy?'

Mary speeds around the perimeter of the zoo, her small body a powerhouse of fur and muscle that flies past the cells of creatures currently beyond her help.

'Scare your fellow inmates will you, missy?'

Kilpenny follows on Mary's heels, horsewhip lashing out before him in arcs of perfect dread. Mary leaps and bounds for her dear life, wondering how long this will continue before one of them tires of the chase.

'Running out of steam, eh missy?'

At the very point when Mary thinks she's unable to muster up the willpower to begin another circuit of the compound, a door opens in an otherwise featureless wall of concrete, revealing a way out of her present situation.

'Close the door, eh, Agatha?'

But before Michael's one-time colleague – now sweetheart – makes sense of the commotion, Mary darts through the girl's legs and into the corridor beyond.

'See what an error you've made, my girl?'

'What on earth is going on, Michael Kilpenny?'

Kilpenny comes to an abrupt halt as he crashes into Agatha and sends both of them to the floor, much to the amusement of the other creatures locked in their cells, whose braying and neighing now reaches a deafening pitch.

It takes Indigo a full hour of furious rapping at the cell door before she manages to gain the attention of a guard. Releasing her, he doesn't ask questions as to how she's managed to lock herself within the room, only insists that she contacts her father immediately to report she's safe. *He's probably yet to notice I'm missing*, thinks Indigo, rather morosely. She winks once to Helen as she exits the cell to enter the dark corridor. The prisoner winks back, and Indigo is certain their paths will cross again before too long.

As she turns away, the young witch has to perform a little sidestep to avoid her left foot connecting with a small creature that dashes past her.

Indigo calls out, 'Mary?'

Kilpenny and Agatha are hard on the creature's heels but slide to a standstill when they come face to face with Indigo.

'Miss Carmichael, is that you?'

'Yes, Michael. Now what exactly are you both doing down here?'

'Your hare, miss, it got out,' he gasps, panting hard from the exertion of the chase.

Indigo can't conceal her disappointment, showing as two ruby red cheeks and scrunched-up fists.

'I can see that, Michael, but how did she *get out* exactly? You were asked to keep a close eye on that hare above all other creatures.'

126

Kilpenny straightens up, still puffing and blowing, and whines, 'I tried, Miss Carmichael, but it *wanted to get away*, do you follow me?'

'I think it's *you* who is doing the following, Mister Kilpenny.'

Agatha suddenly pokes her head out from behind Kilpenny and pipes up, 'Oh, very good, Miss Carmichael, him doing the following, very funny!'

Kilpenny drives an elbow into Agatha's ribs, looking beyond Indigo and into the murky distance of the corridor.

'Do you think you ought to go after the hare then, Miss Carmichael?'

'I do. But this is as far as *you* go, Michael.'

Kilpenny seems genuinely disappointed that the hare has managed to escape.

'Really miss, you'll give chase alone?'

Indigo directs her next comment at Agatha, who seems far more open to instruction.

'Take him to your quarters, before he does himself a serious injury. I'll have one of the others lock up the zoo for the night.'

Harriet continues her tour of the complex at the heels of the professor, her muscles aching for a period of rest. The ceaseless adventuring of the last few days is finally catching up with her and can be seen in dark circles beneath her eyes and in two hollowed-out cheeks. As they walk, the professor reads out his list of house rules for the complex, with the stern warning that if Harriet breaks any one of them she will be punished with a lengthy period in an isolation cell, located far beneath her present position. She is left to guess how many prisoners have already been assigned such a ghastly fate, but suspects there are more dissenters than there are those willing to adhere to his set of rules.

'You're free to treat this as your home, unless you prove to me you need closer monitoring, Miss Gordon.'

Harriet is heartened by the news.

'Do you have any family, Professor?'

'Only a daughter,' he replies, suddenly remembering he hasn't seen her for some hours, 'Indigo.'

At mention of the name, Harriet's spirits lift. She knows the time is fast approaching when the two girls will finally meet in person.

'You'll be good for her,' he murmurs.

'I don't easily forge friendships with those my own age,' warns Harriet.

The pair swing sharply into a large room whose air has the familiar homely smells of a Victorian kitchen, yet somehow less savoury. *More … artificial*, thinks Harriet as she's introduced to a robust woman whose official title, she's been told, is that of head cook.

'Mrs Dalrymple,' the woman splutters, extending a hand of goodwill, her tunic quite stained with the juice of the freeze-dried fruit she has been reconstituting.

Harriet returns the handshake, smiling.

'Harriet Gordon, pleased to meet you.'

As is common when this precocious child is introduced to adults, a flicker of mischief passes between the two, as if they are already accomplices in some foul plan.

Carmichael seems pre-occupied, saying abruptly, 'Mrs Dalrymple, please have one of your staff escort Harriet back to her quarters in the guest wing, once she's done here. I have to make an important call.'

'Of course, Professor, off you go.'

On his way out, Carmichael turns one last time to say to Harriet, 'Tomorrow, we'll meet for breakfast and talk some more of how exactly you came to be here.'

In an instant he's gone, Cook turning to Harriet and saying, 'The professor has a brilliant mind, you know. It's just his heart that needs fixing.'

Harriet climbs onto a stool directly to the left of the range, peering over the rim of the cooking pot.

'May I be as bold as to inquire what it is you're cooking, Mrs Dalrymple?'

'Mush, child, *pure mush* – for the less honoured of the professor's *guests*. And please, call me Mrs D.'

The young witch watches on as the mixture within the pan thickens and turns a dark green colour.

'What's it doing now?'

'Emulsifying, in its tragic quest to become edible food, child!'

Harriet leans closer still, ready to pass judgment on the woman's efforts, but is nudged away by Cook.

'Be careful not to tumble, child.'

'I'm hungry myself, but it must be said I possess not the stomach for your *mush*, Mrs D.'

Cook issues a little laugh. 'You've certainly got a way with words, young lady. But it's not as bad as it looks, or smells, for that matter. Anyhows, it's all the masters see fit to feed those in their care.'

Harriet is intrigued. '*Masters?*'

'Those who pay our wages and made it possible to poach you from your particular river.'

Harriet senses the old woman has details of how the young witch had come to travel through time. But she is entirely unsure how much she should reveal to a relative stranger, opting to say, 'Actually, I'm here to deliver a number of special ingredients to the professor's daughter.'

At the news, Mrs Dalrymple's whole countenance changes, her normally black eyes becoming two stoked embers.

'Ingredients, you say?'

'Yes. They're in my satchel, guarded until such a time when they can be used to aid a fellow witch.'

'I see.'

The old woman smiles, quickly drying her hands on her apron. 'I haven't always been such a rotten cook, you know. It's what I have to work with, these days. I learnt from my grandmother how to cook proper dishes, Miss Gordon. She taught me a number of mouth-watering recipes before she passed on.'

Harriet decides to give the old woman her full attention.

'But dear Earth has become crippled, child. We've used up all her resources. Taken what we want for ourselves and left nothing for future generations. Like the dark-hearted creatures we are, we've had to bury ourselves deep underground, in complexes just like this one, because the Mother Goddess's lungs are choked with soot and carbon; her blood runs with sewage and chemicals; the lengths of her legs – and even the nape of her neck – have been cultivated and developed until there's now no sign of her skin; crops are dead before we've planted the first seed in her diseased soil. And me? I'm left to serve *mush*: modified, starchy mush, packed with scientifically engineered numbers.'

With Mrs Dalrymple close to tears, Harriet unbuckles her satchel and pushes her fingers through the dark interior of the bag. She soon locates the handfuls of herbs and roots she'd only that morning plucked from around the Gordon family grave and holds them out to show the older woman.

'My goodness, child!' says Mrs D, her eyes damp with upset but now twinkling in the murky light of the kitchen. 'Where did you manage to find those?'

The hare's instinct to keep running takes it ever further from its cage and into territory it hasn't seen before. Deep beneath its skin moves Mary Harries, desperate to take command but failing miserably. With every step the hare takes, Mary's control over its actions continues to weaken, her old life rapidly becoming a series of unconnected images and feelings … *A candle, a mattress riddled with lice, a circle of light, an open grave, a cat by the hearth, a black mirror, a twig …*

'Mary, stop at once! It's me, Indigo!'

But the hare fails to make sense of the words, slipping effortlessly past another human – this time, the professor – even weaving a figure of eight around his ankles. He's too pre-occupied though to stop, and his inattention allows the hare to move further into the complex, soon arriving at a set of double doors that cuts short its progress.

On recognising her father, Indigo slips into the crevice of a doorway, its shadow providing her with temporary cover.

'Indigo – is that you?'

The young witch dares not move. He's seen me – or at least part of me – disappear into the alcove, perhaps, she thinks. Or has he sensed my presence, as if he himself possessed the intuitive skills of a Knowing One?

When there is no response to his call, satisfied he was mistaken in thinking his daughter is close at hand, the professor walks on, checking his watch and tapping at the dial in frustration.

Meanwhile, the hare noses at the gap beneath the double doors and decides to press its full weight against them. Finally, and after a few failed attempts, Mary exhibits one last display of control over the poor creature and has it lunge at the hinged oblongs of reinforced steel. This sends it headfirst into the kitchen, paws stretched out before it to cushion the impact of its forward-careering motion.

Harriet is first to spot it, shouting, 'A hare!'

Followed by Mrs D, '*In my kitchen*? How did it get in here? The masters would close me down if they were to find out!'

Harriet moves quickly, saying, 'We must remain calm if we wish to capture it!'

The hare continues to dart this way and that out of sheer panic, soon to realise it's arrived at a dead end.

At this point, Mary Harries allows the creature full control of her faculties, losing sight of the line that separates her behaviour from the ways of the creature.

'Shh, there, there,' Harriet says soothingly, edging close to the hare now it's been backed into a space between the sink and a nearby cupboard.

And then, quite suddenly, the hare's breathing becomes laboured, its heart stepping very close to collapse. Exhausted, it lies flat on its stomach, the very picture of submission.

'By the ears, Miss Gordon, just like so! One hand under its legs and the other round its ears!' shouts Cook, demonstrating for the young witch how to handle the hare.

'Mrs D, step away from your stewing pot!'

The old woman and Harriet suddenly turn to experience the full wrath of Indigo Carmichael, who has entered the kitchen with panic framing her every action. Her whole face is contorted at the sight of Mrs

Dalrymple standing next to a cooking pot, hare in hand, as if to dispatch Mary Harries that instant.

So, it comes to pass that several tributaries meet and form a single river. In Harriet Gordon's sapphire-blue eyes there shine the twin lights of optimism and intellect. In Indigo's eyes – a rich hazel brown – one is given the impression that the challenges of living with limited vision and less-than-perfect lungs make for a more taxing daily existence. However, it's clear to see that she is no less resourceful than the girl from the Victorian era. And yet there is, in Indigo, something of the Mother Goddess's sad plight from bounteous to ravaged. It can be seen in the delicate silhouettes of shadows stationed about each iris and is present, too, in the deathly pallor of her skin.

'Indigo! It is I, Harriet Gordon!'

Indigo, though she knows the space well, moves cautiously through it, feeling her way until she comes face to face with Harriet; in some ways it was easier to see her through the vast chasm of time.

'Honoured to meet you, Harriet Gordon.'

'What exactly am I to do with this creature, then, Miss Carmichael?'

Locked in a trance, the young witches had clean forgotten about the third member of their unique coven: Mary Harries. The whites of the hare's eyes presently point earthwards to the dangers contained within Mrs D's stewing pot.

Indigo steps forward, saying, 'Ah yes, of course, the hare.'

She then procures the affrighted hare from Mrs D and smooths its forehead using her free hand.

'Mary Harries, meet Harriet Gordon, your saviour. Assuming she's managed to locate the ingredients needed for your elixir?'

Harriet takes the hare's paw and shakes it with calm authority, her brow raised in deference.

'The pleasure is all mine, I can assure you, Miss Harries.'

The two girls laugh together before Harriet turns to the important business of sorting the herbs and roots, which she had placed on a nearby chopping board on the sudden appearance of Mary Harries. She looks up at the bemused cook.

'Mrs D, you are hereby required to set aside your menial duties as cook and help create an infusion that will cure a fellow sister of an affliction.'

Mrs D shows concern at Harriet's words.

'*Affliction*, you say?'

'Animagus stasis can leave a victim permanently locked within the body and mind of a witch's chosen creature. Should we leave things as they stand …'

'Of course, Miss Gordon.'

Indigo remembers that the handbook, which will provide some sort of structure to their joint experiment, is presently located beneath her bed. Simultaneously, Harriet asks, 'You found the handbook I left you?' Indigo's eyes light up in recognition of this shared thought and she abruptly leaves the room to go in search of the book, full of high spirits, calling over her shoulder, 'I'll be back shortly. Begin by –'

'– preparing the ingredients,' Harriet finishes, just in time to see her sister disappear through the large double doors that lead back out into the complex.

'What can I do to help?' asks Mrs D.

Harriet answers immediately, 'Well, you can begin by boiling some water. And then you could perhaps explain to me why it is you're not in the least bit fazed by our talk of ancient witchcraft lore and practices.'

Indigo contemplates a great deal during the short trip to her room. Unlike her father, who possesses a mind predisposed to accepting scientific truths above all else, the young witch believes that all life has been designed with some higher purpose in mind. She doesn't exactly understand how she's come to play such a significant role in a plot to reunite fragments of a witch's sacred pentacle, only that she should carry out her duty with the necessary level of commitment. She feels sure that she, Harriet and Mary will soon exchange stories and somehow make sense of the situation. Already, Indigo feels stronger, inwardly and outwardly more confident than she'd felt prior to meeting the first of her sisters. *If that is what we are*, she thinks. She privately suspects Harriet experienced a similar feeling of unification when they met for the first time.

Only on the half-sprint from her room back to the kitchen – moving as fast as she can tap her stick in front of her and clasping the handbook tightly against her chest with the other hand – does Indigo's faith in her new enterprise suffer a blow. She hears her father's voice and stops dead in her tracks.

Yes, there he is, sitting in a high-backed chair opposite his beloved computer. The little light above the machine's display unit is flashing on and off to signify a communication link is running.

'I'm positive the girl is different to the other subjects,' says Carmichael.

Indigo notes the cool edges of Rees-Repton's head filling the monitor, before she withdraws back into the shadows.

Rees-Repton's voice is sullen.

'How exactly did you manage to locate her, Professor?'

Carmichael clears his throat before answering, his swivel chair moving gently with his weight.

'I don't know. Something told me ... A voice, perhaps ... I know it sounds odd, but it's as if she called me to the portal.'

'A powerful witch indeed,' Rees-Repton growls.

'More importantly,' the professor adds, 'she has the pentacle fragment hanging about her neck, displayed for all to see.'

Rees-Repton's image increases in size, as if leaning forward to search out Indigo and any other eavesdroppers within range, before whispering, 'Make sure the fragment "falls into the wrong hands", Professor.'

Indigo's heart sinks, unable to accept her own father has allowed himself to become a puppet of Sentinel Technologies.

Rees-Repton's voice draws her back from her thoughts.

'I sense you're straying, Lance.'

'Not at all,' Carmichael assures his superior. 'It's just … I can't help …'

Rees-Repton cuts in, 'You're thinking perhaps the woman you have under lock and key is not enough? That the girl's appearance offers some proof that time travel within a single dimension is actually possible? And you're now considering the unthinkable.'

Indigo leans towards the edge of the door, the weight of the book beneath her arm making it ache.

'The *unthinkable*, sir? I cannot guess what you mean by using that word,' remarks Carmichael, his voice close to cracking.

Rees-Repton continues, 'Why, nothing other than using the pentacle fragment to locate the four remaining pieces, Professor. And then, once complete, harnessing the power within the sacred pentacle to reverse the direction of time itself.'

Indigo lets out a little gasp, only partially recovering enough to hear her father say to Rees-Repton, 'That's a myth, Oliver, a silly story that did the rounds at boarding school. We were kids back then and prone to believe such nonsense.'

A disgruntled Rees-Repton issues his final words on the matter, his delivery crisp and without sentiment.

'You would sacrifice everything to be with her again, wouldn't you, Lance? Yes, even your own daughter.'

Indigo slips away from the open door, her head full to bursting with information and her heart completely broken.

○

Within the hour, Mrs Dalrymple begins to prove her worth as cook of a different sort, as she assembles the ancient infusion detailed in the handbook. Indigo reads aloud from the yellowed pages, as if peeling multiple skins from the body of a snake.

Harriet is resigned to keeping the hare firmly within her grasp, its tiny heart outpacing her own pulse three to one. 'Not long now, Mary Harries,' she soothes, the creature's delicate nostrils twitching as they trace faint odours on the air. Clover, beta vulgaris, burdock root and borage – the various fragrances intermingle until a single scent rises from the pot like a curse, ripe for utterance.

Indigo suddenly says, 'Oh dear, the recipe states the beta vulgaris should be distilled essence.'

'We simply don't have time to make that,' remarks Harriet.

'We shall have to hope,' Indigo continues, 'that in one as young as Mary, the method for creating the infusion does not have to be strictly followed in order for it to prove successful.'

Mrs D now cuts in with, 'You could try using the power of the pentacle, Miss Carmichael.'

Harriet and Indigo exchange uneasy glances, before Cook adds, 'I told Miss Gordon while you were out collecting the handbook, so you'd best know yourself. I'm a direct descendent of those who once witnessed the forging of the sacred pentacle. I'm what's known as a Watcher.'

Indigo is relieved to discover that Mrs D possesses intimate knowledge of pentacle lore, as well as its true, but as yet unspecified, purpose.

'There are Watchers everywhere apparently,' Harriet puts forward, as if she were one herself.

Even with this recent revelation, Indigo fails to see how the pentacle fragment could be of use in terms of the beta vulgaris plant they have in their possession, pointing such out to the others around her.

'Well,' Mrs Dalrymple says, 'the pentacle responds to the subconscious desires of its keeper. It's an incredibly powerful object, miss, especially when used in combination with a second object bound to it by the same ancient magic.'

'The athame!' shouts Harriet. Hurriedly handing the hare, which for some time has been lying passively in her arms, to Indigo, she scrabbles under her skirt for a second or two before producing the ancient blade. The old woman grows stern for a second, warning, 'The athame is bound to the sacred pentacle, Miss Gordon, and can never be the property of the witch overseeing its safe-keeping. Hand them to your sister, if you please, and the pentacle fragment, also. If she is the Last of the Knowing Ones, she's rightful keeper of both objects.'

Harriet doesn't know what to say. She wonders if she has merely acted as some elaborate vehicle to transport said artefacts across almost two hundred years, to be rewarded with nothing more than an instruction to hand them over to a girl she'd first captured in paint form and only met for the first time this afternoon.

'But I'm also a witch,' says Harriet, gripping the fragment to her throat and turning the athame over in one hand.

'That you are,' agrees Mrs D, approaching the girl and stroking her hair with the tenderness of a mother, 'but the prophecy states the sacred pentacle can only be reassembled by the last of the great witches. It now looks increasingly likely that honour will fall to Miss Carmichael here.'

Harriet is quietly incensed, but her better sense of propriety allows her to submit to the Watcher's wishes, dutifully exchanging the hare for the athame and pentacle fragment.

Indigo accepts them with half a spirit, mindful of her sister's upset and not wishing to aggravate it any further.

'Miss Carmichael,' Cook says. 'Accept these sacred objects into your life and use them sparingly, for unlocking the great, ancient magic locked within each of them will alter you in unimaginable ways, and not always for the better. With great power, comes great responsibility.'

Mrs Dalrymple now urges the young witch forward to the stewing pot, which has by now become a bubbling cauldron. Indigo places the pentacle fragment about her throat – the chain on which it hangs warming instantly to her skin – while Harriet looks on with a simmering envy. Indigo then stands above the pot, her left hand bunched with beta vulgaris and her right hand gripping the athame. Led by instinct and an assuring nod from Mrs Dalrymple, she stirs the mixture with the tip of the knife, creating a whirlpool in the liquid that spins anti-clockwise against the edges of the pot. And then, as the beta vulgaris falls through air to reach its destination at the centre of the circle, steam rises from the infusion and melts the roots, stalks and leaves of the plant. It enters the body of boiling water as a distillate, the powerful magic forming a bridge between the *possible* and the *impossible*.

'Now you can help,' whispers Cook to Harriet and pointing to the handbook with evident glee. 'Locate the relevant spell to reverse an animagus stasis curse.'

Harriet perches on a stool at the long counter, the precious handbook in front of her. With some difficulty, as her left arm is already employed in keeping the hare on her lap, Harriet flicks through the pages she'd once pored over with an insatiable appetite to devour every word set within its borders.

'Here,' she says at last, the hare reaching its nose forward and sniffing at the mouldy tome. 'Should I read it aloud?'

'Now, would be good,' nods Cook. 'Let's see if this hare is more than just a hare!'

'Eko, Eko, Azarek,' Harriet begins, her words tumbling forth from her lips. 'Eko, Eko, Zomelak, Eko, Eko, Cernunnos, Eko, Eko, Aradia!'

Here she pauses for the hare in her hands to receive a spoonful of the magical infusion, administered by a smiling Mrs Dalrymple.

Harriet continues, watched closely by Indigo who seems lost to the spectacle of the ritual.

'Oh, Crafters of Heaven, oh Crafters of Hell,
Lend your power unto our spell.
By all the might of Moon and Sun,
Chant the spell and be it done!'

Harriet thrusts her right hand skyward, instinctively releasing the spell into the universe to do its work.

'Well done, girls,' says Mrs D, looking rather exhausted from the ordeal.

The hare suddenly bucks and somersaults out of Harriet's grasp, leaping for freedom and bounding across the kitchen's many counters.

'It mustn't get away!' Indigo cries out, the athame thrust out before her as if to underscore her point.

'It's happening!' shouts Cook. 'Its ears are shrinking … Its legs are changing shape … Its paws are becoming hands … Its hair is turning to smooth skin!'

'Mary Harries!' Indigo confirms for everyone as the hare's transformation nears completion and it suddenly reverts to a twelve-year-old girl.

'Incredible!' says Harriet, noticing only then the girl nestled in one corner of the kitchen hasn't the faintest idea where she is or how she arrived there, but is scrabbling frantically at her chest as if in search of some precious object.

'Her pendant, of course!' Indigo guesses, approaching Mary. 'I used it to become a mouse and I expect it is where I left it: in Father's broadcast portal room.'

Harriet stares into the eyes of creature-turned-human, Mary's rag dress and moth-eaten cloak drawing a little sympathy from the more privileged of the two girls.

'My name's Harriet,' she says, offering the hand of friendship. 'Hello, Mary.'

'Don't crowd her,' warns Cook. 'Give her a little space.'

Indigo soon has the group ready to depart the kitchen, wondering to herself if her plan is a sensible one after all. She tells Harriet, 'We can collect Mary's pendant on the way to my room.'

All set, the three witches are soon tiptoeing into the corridor that will take them one step closer to realising their collective destiny – but also send them headlong into dangers they thought were the premise of storybooks and nightmares.

Sisterhood

Nightmares of varying strength and character plague one particular sister of the broken pentacle. She's been asleep for hours, watched over by Indigo and Harriet, carrying out a shared vigil. Every now and then, Mary tosses and turns, *like the raging seas beyond the walls of the complex*, thinks Indigo.

'Abe!' Mary cries out, eyes flickering open and showing she's finally returning to the present. Mention of the name has the effect of drawing the two girls to her side.

Harriet whispers to Indigo alone, 'As in *Abe Aderyn*?'

'I would imagine so.'

Harriet strokes the backs of Mary's hands, as she might the paws of a sick animal. 'The same Abe she later comes to marry and with whom she helps start our handbook?'

Mary draws her knees tightly to her chest, now fully awake. '*Marry?*' she says.

Indigo is quickly on her feet, of all things panicking over the lateness of the hour. 'Goodness, we'll be late for breakfast!'

Harriet tears herself away from Mary, whose unblinking stare she is finding quite unsettling. 'We'll explain everything once you've had chance to … adjust,' she assures her sister, squeezing her shoulder. 'If it's any consolation, most of my family passed away in the blinking of an eye … just like that!' Harriet clicks her fingers for effect, stressing each syllable in *just like that*.

Mary stands, rising to confront her. 'So were my family, Harriet, but the plague took them!'

Indigo steps between the two girls. 'Let's agree that we have much in common. We've all lost parents, in one way or another, and that makes us into sisters of a sort. We certainly can't spend our first days together quibbling over whose situation qualifies as the most awful.'

Harriet immediately backs down, offering Mary the hand of friendship, which her sister takes with some reluctance.

Mary says, 'I'll wait here until your breakfast is over, but no longer. I intend to leave this place as soon as possible.'

'*Leave?*' asks Indigo. 'And go where exactly?'

'Well, I'm no longer a hare and, as grateful as I am to you for saving me from a fate worse than death, I've not returned to human form to be locked away beneath the earth for very much longer.'

Indigo looks again at her watch.

'I can't explain properly now, Mary, but you mustn't go against my wishes and attempt to leave the complex without the correct equipment. The air above ground is toxic, potentially lethal. Like one of your plagues, only worse.'

Harriet provides further guidance.

'She means the world outside of here is poisonous, Mary, like a disease of the lungs.'

'Okay then,' Indigo says. 'Now remember, we'll be back as soon as breakfast is over. We promise.'

Mary issues a half-nod, Harriet managing to place the *Handbook for Witches of the Broken Pentacle* squarely in the girl's lap, before being whisked out of the door by a rather flustered Indigo.

Alone, Mary turns the volume over in her hands. She grips the book's outer cover and peels it back to reveal the first of its pages. Thank goodness her mother had taken the time to teach Mary the basics of reading and writing; a privilege not afforded many children her age, especially girls.

'My name is included here,' she says to herself.

Her eyes widen even further when she deciphers a name positioned next to hers: *Abraham Aderyn*.

She promptly closes the book and throws it to the floor, the text skidding away from her and landing heavily against a distant wall.

'The magic here is dark in nature.'

Before she knows what she's doing, she's up on her feet and heading for the door.

○

Harriet is first to break the silence as the two girls make their way to the fort's dining room.

'I worry about Mary.'

'She'll be okay, I'm sure of it. She just needs more time to adapt. Not all time-travellers are as experienced as you, Harriet.'

'I mean, it doesn't exactly help she belongs to the seventeenth century either,' Harriet explains. 'For you and I are closer in terms of ideology, education, culture –'

Indigo stops mid-stride.

'You mustn't do this, Harriet.'

'Do what?'

'Draw the two of us together in an imagined conspiracy and leave Mary to one side, as an outsider. It's not at all helpful and I wonder about your intentions.'

Harriet rises to the challenge of defending herself.

'I'm expressing an opinion that's all! Quite simply, that you and I appear to have more in common than we do with Mary, for example.'

Indigo shakes her head as she marches off from her sister.

'You forget that the athame and the sacred pentacle, besides many other magical tools, once belonged to Mary. She's a more powerful witch than our collective might combined.'

'I doubt that,' Harriet scowls, soon back at Indigo's side. '*You're* the Last of the Knowing Ones, not she; no, nor I for that matter!'

Indigo now feels able to decode part of the message lingering behind her sister's words.

'You're jealous, that's it! You think that by keeping me close, I'll call on you in my hour of need, rather than poor Mary! And what then? Do you plan to take them from me? You never did want to surrender the articles to me in the first place. I saw your expression when you were asked by Mrs D to hand over the pentacle fragment and the athame.'

'Nonsense,' says Harriet. 'I would never stand in the way of a more resourceful witch – or one more adept at the Craft.'

They now approach the dining room, where Indigo can clearly see her father sitting at the far end of the table. There's a woman with him: it's Helen Carmichael, her mother's doppelganger and replacement.

'Who's that?'

'Another of Father's prisoners,' Indigo says quietly to her sister as they take their seats at the table, opening cream-coloured napkins and spreading them on their laps, 'otherwise known as *Mother*.'

'But last night I thought you said she was –'

'She is,' Indigo turns her head to face away from her father as she whispers, 'but I want Father to continue thinking the exact opposite. That way, we should be able to help her, as well as a number of others in a similar predicament.'

'Very good,' Harriet smiles, affording a little wink.

'I trust you both slept well?' asks Carmichael.

'Very well, thank you,' the girls say in perfect unison.

'My goodness,' he laughs, 'you could be mistaken for twins!'

It takes Mary a great deal of time and cunning to find her way out of 'the burrow', as she terms it, and into the open air above ground. She has to use the homing instinct she's relied on for much of her young life, charting a course through the maze of concrete and glass. As a Knowing One, she has the ability to respond to instinct first, intellect second and wonders if this is where her sister, Harriet Gordon, was going wrong.

Despite the presence of the fort – much of it now in an advanced state of ruin but not even built in her own timeline – Mary knows the outcrop of land at once, from her days as citizen of Tenby town. 'Harrowing Point!' she exclaims in recognition.

But as she attempts to fill her two lungs with the normally invigorating coastal air, she doubles over in a coughing fit, pressing a hand to her mouth to prevent the contents of her stomach reaching the edges of her throat.

'What sinister magic is this?' she thinks.

Part-recovering, she sees now how time has not been kind to the landscape. The grasses and flowers of her youth now bend away from the sky, lowering their heads in shame or because of some unchecked sickness in their roots. The great woods and forests that once bordered the coastline are now absent, only clumps of vegetation remain to signify to the girl anything but barren rock had ever thrived here.

'What disease worse than the damned plague came to Tenby?' she gasps, out loud.

'Man,' trills a voice behind her.

It's Indigo, a small glass mask covering her mouth and eyes; Harriet, alongside her, is kitted out in identical equipment.

'I told you not to leave the complex, Mary. Here, take this,' Indigo says, handing Mary a spare oxymask. 'They will allow us to stay outside for up to an hour.'

Mary wonders if one of the nightmares from the previous evening has now been reignited in her mind, so unsettling does the whole scene seem to her.

With a degree of tenderness, Indigo takes each sister by the hand and makes an unbroken chain. She leads them to the edge of the Point and down towards the beach, outlining for them all that has happened to Tenby and its people in the last hundred years or so. Her history isn't able to go back much further than that, but her storytelling cannot fail to engage her audience of two. Tales of civil wars erupting all over Britain because of rising oil and food prices; climate change that became impossible to manage as the earth's population escalated beyond control; terrorism and counter-terrorism; mass migration north and south away from a cinder-hot equator and the continued melting of the polar ice caps; the religious conflicts that shortened millions of lives and the scientific breakthroughs that extended the lives of a privileged few. She finds she has to stop every so often to explain certain terminology, not only for Mary, but for Harriet, also. By the time she's finished, her throat hoarse, the three witches stand aghast on the polluted, dark sand of North Beach with the fort – itself a misshapen shadow of past splendour – looming above them.

'Can we go into Tenby?' asks Mary.

Indigo nods, 'Well, we have a little time while the tide is out.'

Harriet gives Indigo's hand a conciliatory squeeze, proof she wants to be friends again and a sign it's also her wish to explore the town she's already seen transformed once before – that time shaped by the impact of war.

Indigo checks the dial on her watch: ten minutes have elapsed already, leaving the group another half an hour of oxygen before they would need to think about heading back.

'But we stay together, agreed? If anything or anyone takes you by surprise, no one screams or panics. You're in my world now and I can handle most things it can throw at us.'

'*Most things?*' Harriet asks, allowing Indigo to take the lead as they mount the long ramp from beach to cobbled streets.

Tenby is a ghost town where no living soul occupies its streets out of mischief or necessity. It stands forgotten and abandoned, many of its little houses and cottages burnt out; the broken panes of windows reflecting dour sunlight back at the rolling sky. Roofs have tumbled in or have been salvaged for lead. Here and there, seagulls roost on wrecked chimneystacks, their glassy eyes marking out the three sisters as they make their way up the high street and into St Mary's Square.

'It's awful,' Harriet says after a period of prolonged contemplation.

'More like hell opened up,' Mary adds, bending to retrieve a doll's head from the gutter, reminding her of the corpses she inspected each day with Farmer Stevens.

'This is home,' says Indigo.

The girls now huddle together and quietly sob for all they have lost and all that now seems irrecoverable.

'I wonder if Rowan Cottage is still there?' asks Mary.

Harriet answers, her voice quite brittle, 'It was a graveyard the last time I saw it.'

The two witches turn to their guide; two sets of eyes fixed on Indigo.

She merely says, 'You can see for yourselves what's become of it.'

In the years since Harriet's last visit, Tenby cemetery has suffered almost as much misfortune as the surrounding town. Many graves now lie open to the sky, their coffins having been exhumed – no doubt by criminals looking for jewellery, trinkets, heirlooms or even spare monies buried with the dead. The bare skeletons of adults and children have been cast to one side on open ground, once easy pickings for carrion, long since moved on.

Mary doesn't flinch, for she'd once tiptoed amongst the decaying and the dead. Harriet though, with her customary nineteenth-century fear of all things related to death, averts her eyes, Indigo helping her sister traverse the grisly terrain.

'My Gordon headstone appears to have gone,' Harriet manages after a few minutes of fruitless searching.

Indigo says, 'If constructed of marble or granite, it would have been worth something to someone.'

'But my family's headstone has gone,' Harriet says, becoming quite distressed. 'There's no record a Gordon left any kind of impression on history!'

Indigo loops a comforting arm around Harriet, noticing only then Mary has wandered off to a set of very timeworn gravestones at the far end of the cemetery.

Harriet and Indigo are soon by their sister's side, their presence indicating their concern. The young witch's breathing has quickened, her glass mask having no time to clear its interior of condensation, before extinguishing more air.

'On Queen Victoria's head a crown!' Harriet cries, noticing then the gravestone at Mary's feet with the following message:

Here lie the bodies of
Abraham Aderyn and his good wyfe Mary Harries.
Peacefull in their joint and eternyl reste.

'I saw our names together in the handbook,' Mary begins, 'and here they are again! Only it's now clear to me I eventually marry a boy I met one afternoon many hundreds of years ago! What can it all mean? Am I standing above my own dead body?'

Harriet steps forward, her face pained with knowledge she feels she has to share.

'Actually, I met a descendent of yours, Mary, a boy of the Aderyn and Harries' line of witches. I met him while here in Tenby. Back in 1943, actually.'

'When were you going to tell me this?' Indigo asks.

Harriet is angry with herself for the omission. In terms of gaining the trust of her sisters, she's back at square one.

'He was the one who gave me the handbook we know and use today. He also confirmed for me who we are and why it is we've been brought together.'

Mary and Indigo now face their sister, eyes sparkling with excitement. They wait for Harriet to surrender more information – toes tapping, arms folded, mouths silent.

'Well,' Harriet begins, 'what I am about to tell you is really quite incredible. But it would appear that Indigo and I are successive incarnations of a single witch – actually, of our sister of the broken pentacle: Mary.'

As both absorb the revelation, Harriet continues, the wind now picking up about her and howling through the graveyard like phantoms have been set loose.

'And Indigo, I think the Mother Goddess has waited patiently for the arrival of your father. His brilliant time machine has brought all three of us together, you see. Technology and ancient magic combined to bring about the dawning of a new age.'

The witches marvel at Harriet's ability to draw conclusions where their inquiries had only ever led them to brick walls.

'How then do you explain the inscription in the handbook?' asks a bewildered Mary. 'Or *my name* appearing on this headstone?'

Harriet has an answer for her sister.

'I can only guess that, at some point in the future, you'll be presented with the opportunity to travel back to Tenby of the seventeenth century and, willingly or not, you decide to go back.'

Indigo steps forward and faces Harriet, upset and keen to cut the conversation short.

'Enough of this, sisters; we run short on time and I refuse to entertain the idea we'll ever again be parted from one another. We're together now, forever!'

But here, the wind's fearsome howl becomes the actual growling of two enraged dogs. To be precise, a pair of great pit-bull terriers, snarling jowls and knives for teeth, suddenly rearing up from behind Mary's headstone and leaping at the sisters.

Transforming into their animaguses, the witches evade the attack. With the witches reduced in size, the dogs miss them entirely and collide mid-air, their elongated skulls connecting and drawing pained whimpers and howls from the animals.

Harriet, as fox, quickly brings her jaws down on loose skin about the hare's neck, Mary in turn using her two front teeth to pluck Indigo, the mouse, cleanly from the grass. Thus arranged, the more powerful of the creatures, Harriet, races clear of the cemetery. The weight of her two sisters is making her lower jaw ache but she dares not rest. *Not just yet*, she tells herself.

Behind her, the dogs have recovered and can be heard picking up the sisters' trail.

Out in the open, a fox, a hare and mouse would be easy prey for dogs of the pit-bulls' size and temperament, so the witches dive through a partly shattered window into a fisherman's cottage.

In the grim interior, the smell of rotting excrement lines the nostrils of the three animals, the damp floor and walls making the building wholly unappealing. Outside, the dogs appear to have lost track of the witches. But the pads on their paws can be heard as they prowl back and forth, connecting with gravel puddles of water just beyond the brick walls of the cottage.

As one, the sisters revert back to their human forms – their five senses somewhat inferior to those of their respective animaguses but such magic has served its purpose for now. Mary presses a finger to her lips to indicate they shouldn't make a sound. Only when Harriet dares peep through the gap in the window that had previously allowed the witches entry, is she met with the crumpled muzzle of one of her pursuers.

She screams, Indigo instinctively pulling her sister away from the gap, pointing then to a staircase at the far end of the room.

The dogs launch themselves at the frailest of the cottage's windows and enter the building to the sound of smashing glass.

Harriet and Mary are soon in the room at the top of the staircase, breathless and exhilarated. Behind them trails Indigo, acutely aware she's holding the group back.

Seeing her sister's distress, it is Harriet who cries, 'Mary, you have to help us!'

The dogs are now at the base of the staircase and scrambling over one another to reach the witches.

Mary steps to the head of the stairs, simply raises a slender hand before her and breathes the words, 'No evil can enter here; all evil is turned back.'

The two dogs suddenly pause and sniff at the air as if some greater threat now occupies the first-floor room where the sisters stand grouped together.

'What are they doing?' Indigo asks, her voice barely a whisper.

'Thinking,' Harriet guesses, 'about what to do next?'

Suddenly – and with terrifying ease – one of the dogs bounds across the first seven steps to reach the middle of the staircase. The sisters tumble back as one, only then to hear the hound cry out in agonising pain.

'The spell, it worked!' Mary shouts, surprised at her own skill.

As she'd hoped, her magic has forged a weakness in the staircase's structure, the dog falling to the floor below as if made of lead, not flesh and bone. In its wake, it leaves a perfect circle of air, a thin plume of debris and smoke climbing into the ceiling space across from the sisters.

'They can't reach us now!' Harriet cheers, only then stepping back and losing her left foot to a fresh hole in the floor.

She cries out a second time and it's Mary, now, who rushes to her friend's aid, snatching her clear of the gap. But, alas, Harriet loses one of her boots.

The dog below soon makes light work of the object, tearing it apart in its huge jaws.

'Mary,' Indigo shouts, quite breathless, 'I think your spell has become unstable. We now have a cursed house on our hands!'

It's true; all about them, holes begin to appear at random intervals across the floor of the room and the sisters are now required to cross the space if they intend to reach the next staircase beyond.

On the floor below, the dogs roam, expecting at any moment for one of the holes to carry a girl directly into their salivating jaws.

Harriet says, 'We need another spell, Mary! One that will carry us to the staircase over there and preferably in one piece!'

'I'll do my best, but it's not in my nature to conjure dark magic. The only tricks I know, I learnt from my mum and grandma Nancy and I doubt any of them can save us from such savage dogs.'

Unexpectedly, a hole opens up beneath Indigo and swallows her almost completely, the floor soon level with her armpits.

'No!' she screams, her sisters hauling her up in time to bring all three of them back onto solid floorboards, if only momentarily.

'There is a very *old spell*,' Mary says, remembering one that always proved popular at children's parties.

'Whatever it is, you have my permission to use it!' Harriet pleads, almost disappearing down another of the cursed holes.

As with any ritual, Mary gathers her thoughts together in order to call on the help of sacred, hidden spirits.

'Of the petals counted and spun on the stalk,
Turn the upside down to right,
Of owls and sun gods switching sides,
Turn the upside down to right!'

At the final syllable of the final word of the spell, the cottage begins to tremble.

'What have you done, sister?' asks a bewildered Harriet.

Mary takes each of her sisters by the hand and nods towards the second staircase at the other side of the room. Before them, it seems to drop a whole floor, an entry-point suddenly appearing in its place and a way opens up that will lead them back downstairs. Indeed, all across the room, holes that had once barred their passage now appear on the ceiling above them, a set of clouds promising a deadly downpour.

'Run!' Mary yells.

The sisters at her side need no further encouragement, although Indigo holds onto Harriet for guidance and support. As one, they speed across the space of ceiling made floor, quickly reaching the staircase at the other side of the room.

'Oh dear, I didn't think that would happen,' says Mary, quite humbled by the entire adventure.

Behind them, two holes in the ceiling now fill with dog; pit-bulls freefalling ungracefully through space to reach a patch of solid ground just a few feet from the sisters. The vicious creatures shake themselves free of dust and plaster, growling as they do so and preparing to launch a fresh attack.

'How long is the spell meant to last?' Indigo asks.

Mary says, 'Only a short time; it's merely a trick!'

The staircase next to where the sisters stand turns a hundred and eighty degrees and leads, once again, to the cottage's attic space.

The pit-bulls fall foul of two fresh holes and are swiftly returned to the floor beneath the sisters, much to the dogs' dismay and to the girls' collective delight.

Indigo takes a moment to look at her watch. 'Oh dear, we've less than ten minutes to get back to the complex. Our air is about to run out!'

The dogs eventually return to their master, a tall slip of a figure perched high on a hill where Tenby's castle once overlooked the Point and grand sweep of beaches to the north and south. They cower before him, one gnashing at the heels of the other, their tails mere shreds of muscle and fur.

'Oh, stop it, you two,' Rees-Repton says, 'and at least have the decency to face me as yourselves. Quickly, before I have you impounded in some Goddess-forsaken kennel.'

The two dogs immediately transform and become Maxwell and Anton, the bruised and battered sons of Oliver Rees-Repton.

'Any *positive* news to report?'

Anton looks at his brother, who is staring off into the distance. As ever, the dutiful half of the pair licks his lips before delivering the bad news.

'We tried *not* to let them get away, Father.'

Rees-Repton laughs.

'I can see that, Anton, but *who* exactly did you let *get away*?'

Maxwell now steps forward to say: 'You should know there are now three of them.'

'Three?'

'Yes; the two girls have been joined by a third, more powerful, witch they refer to as Mary.'

'Very good,' Rees-Repton says. 'Now pray tell, what do you think I should do next?'

The twins don't like their father when he seeks advice from his sons in this way, for a period of sarcasm usually precedes a bout of intense physical and mental torture for one or both of them.

Maxwell smiles and advances with a comment, 'I think you should stop playing games, Father, and tell us why it is you're allowing a bumbling professor and his no-good daughter to enjoy the run of a complex funded by our family.'

Rees-Repton looks out across the bay, his long fingers neatly folded until the knuckles overlap on both hands.

'That *bumbling professor*, as you so inaccurately call him, has a powerful machine that might yet bring the missing pieces of the sacred pentacle out of hiding and into our possession.'

Anton and Maxwell admire their father when he speaks this way, directly and without affectation.

Rees-Repton continues, 'The fragment presently wound about the neck of the Carmichael girl will complete the set and, with the pentacle made whole again, I will become the most powerful witch this sorry planet has ever known.'

Thrilled, Maxwell and Anton chorus together, 'What then?'

Rees-Repton nears the edge of the cliff, his footing close to being lost beneath him. When he speaks, his voice is as stiff and as sour as the air about the headland.

'I'll forge a new one for us, boys, just as this tired one was once created by a now dead Mother Goddess. And before leaving this globe of putrid compost, I'll ponder the fates of any surviving mortals I come across. And then, *when they least expect it*, I'll use the sacred pentacle to bring their reign here to an end with a great, all-consuming, black-hearted apocalypse.'

Still wary of dangers at street level, the sisters make their way from rooftop to rooftop, in a desperate bid to reach home before the air in their oxymasks runs out. To add to their problems, Indigo knew the tide would soon start to turn. At its highest, it was capable of cutting the Point off from the rest of Tenby for hours on end.

Despite her being the least physically agile of the girls, Indigo leads the group, for she's most familiar with the landscape of chipped tiles and collapsed chimneys. Harriet follows next, nursing her disappointment at proving deficient in spellcasting and having to rely solely on Mary to provide the three of them with a method of escape from the wild dogs. Harriet wonders if she's worth anything compared to her two sisters, as she lacks those qualities normally associated with a practising witch. Mary brings up the rear, her whole outlook renewed by the successful handling of powerful magic.

'We're nearly there; just a little further,' Indigo calls over one shoulder.

But, no sooner are her words on the wind, Mary begins to cough and splutter.

'I think she's running short of oxygen,' says Harriet, realising her own breathing has become rather more laboured, too.

'But we're not home yet!' calls Indigo.

Harriet joins her friends in the search for clean air, she and Mary now wheeling between one edge of the roof and another.

'Careful, sisters,' Indigo calls, 'or you'll fall to your deaths.'

Indigo looks out across the uneven horizon of roofs and stacks, guessing the group still have another half a mile or so to cover before they'll reach the steps of the Point.

'The athame,' Mary says at last. 'Do you have it with you?'

'Of course,' says Indigo, doubling over in a coughing fit herself and drawing the last of the air from her mask. With an already weak chest, she'll most likely be the first to die.

Harriet helps her sister to her feet.

'Give it to me.'

Indigo removes the witch's dagger from her belt and hands it to Harriet, meeting her gaze for a second.

'If you don't trust me,' Harriet warns, 'then say so now. I've handled it on other occasions and always profited from its use.'

'I trust you,' Indigo manages between coughs, 'to do right by us, sister.'

With speed, Harriet has the athame held out ahead of the trio, the air before them sliced in a single loop and enclosing them.

'There,' Harriet says, the athame quickly returned to its owner.

But the toxic atmosphere quickly overpowers the protective sphere, the sisters enjoying only temporary respite from the deadly air.

Composing herself, Indigo removes the pentacle fragment and holds it out towards Mary, barely any breath to issue her final commands.

Mary asks, 'What would you have me do with it?'

Harriet examines the markings on the surface of the fragment.

'There: the crescent moons, Mary! What do they represent in ancient Craft lore?'

Mary appears confused.

'I don't know. The pentacle was ancient before I was born.'

'*Think*, Mary,' Indigo manages. 'The sacred pentacle was entrusted to your family long before it was unmade – surely you know something?'

Harriet paces around the circumference of the circle, only after three revolutions hitting on an idea.

'What if the athame and the fragment are in some way connected?'

Indigo retrieves the athame from her belt, showing her sisters the strange run of symbols along its hilt.

'Of course – it's a code!' Harriet enthuses, drawing the athame and the pentacle fragment together. 'The world is made up of four sacred elements, sisters: Air, Fire, Water and Earth. I learnt that much from my governess.'

Mary and Indigo nod to show they're in agreement.

Harriet is excited now, her voice rising a whole octave, 'One of the symbols on the athame corresponds with the symbol on the pentacle fragment, I'm sure of it!'

Indigo lifts her head to speak.

'But there are five symbols, Harriet. Which one could it be?'

Harriet is not fazed.

'The fifth one is a five-pointed star, denoting a secret element as yet unknown to us, so let's discount that one for a second.'

'The circle's barrier is beginning to fade,' chokes Mary.

'So,' Harriet says, 'if … and … therefore …'

'Harriet,' Indigo says, 'it's just a theory!'

Harriet turns on her sister, great authority suddenly edging her voice, 'All knowable facts once began life as theories, sister!'

'All the same,' Indigo says, 'here's a *knowable fact* we know to be certain: we're running out of air.'

'Eureka!' Harriet screams, rousing poor Mary from her stupor.

'What, sister?' Indigo asks.

'That's it! The two shapes can be overlaid, one atop the other, to create a third shape and that should always be a circle of some description, the symbol of the Mother Goddess!'

Harriet turns to Mary, lifting her face until she can see directly into her eyes.

'Mary, can you hear me?'

'She's passing out,' Indigo says. 'Mary, we need a spell from you – and one that can harness the power of Air.'

'Air?' Mary asks, drifting in an out of consciousness.

'Yes, Air,' Harriet repeats. 'I'm certain now the fragment we have in our care and the athame are bound by the same sacred element.'

Mary's eyes narrow and her hands roll into fists.

To Harriet's left, Indigo is now slumped in one corner of the protective circle, her lungs quite spent.

'Indigo,' Harriet begs. 'Don't give up! Say something – *anything* – just stay with me!'

Mary draws Harriet's attention with an outstretched hand.

'The pentacle and the athame,' she whispers. 'Give them to me. I have a spell I should like to try.'

Without delay, Harriet hands both objects to Mary, tears of frustration and elation lining her eyes.

'There you go, sister.'

Mary clutches them to her chest, the words of a long-forgotten verse slipping from her lips.

'Marvel beyond imagination, soul of infinite space.
My two faces are life and light,
For Air is life and giver of life,
Now again I call upon the seed and the root,
The stem and the bud,
Now again I must beg purification.'

At the utterance of her spell, Mary falls limp in Harriet's arms, as if nothing appears to have worked.

'Sorry, sisters,' mumbles Harriet, slumping to the ground, finally succumbing to the poisonous air.

Then Mary and Indigo both manage to open their eyes and look up from their positions on the ground.

'Sisters, look!' says Mary, the athame's unique second symbol glowing brightly and the pentacle fragment's two crescent moons shining just as fiercely. Harriet's eyes snap open as she instantly revives. 'I was right!' she shouts, bounding about the edges of their protective circle. 'The element of our pentacle fragment is Air! Lovely, life-giving, breathable air!'

It's only now the sisters witness the true potential of the pentacle. Mary's spell has called upon one of the four great elemental spirits to assist them, and Air – a force of considerable power and majesty – comes to the rescue. It brings forth gallon upon gallon of restorative and revitalising oxygen, filling the airways and lungs of the three girls and raising them to their feet.

As they reach the safety of more stable ground, the sky above the town clears of a pernicious smog that has hung low and heavy over it for many decades. The magic sweeps before the sisters like an invisible prayer of hope and goodwill, replacing every toxic particle with three times the quantity of oxygen.

'Already the plants look a little less sad,' says Mary, regaining her spirits.

The pentacle fragment shines on as it continues to filter the putrid air around them.

'Imagine, if you will,' says Harriet. 'A time when we've found a way to unleash the magic within the remaining fragments.'

Indigo pauses, having led them successfully to the steps of the fort. In an hour or so the advancing sea will claim the spot of sand they currently occupy. She smiles at her two sisters, saying, 'We could clear the waters, feed the soil and bring light to a world that, in my lifetime, has only ever known darkness and death.'

'A wonderful vision,' Harriet nods, pushing past her sisters to reach the top of the steps before them.

'I win!' Harriet declares on reaching the summit, punching the air in a display of unchecked happiness. But she looks back at Indigo and privately remonstrates with herself for displaying such insensitivity. Her sister has only advanced a few feet, her delicate lungs still struggling to provide her muscles with the oxygen they require.

'The grey skies are moving on,' says Mary rather mournfully. 'Like storm clouds they drift, finding shelter elsewhere.'

As one, the sisters regard the lingering grey horizon to the north; it appears only Tenby is enjoying the purifying magic of the pentacle. They sense their work has only just begun.

'We must make it our priority to obtain the remaining fragments, sisters.'

Harriet and Mary stare at Indigo, a girl like them whose voice now hums with the winds of change.

Indigo continues, 'I have a plan. Harriet. It's high time you asked my father to show you the inner workings of his accelerator engine. You can witness first-hand how he's managed to manipulate time and space and turn it to his advantage. Of us three, I suspect you have the intellect, patience and fortitude to cope with such intricate knowledge. Make lots of mental notes, sister, of everything you see and everything you think will prove useful in our quest to re-assemble the sacred pentacle.'

Harriet is overjoyed at being trusted to undertake a mission of such importance. In fact, only on reaching the doors leading back underground does she think to ask a question of her own.

'What will you and Mary do?'

Mary has no idea, looking to Indigo for an answer.

'We've reading to do,' Indigo says. 'I suspect our handbook contains a number of clues to the whereabouts of each fragment. We're going to try our hand at a little code-breaking, aren't we Mary?'

'Beyond recognising letters that make up people's names and a few basic spells, my reading is far from magical, sister.'

Indigo is undeterred, looping a reassuring arm around her sister.

'Symbols then, for you. We shall begin with symbols, Mary, then make our way to words: small steps leading to strides. After all, if we're to believe the handbook is a genuine article, you'll one day become an author in your own right.'

The Unmaking of the Pentacle

That very afternoon, the professor accedes to Harriet's request to have him show her the lower levels of the facility, where Indigo claims the true magic of the accelerator engine can be surveyed. He leads the two of them down a winding staircase, corkscrew-fashion, for maybe half a mile or so, before Harriet speaks.

'We must be far beneath the seabed, Professor.'

'Absolutely, Miss Gordon. It seemed to me to be the safest place to house a machine as powerful as my locator.'

On they descend, the air about the young witch's shoulders turning icy cold and bringing a region of goose bumps to her skin.

The professor seizes the opportunity to speak further.

'I want to explain something to you, Miss Gordon.'

'Do call me Harriet,' she smiles, her left hand gripping the safety rail.

'Very well. I've been a bad father, Harriet.'

The young witch says nothing, allowing Carmichael space to add detail in his own time.

'I've also been a bad husband. Indeed, in my time I've been a bad son and, if I had known siblings, I'm sure I would have made a lousy brother, too!'

Harriet feels a certain degree of sympathy for the professor, so stung does he appear to be by his own words.

'I am, though, a remarkable scientist and my skill is something I can always rely on when I fail to engage, connect and socialise with those around me. You see, science has never failed me, child! In many ways, it's been the best, most reliable friend.'

A short minute later, the staircase ends and becomes a viewing platform overlooking a crater of considerable size. Harriet is amazed. She can see nothing below them but a circular depression of smooth rock. She peers over the edge of the railing and realises there's actually a glass panel of some thickness separating her from the expansive region beyond.

'Extraordinary,' she manages, the professor already off to her left, tapping away at a keyboard.

'This, Harriet, is my locator. Its main purpose is to feed the accelerator engine high above us.'

'Feed it *what* exactly?'

'Dark energy.'

Harriet watches on as Carmichael begins inputting instructions into the terminal, his little screen ablaze with row upon row of letters and numbers.

Out beyond the platform, something rumbles to life. Harriet can feel it in her bones and instinctively backs away from the railing.

'Never flinch from science,' smiles Carmichael. 'It will not hurt you, unless you prove unequal to the task of controlling it, Harriet.'

She watches on in disbelief as the crater thrums and warps, here and there little pinpricks of light beginning to punctuate the mammoth darkness.

'A globe!' shouts Harriet.

'Remember yesterday, when I told you about time and space acting like pages in a book? Well, my locator is the letter knife that finds a specific entry in a particular book.'

Harriet nods.

'I see that, yes, but a book that is shaped like a globe, a miniature copy of Earth.'

The crater is actually a titanic plate on which is balanced a huge ball of swirling dark-hearted stars – *a world in negative*, thinks Harriet – whereby shadowy blots of matter are framed by areas of brilliant white light, moving between them and around them.

Carmichael finds he has to shout above the increasing din.

'The dark spots you see are called *black holes*.'

He watches Harriet approach the railing a second time, no doubt to gain a closer look at the locator. He is just able to hear her say, 'What are they made of?'

Carmichael continues tapping away at his keyboard, while talking over his shoulder.

'It was once thought they were dead suns – stars that had collapsed and wandered the universe seeking out particles of energy they could feed on and eventually destroy.'

Harriet shivers at the thought of such.

The professor goes on, 'In fact, many scientists have published extensively on gargantuan-holes, some of them big enough to swallow a million planets like ours, suns and even entire galaxies. But I took a different view of things – seeking *micro-holes* in hard-to-reach places – and discovering thousands of them hanging in the air around us. Some of them are so small they float back and forth between particles of matter itself. They are so infinitesimally slight, some could avoid detection by even the most powerful machines known to man.'

Harriet is a little reassured.

'And you collect them here, in your ... locator?'

The professor laughs at the notion.

'Forgive me child, I mean not to mock you. Not *collect*, exactly – no. Black holes don't take kindly to being contained, you see. The locator merely helps me record the co-ordinates of active black holes.'

Harriet approaches him at the terminal.

'How many have you recorded, Professor?'

Carmichael licks his lips.

'Oh … around 35,000. But that doesn't include those that led me to the 200 prisoners in my care.'

'I'm number 201, aren't I?'

'Yes, Harriet, you are.'

The great machine now moves up a gear and sends the menacing stars high into orbit.

'What's it doing, now?' asks Harriet, her voice becoming insubstantial.

Carmichael's eyes widen in childlike wonder.

'It's just found another active specimen, and I have to work quickly to note its co-ordinates!'

The numerous spheres of spinning dark matter finally merge until they become a single black hole suspended high above the crater of rock, taking Harriet's breath with it.

'How does it know where to look?'

'That's the easy part. I was the first scientist to discover they grouped around tiny corridors connecting different universes. Meaning that when I found a black hole I usually discovered *a new universe.*'

Harriet's eyes grow wider, daring herself not to blink until the locator settles back down – which it soon does, having acquired the location of another black hole for the professor's collection.

'Are my co-ordinates in there, do you think?'

'They may well be,' says Carmichael, completing his work at the terminal. 'But nothing has registered in the system, as yet. Yours is a fairly unique case, Harriet. You're of *this* universe, if not strictly of *this* time, and it could be you used a light-hole to reach us. It's a variety of star so rare I never expected to come across one in my lifetime. Perhaps your appearance in my broadcast portal is proof of their existence …'

Harriet doesn't respond at first, quite lost to the whole experience. Only on regaining her composure, does she dare mention a theory that's been on her mind the last few minutes.

'A black hole may be a way of returning home as much as it is a way out, Professor.'

'What's that?'

'Nothing – I was just thinking out loud. I must say, I've seen quite enough for one afternoon.'

'Very well, Harriet. Although I did mean to ask why you're no longer wearing your rather unusual pendant?'

'I made a gift of it, sir, to your daughter.'

'I see. And may I ask where you acquired such a unique item of jewellery?'

Harriet is already tackling the steps that will eventually lead her back to the surface, shouting over her shoulder, 'It emerged from thin air itself, Professor … like a magic trick of the Victorian era!'

Harriet arrives back at Indigo's room to discover her sister sitting cross-legged on the floor, flicking back and forth through a tatty-looking book she is resting on her lap. From what's left of the binding, she recognises it immediately as once belonging to the Gordon family library, although she's not sure of the title. *My father is probably turning in his exhumed grave, to see it in that state*, she thinks.

'What is that you're reading?' she asks, cocking her head sideways to see.

'Oh, sister,' says Indigo, looking up dreamily, 'it's *The Illustrated Guide to Welsh Wildflowers*. I found it mouldering away in a storeroom with a load of other books. Just imagine, Harriet, now the air is clean we may see beautiful flowers like this growing on Forgotten Point again, for the first time in decades!' Indigo puts the book aside and slumps back on a cushion, still exhausted from the morning's exertions.

'So, how did you get on with my father?' she asks.

Harriet, realising for the first time how tired she is herself, answers, 'Well, we'll most probably be able to get your replacement mother back home, as well as the other prisoners.'

The news draws Indigo to her knees, her whole frame stirring to life.

'Really? Do you think so, sister?'

'The science was a little confounding at first,' explains Harriet. 'But, after spending time with your father, knowledge of how to operate the machine quickly became my own.'

Mary remains asleep on the ground, her head propped up by a number of children's books that had once formed part of Harriet's prized collection.

'It all proved too much for her, I'm afraid,' explains Indigo.

Harriet collapses on the floor beside her sisters, her mind buzzing with information it seems unable to fully process.

'So, tell me what you found in the handbook?'

Indigo summarises what little progress has been made to this point.

'The handbook contains a great deal of spells and incantations, but very little in the way of clues concerning the whereabouts of the other fragments. The only pages of note are these few here.'

Harriet slides across the carpet, closer to Indigo, who opens the handbook on the floor between them, her index finger making heavy work of finding the pages in question.

My sister's eyesight really is very diminished, thinks Harriet.

The first page of interest contains a map of the known world – dated 1752 – shrunk to fit the small area of moth-eaten paper. The opposite page contains a series of markers.

'Like a dot-to-dot design', remarks Harriet.

'I wondered at first if this second map is of the constellations.'

'It's not?'

'No,' confirms Indigo. 'I consulted a number of books on astronomy shortly before your return and I'm afraid to say none of them match the patterns on the page.'

Harriet suddenly stumbles on an idea.

'Do you possess any tracing paper, sister?'

Indigo slowly stands, her legs stiff from sitting cross-legged for hours, and hobbles across to her desk – her hand soon falling on a few stray sheets. 'You're in luck! And a pencil, too!'

With the objects soon in her charge, Harriet carefully lays the tracing paper against the second of the pages and, using the pencil, indicates each of the unusual markers by scratching a tiny cross in the surface of the tracing paper. As she concentrates, her tongue protrudes from one edge of her mouth, making Indigo smile.

'There,' announces Harriet, turning the tracing paper over and pressing it against the opposite page. 'I think we've just found the locations of sacred sites related to the broken pentacle.'

Indigo does not agree entirely. 'It's a little confusing still … The markers are scattered randomly all over the world and the handbook clearly states there are only five fragments that make up the sacred pentacle. Why don't you try joining some of the dots that are grouped together?'

Harriet agrees to test the theory and within minutes the two sisters fall back on their haunches, able to see for the first time five distinct shapes staring up at them from the paper:

A pair of crescent moons.
Two snakes.
A horned bull.
Two pyramids.
A pentagram, or five-pointed star.

Indigo is first to speak.

'We know the crescent moons symbolise the sacred element of Air, and look, sister –'

Harriet cuts in, 'I see it! Our pentacle fragment was originally sent to America for safe-keeping, possibly with the athame.'

Indigo uses her basic knowledge of world geography to indicate the proposed locations of the remaining fragments.

'So, it seems the two snakes are over South America … The horned bull has to be somewhere near the North Pole. And the two pyramids are over Egypt in Africa. Which then means –'

'The five-pointed star is located in the middle of the North Atlantic,' says Harriet. 'But how odd …'

'Odd?'

'I've a strange feeling about all of this, sister. You see, St Catherine's Fort, above us, is identical to one built in Bermuda, a region of tropical islands positioned near to where the pentagram falls on the map, said to be the gateway to a region of great mystery and danger. One of the islands, Saint George, even has an area called *Pembroke Parish*!'

'The area beyond this complex is known as *Pembrokeshire*,' Indigo smiles. 'Anyway, how do you know all of this?'

Harriet turns to her sister and declares in a sprightly fashion, 'Oddly enough, the Gordon's annual cruise docked in Bermuda last summer on its way back from New York. That is … *last summer* over a hundred and eighty years ago! Through Daddy's connections, we were invited to stay overnight at the fort and, I must say, it's not dissimilar to the one located above us.'

'What are you two plotting now?' asks Mary, emerging from her sleep.

Indigo and Harriet soon confess all to their sleepy-eyed sister, whose unwillingness to become excited at the prospect of travelling to all corners of the planet in search of missing pentacle fragments appears as a series of yawns.

Indigo continues, 'There are two more pages I want to show you, sisters ...'

'What, another map?' groans Harriet.

'Yes, but this one is of Britain,' replies her sister. 'Also dated 1752 and likely completed by the same hand.'

The map in question is spread liberally across two pages of the handbook and contains a series of interconnecting lines covering the whole of the British Isles.

'Like a spider's web,' deduces Harriet.

'I wonder,' says Indigo. 'Whether my father's locator and this map are somehow connected,'

Harriet pursues her sister's theory.

'A map of every black hole in Britain?'

'No, quite the opposite,' says Indigo. 'Perhaps these are points on the world map where the Mother Goddess's elemental energies come closest to the surface.'

Harriet suddenly recalls a conversation she once overheard between her parents – innocent-sounding back then but now carrying great significance.

'There are ley lines encompassing the entire planet, sisters. I once heard a scholar tell my parents about them.'

Indigo clenches her right fist, as if she's caught prey in it.

'Ley lines, of course – marking out the lay of the land, eruptions of positive energy! The handbook mentions them in relation to ancient druidic lore and says that such lines were sources of powerful magic to early users of the Craft.'

Mary suddenly finds she's able to contribute to her sisters' conversation.

'Open the lines to the vortex and see,
What divine providence intended for thee!
Snap shut all the dark holes and enter Her light,
Or draw down the sun to bring out the night!'

Excited, Harriet faces her sister, book in hand and quite giddy.

'Do you know something about these?'

Mary takes one look at the map, her finger marking out a defined route.

'Follow the lines of the vortex … Tenby, Avebury, then onto Stonehenge.'

Harriet jumps to her feet.

'The fragments aren't just going to come to us. We have to bring them out of hiding!'

She flicks through further pages at great speed until she arrives at the very last page which, curiously enough, contains a palmprint of red ink – or blood perhaps. It's the same size as hers and with a set of gruesome fingerprints to match. Taking Mary's hand for a second – and largely against that sister's will – Harriet places it against the outline of the hand, revealing it to be a perfect match.

Mary flinches, drawing her hand away from the handbook.

'What can it mean?'

'Stonehenge will have to wait,' Indigo says, rising to her feet to join Harriet and Mary. 'First of all, we're going to help Mary find out what happened after she stepped into the portal; what became of the life and people she left behind … And maybe why it is her handprint came to be included in the handbook, at all.'

The sisters time it well, so that same evening they're able to access the accelerator engine room without any issues, making use of that narrow passage of time between the lab technicians going home and the cleaners arriving. It is Indigo who takes the lead, both knowledgeable and skilled in using the tuning discs to locate specific people or objects elsewhere in time.

'So,' says Harriet taking it all in as she stands next to Indigo. 'The locator below us is connected to this machine?'

Indigo blows into her palms, as if clean hands were the secret to forging and sustaining a connection with time periods currently beyond her reach. 'Yes. Now, Harriet, please step aside and let Mary join me.'

Harriet raises her eyebrows at the request, eventually stepping to one side.

Beyond the five glass plates – each now aglow with electrical energy and starting to revolve in various directions, both to and away from one another – the accelerator engine powers up, its corridor of lasers chuntering and hissing as if carrying out a factory reset.

'Don't be afraid,' says Indigo to Mary. 'This is what helped transport you here from Tenby of 1650.'

'Albeit as a hare,' Harriet interjects but fails to ruffle Indigo's cool resolve.

Mary appears not to have heard the comment either, adding, 'Please, just tell me what I need to do, sister. My head and heart are all over the place.'

Indigo then reveals the pentacle fragment, raising it in the air for both sisters to see, and all marvel again at the fact the unassuming object could harbour such incredible magic within it.

'When the engine is ready, I'll place this on the same glass plate I've used previously and know works – the middle one. Mary, when prompted, you step forward and hold it there: simply place both hands against the circumference of the plate, with your thumbs pressing down against the edge, like so.'

Indigo and Mary practise together, Harriet watching on as one sister leads the other, as if they were newly engaged in learning a dance for the summer ball. Mary smiles throughout. *But such is a nervous reaction to being in the presence of wondrous modern science*, concludes Harriet, still feeling very much left out.

'You'll master it in no time,' says Indigo, walking away from one sister to join the other at the console.

'Is she going to be able to handle what the locator reveals to her?'

'With our support sister,' says Indigo, refusing to make eye contact with Harriet.

Within seconds, the engine's lasers accelerate, turning clockwise around the dark corridor, until they begin to lose their definition.

'Look! Our light ring, sisters!' shouts Mary over her left shoulder.

Indigo hollers back, 'Concentrate on the plate, Mary! Don't worry about us. And look beyond the light ring if you can. Focus on your last moments with Abe, out on Forgotten Point. Try to recreate the feelings you experienced the moment you crossed over and left him behind, along with your entire world.'

Mary tries again, taking on board her sister's advice. She quickly becomes a silhouette to them, as if the engine were in the process of consuming corporeal matter at its borders, including the young witch.

Of course, Harriet thinks, making a mental note to develop her theory at some later point in time, black holes are more than just dark energy. They're generated by negative experiences and feelings: grief, disappointment, loss, regret. Black holes are all around us – the professor said as much – and small wonder with the world the way it is!

Indigo turns serious for her final remarks.

'One last piece of advice, Mary. Be mindful of interacting with anyone that appears in the light ring. And the same goes for us, Harriet, watching events through the broadcast portal. These are not just images of the past, they *are* the past, being played out in real time, and can be altered by us if we interfere even in some small or seemingly insignificant way. We must do our best to remain *passive,* to let the images play out for us as if part of a moving painting, a series of photographs, or something we refer to as *films,* in my timeline.'

In a matter of seconds, the first episode presents itself to the sisters, Mary having successfully used the fragment and glass plate to locate a downcast Abe Aderyn. However, he's not abandoned on Forgotten Point, as Mary had been expecting to see, but alone on a shingle beach in the cold light of a new day ...

... Abe is on his knees, having emptied Mary's velvet bag, magical instruments strewn before him on the sand. In amongst them, the Harries family's sacred pentacle shines in the inky light of early morning. Abe presses his fingers against the centre of the pentacle's design, producing a life-nourishing wave of energy that takes him and the sisters by surprise, surging out across the sheet of sea stretching between Caldey Island and Tenby town ...

... In the next scene, Abe and Farmer Stevens are sat opposite one another in a sparsely furnished interior. The sisters lean forward as one, eager to learn more.

'I live here by myself,' Stevens says, handing Abe a tankard of ale that bites at the back of the boy's throat as he drinks.

Abe's eyes dart into corners, looking for signs of life.

'I lost my wife and child, which is why I returned home to Tenby,' adds Stevens.

Abe squirms a little in his seat.

'And I'm not really a labourer, boy. Although it's a trade preferable to that of witchfinder ...'

Abe's voice prickles with anger.

'Someone like you hanged my father, strung him high because he dared to love my mother, a practising witch.'

The sisters take a moment to stare at one another in disbelief, before turning back to the portal.

Stevens says, 'I'm sorry for your loss, boy.'

Abe makes no reply.

'It was my job to gather evidence,' Stevens continues, drinking more of the ale.

'Evidence?'

Stevens merely nods, 'The witchfinders of London needed only grains of truth to bring a case against someone. It was my job to make sure evidence couldn't be challenged by the friends and family of a suspected witch.'

Abe lifts his eyes for a moment, 'I'm guessing the finger of suspicion eventually fell on someone close to you?'

Steven's blue eyes become two shadows. 'Very good, boy. Yes, you're right. It fell on my dear wife, and on the four-year-old girl in our care, Emeline, someone we came to love more than life itself.'

With nothing to say, Abe takes a sip of his ale.

Stevens says, 'Looking back, I can see it was Emeline who brought us bad luck. We tried in vain to have a child of our own and then, one day, she turns up on our doorstep, round face like a button, blue in the cheeks from being abandoned mid-winter. We loved her the first moment we set eyes on her!'

Abe motions for his tankard to be re-filled, which Stevens does without question.

'You think Emeline was a witch?'

'I'm sure of it,' says Stevens. 'At first she performed little acts of magic to make our lives easier.'

'That's common among our kind,' smiles Abe.

Stevens speaks on, 'I'd return to the room to discover it'd been cleaned from ceiling to floor, with only Emeline sat there in the middle of the carpet.'

'And money would suddenly appear in your pockets?'

The farmer's eyes widen. 'Yes. Spare change at first, then whole nuggets of gold in my shoes each morning as I rose to start the day.'

'Did you talk to your wife about it?' asks Abe.

'Of course,' Stevens replies. 'But Hannah was a devoutly religious woman and believed our good fortune was being sent to us from above.'

Abe says nothing, allowing Stevens to continue.

'Only when Emeline began to mix with girls her own age did it become apparent to us she was, let's say … *different*.'

'What happened?'

'Well, one afternoon I returned home to find Emeline and five of her friends hanging upside down from the ceiling. They were arranged like bats, I tell you. I was shocked, of course. Only Emeline found the trick in any way amusing. The other girls were screaming to be freed of the magic's influence.'

Abe looks over the rim of his tankard. 'It's a common spell among our kind. She would have meant no harm by it.'

'That 'common spell' brought my home to its knees in the weeks that followed, boy.'

'It seems we have both lost a great deal,' says Abe.

'On that much we can agree,' says Stevens, clearing away the dry tankards. 'Now tell me what happened to Mary after I left her on Caldey. I've watched the wharf each evening since her departure. You see, Tenby is presently in the throes of the most confounding miracle, and I suspect you, or her, may well be responsible …'

… The pair are then seen visiting Rowan Cottage, producing a little tear in Mary's eye which actually sharpens the quality of the image for a second. Mary is forced to tolerate it sliding across the curve of her cheek like a snail's trail, afraid to remove her hands from the glass plate and risk disrupting or breaking the connection. In these scenes, Abe and Stevens confront a plague-infested Nancy, confirming that the old woman had been the originator of the curse.

'Until quite recently I thought Mary was the Last of the Knowing Ones,' says Nancy.

Stevens and Abe remain silent, allowing Nancy to continue.

'Such was told at her birth, by prophets of the old lore. That with Mary's death, no witch would again be privy to events *yet* to occur.'

The news makes Mary take a step away from the glass plate, requiring Indigo to urge her sister back to retain a connection, which she does after a few seconds.

Nancy's voice is barely a whisper, 'The night she left this very cottage – no doubt to meet with the fairies on Harrowing Point – Mary told me about a girl she saw in leaves at the bottom of her cup.'

Abe slides forward in his seat, as if enchanted by the words of a storyteller, 'What did she see?'

'Another Knowing One, of course: meaning that our Mother Goddess was still not yet ready to trust witch or mortalkind to live without Her assistance.'

At this point Harriet stares at Indigo, who offers her sister a broad smile in place of actual words.

'I'm confused,' Abe admits after some time.

Nancy's pock-marked skin stands out in the half-light of the kitchen. 'It's simple, boy. Each generation of Harries possesses the skill to read the future.'

Stevens asks, 'So where do you think Mary has gone, old woman?'

'I suspect a Knowing One called to her from across time.'

Abe rises from his chair.

'So, she's somewhere in the future, with a descendent of the Harries clan? That could mean she's not coming back!'

'I don't know about that,' Nancy offers, her face twisted with upset. 'But I do know the journey she's on has taken her from me.'

Stevens stands and joins Abe, as if preparing to leave.

'At least Mary took her tools,' Nancy adds.

Abe nods to the old woman, reaching into his satchel and taking out a velvet bag. 'I have them here,' he says.

'But she's powerless without them!' Nancy gasps. Her veined hands reach out, her eyes little pinpricks of light. 'One in particular would prove useful in the battle between opposing magical forces.'

'The pentacle,' Abe offers, removing it from its cloth casing and showing it to the old witch.

Stevens watches on, dumbfounded.

'Her parents never got chance to tell Mary just how powerful that pentacle is over others of its kind. They died, you see, from the plague.'

'Which was really a curse created by you,' Abe says. 'And you didn't think to tell Mary, about the pentacle, at least?'

Nancy then says, 'I wanted her to live as normal a life as possible, you see. I intended to tell her later, once she was old enough to handle the responsibility. They'll come looking for it now it's out in the open and without its protector.'

Here, she casts a curse-filled look in the farmer's direction. 'Your friends will come to Tenby and they'll use its power for themselves. And all done in Cromwell's name.'

'It's not safe here,' Abe determines. 'But where should we take it?'

Nancy smiles at last. 'That, I do know. The sacred pentacle must be *unmade* where it was originally *made*.'

Stevens suggests, 'You should leave it here, Master Aderyn and return to your home. It's no concern of ours what comes of this parting of young Mary and her family's pentacle.'

'You're wrong,' growls Nancy, rising now to her feet and bearing down on Stevens. 'The sacred pentacle was created to protect each and every living soul. And until now it did its job. What comes of the separation between this object and its true owner affects every single one of us: all those that live now and those *yet* to live.'

'We'll unmake it,' Abe assures the old lady. 'Until such a time when its pieces can be reassembled and its true power can again be wielded for good.'

Nancy nods, 'You must head east – back into England.'

'What's there?' asks Stevens.

'Stonehenge,' replies Nancy, her voice fragile. 'A great stone circle, many thousands of years old, erected by an ancient cult and more powerful than even the object entrusted to you by my granddaughter. It is said that Aradian Crafters forged the sacred pentacle at the very centre of the circle – and it is there it must be unmade.'

Stevens turns to Abe.

'I've never been to Stonehenge, although I do know Avebury, which lies a little further north, a village that happens to lie within another great circle of stones. It might be best to head there first.'

'Anything else you want to tell us, Witchfinder?' asks Nancy. Abe fixes his gaze on Stevens.

Stevens brings his brow down over his eyes, as if to conceal them, 'I have passed through it many times on my way from London to home, that is all. Be satisfied with my answer, old woman …'

… In the next scene, Stevens and Abe share a single horse, a beautiful piebald mare named Cottonfloss, which Mary recognises as belonging to the farmer. Fragmented images appear in the lens of the broadcast portal as farmer, boy and horse navigate a series of rolling fields, meadows and dales, revealing to Indigo and Harriet snippets of an unspoiled world, of natural beauty and serenity …

... Abe and Stevens are next seen riding through a raging storm, forked lightning tearing through trees to the left and right of them. Mary watches on, having to remind herself not to make her presence known. She instead speaks to Abe using the power of thought alone. *Use the black mirror, boy,* she urges him, sounding out in young Abe's head as the voice of his own subconscious mind. In a second, Abe slips from the horse's back and strides away to a patch of open ground between half a dozen great oaks. Stevens cries out for the boy to see sense and get back on Cottonfloss. Abe, though – perhaps still being guided by Mary some four hundred years or so removed from the scene – raises the black mirror high above his head and skilfully uses it as a conductor, drawing currents of deadly electricity from the sky above him and capturing each tendril in the mirror's glass surface, until the storm moves on. By the time Stevens gets to Abe, he sees for himself the boy's act has cost Abe an aspect of his youthful good looks: the boy's once auburn hair has now turned a hoary white from root to tip ...

... Next, the pair arrive at a settlement that an old wooden sign states to be Avebury. The sisters marvel at the tall, upright stones encircling the whole village like a set of fearful-looking teeth. Rather worryingly, Abe seems to have his hands bound behind his back, as if he were Stevens' prisoner. Mary bows her head when Stevens approaches a clerk to the court, accepting a bulging bag of coins for his work in capturing another witch.

'I have secured a boy-witch from Pembrokeshire,' says Stevens, drawing a smile from the clerk …

… In the next scene, the farmer is alone with an older man, whose grey skin shimmers in the candlelight.

'You've performed your task most admirably, Witchfinder.'

'My thanks to you, Lord Rees-Repton.'

At mention of the name, Harriet and Indigo exchange concerned looks. It is obvious to them both that members of the same family occupy several timelines and all with one purpose in mind: to track down the sacred pentacle and take possession of it for themselves.

Rees-Repton's voice seems to crawl across the table that separates him from his guest. 'The young man is now safely under lock and key. You should know it's my intention to have him stand trial as soon as tomorrow and see him hang before sunset of the same day.'

'He has no great skill as a witch, Your Lordship.'

'He's a witch, Stevens, and must therefore carry the penalty for practising the Craft.'

Stevens pauses before adding a further remark. 'During my investigations, I have come to learn a great deal about the nature of the sacred pentacle and have noted that misery and suffering seem to follow it wherever it goes, my lord.'

Rees-Repton finally makes himself visible among the smoky atmosphere of the room. The sisters see a pair of bulbous, watery eyes and a mouth that presses up and out in a triangle of perfect menace.

'Don't lose sight of your mission, Witchfinder, or your final reward shall go to someone else. You've procured *all* the articles, I take it?'

'All but the girl's broom, my lord. The rest are contained within this bag.'

Despite his disappointment in not yet acquiring the broom, Rees-Repton cannot conceal his excitement as he watches Stevens produce a number of objects. Stevens sets them out along the gnarled oak table, arranging them left to right in the following order: the cords of charm, the black mirror, the athame and, finally, a pentacle.

'Why is he handing over my family's pentacle?' whispers Mary to her sisters.

Harriet shakes her head, saying, 'Trust me, Mary, that's not the real one. It's a fake, a copy. Abe and Stevens must have hidden the real one on the way to Avebury, although the portal hasn't shown us exactly where, yet.'

As if able to hear the girls, Rees-Repton brings the pentacle close to his right eye, checking it for authenticity. 'My family have pursued this since time immemorial, but it always managed to evade us – that is, until now.'

Stevens licks his lips as he forms his next deceit, 'The boy's mission was to unmake it where it was made. Possibly here in Avebury or a place called Stonehenge, Your Lordship. Do you know which one?'

Rees-Repton's eyes narrow until they almost disappear.

'You seem to be developing an unhealthy interest in magical practice, Stevens. Remember, you're a witchfinder, not a witch.'

Stevens shifts uneasily on his heels, drawing the attention of the judge.

'Fear not, man. I know you're a God-fearing Christian. And one that'll be handsomely rewarded for his work, don't you worry.'

'I was thinking I should like a property of my own: a little cottage I thought, set by a river, but just high enough for the water to be fresh and the salmon to be plentiful. I would live simply and within my means, work the land and pay my taxes on time, my lord. I wouldn't trouble anyone for company or tell a single soul of all I've discovered after working closely with you.'

Rees-Repton doesn't allow himself to be seduced by the qualities of the witchfinder's descriptive powers.

'You will receive gold, and a lot of it. What you choose to squander it on is no concern of mine. For now, I bid you goodnight, Witchfinder.'

Stevens bows with mock reverence and promptly leaves the room, aware Rees-Repton's interest could not be torn from the magical articles ranged before him on the table, particularly the counterfeit sacred pentacle that glistens and gleams as if imbued with actual magic …

… In another scene, Stevens manages to visit Abe in his cell, moonlight trickling in through a narrow slit in the brickwork. Abe and Stevens discuss the fact that the two of them still intend to 'unmake' the original pentacle, if they can somehow get to Stonehenge …

… Court commences the very next day. Mary, Harriet and Indigo look on in horror as a number of women and children face trial, suspected of using witchcraft against other villagers. One after another is condemned by the same Lord Rees-Repton that featured in the previous scene.

Shortly, Abe enters court to take his place on a stool, set before a large audience.

'Case number 461, The People versus Abraham Aderyn of Caldey Isle, Pembrokeshire,' calls the clerk.

'He looks frightened,' whispers Mary, as if to herself.

'Your name, please – and state it clearly for the court,' orders Rees-Repton.

'Abraham Aderyn.'

At last, the young witch sees the familiar figure of Stevens make his way from the rear of the court to the front. His gait is rather uneven, his brilliant flash of orange hair tied back in a ponytail.

Rees-Repton says, 'Witchfinder Stevens is here today as a representative of the people and will produce evidence in accordance with the rules of my court.'

Stevens takes a deep breath before regaling the gathered company with a tale of how he had, through sheer dogged determination and investigative rigour, managed to unearth a cult of considerable size while working in the seaside town of Tenby, Wales. He'd witnessed the dark intent of the community as all manner of curses and spells besieged the local population, resulting in a deadly plague that ended the lives of many hundreds of innocent citizens. He next tells of how he successfully tracked the source of such evil to a population of renegade witches on the Isle of Caldey, a member of which sat before the court that afternoon: one Abraham Aderyn.

'The boy is an untrustworthy witch,' declares Stevens. 'And one whose powers have notoriously been set against good people, with no purpose other than to inflict harm for harm's sake.'

'Lies!' shouts Abe, rising from his stool to challenge the witchfinder.

'Order! Order!' Rees-Repton calls out, seizing the opportunity to cast a spell over the young man, so that every time Abe moves to speak he finds his tongue and lips will not work in tandem and produce speech.

'Please continue,' says Lord Rees-Repton.

Prompted, Stevens details for the court how he had come to be in possession of a number of magical instruments, each now paraded before the assembly by one of the clerks. Rees-Repton's black eyes flash silver when they alight upon the athame and the sacred pentacle, as if some dark aspect of his character has been stoked.

Rees-Repton then says to Stevens, 'I take it that, in your time with the suspect, you saw him use many, if not all, of these wicked instruments?'

The judge waits for his question to be answered, but Stevens seems instead to focus on Abe. 'The subject is presently unable to defend himself, Your Honour. Might the court reconvene in, say, half an hour?'

Rees-Repton barks, 'Witchfinder Stevens, on whose authority do you have it that my court should reconvene as and when *you* desire it do so?'

Stevens remains silent, drawing quizzical looks from each of the three girls, silent and helpless in the broadcast portal room, many hundreds of years into the future.

'Well? Speak, man!' orders the judge.

The public now engage one another in conversation, amused as they are by the turn of events. The thrill of such theatrics is precisely the reason they attend in such high numbers. Here and there, citizens rise from their seats and call across the space for order to be restored.

Rees-Repton's gavel promptly falls to work, executing stroke after stroke, his great booming voice regimenting the babbling mouths of people back to the silence whence they came.

Desperate to re-engage Abe, Stevens stands directly before the boy, the athame balanced on the witchfinder's upturned palms. 'Do you recognise this article, young Master Aderyn?

'Stevens, I order you to step away from the defendant!' warns the judge, his voice rising in pitch and gaining in intensity.

'Why, it's a magical athame,' Abe replies, his eyes now quite dry, his colour fully restored. 'It's the essential tool of any witch, enabling its owner to cast a circle of protection.'

Harriet and Mary almost move to cheer until they are silenced by Indigo with a single, withering look. As one, the three girls resume their positions at the portal.

'Then cast away, my friend, for we are now in dire need of its protection!' shouts Stevens.

Rees-Repton's eyes widen, as if a reptilian aspect of his character has been stirred from its slumber. He stands to the vertical, his great hands made into fists of unexploded anger.

'Witchfinder, you'll pay for this deception!'

Stevens appears to ignore the threat, stepping towards the young witch who now grips the athame tightly about its handle and carves a circle from the air itself. This is done so swiftly that the two friends are quickly enclosed within the shape's circumference.

At witnessing magic, people scream and shout before scrambling for the room's exit.

A crimson-cheeked judge yells, 'Arrest them both!'

Rees-Repton then casts a terrible spell on various keepers of the peace, swords and rapiers rising involuntarily from their hilts to hurtle at speed in the direction of man and boy locked within their magic bubble. A few miss their targets, landing instead in the backs of fleeing citizens - each victim falling to their knees and issuing their final breaths.

The sisters watch on in horror as violence ripples through the court.

'Rees-Repton is working his way towards the remaining objects,' warns Stevens. Abe agrees with a nod but much of his energy is being spent maintaining the sphere's defences.

A small army of benches now rise from the ground until they hang suspended in the air.

'He's barring our way,' says Stevens. 'We can't get around such an obstacle. We must retrieve Mary's objects at some later point in time. Our circle will not last much longer!'

On cue, Abe's eyes now droop and close, the athame falling to the expanse of floor and drawing the attention of Rees-Repton.

Furious, the judge yells, 'Witchfinder, know this: I'll hunt down every last one of your kind until not a single Stevens remains alive. I'll hang them all, do you hear me? Or I'll burn them, or drown them, for this act of treachery. Mark my words!'

'I hear you, judge,' Stevens says at last, lifting the inert body of Abe over his right shoulder while retrieving the magical athame from the floor. 'But hear me, too. There is a greater power at work here, moving between us and through us, a force so powerful it'll make a hero of this young boy. He will play his part in a story that will linger long in the memory of men and women, centuries beyond today. And know this, too: I now serve an authority greater than yours. I'm no longer your servant …'

… The setting changes for the next scene, revealing a different stone circle to the one that runs the circumference of Avebury.

'Stonehenge!' cries Harriet, drawing a stern look from Indigo next to her at the portal, but thankfully not heard by Abe and Stevens. They are too busy pacing around the interior of the circle to think Harriet's utterance is anything more than the wind, passing through one of its doorways.

Eventually, Abe and Stevens come together at the centre of the circle, to stand either side of a small boulder with a flat and unnaturally smooth top.

'This one's more like a plinth,' says Stevens.

Abe bends down until his eye is level with the top of the stone, his right hand travelling left to right across the cold surface. 'I can just feel a shallow dip, here,' he says.

Stevens bends down to mirror the young witch's body language. 'Is it a circle, like the pentacle?' he asks.

Abe retrieves the sacred pentacle from a pocket in his jacket.

'The pentacle didn't show us where they hid it before reaching Avebury,' whispers Harriet to Indigo. 'But they have it now.'

The sisters huddle closer together around the portal screen, watching in silence as Abe rubs the silver disc with one edge of his shirt, until it is able to reflect the amber light of dawn.

Stevens meets Abe's eye for a second as the young witch prepares to lower the pentacle into the circular impression. 'Go on, boy. I have your back.'

Nothing appears to happen at first. It is just any old witch's pentacle perched on a lump of stone in the middle of a vast, open plain.

Only when man and boy stand upright and step away from the plinth does something seem to stir, beginning as a distant rumble, then travelling slowly and steadily up through the earth to reach the surface.

'Look,' says Abe, raising a hand and pointing directly at one of the stone doorways.

And there, for all to see – including Mary, Harriet and Indigo – the fabric of one entranceway seems to be pulled inwards to its centre. It bevels the rectangle of space, until a brilliant light yields a ghostly apparition whose shape resembles that of a human child. Indeed, light itself marks out the hollows of its cheeks, the gaping zero of a mouth and two ghastly, sunken eyes.

'Look! There are more!' Stevens warns, four other doorways igniting with spiritual energy and disgorging more unearthly shadow people onto the ground around the site.

Abe watches as one of the spirits sails across the space towards the pair and suddenly merges with Stevens, the film of its skin slipping over the older man's figure like a blanket of the finest silk.

'We speak through you and with you,' Stevens' figure intones; he has become a puppet, used by the first of the Crafters to convey their welcome message.

'My name's Abraham Aderyn,' stutters the younger man, transfixed.

'We know who you are, Master Aderyn!' ...

Mary looks over her shoulder at her sisters, who merely nod to her, as if requesting she hold her nerve a while longer.

… Abe shifts uneasily on his feet, catching sight of a second spirit who deposes the first from its place in Stevens to register its voice – this one decidedly more feminine than the first.

'Five made the Circle and Five shall unmake it.'

Abe asks, 'What are your names?'

A third spirit, slighter in form, slips into the gap left by the second one. Stevens briefly re-awakens, before being plunged back into a world of indifference as the spirit speaks through him.

'We are Fire, Earth, Water and Air!'

On hearing this, a fifth spirit dives headfirst, from the highest of the stone plinths, into the human vessel that is Stevens and turns the farmer's eyes opaque white.

'And I'm the Girl Child with the Hidden Name. Pleased to make your acquaintance, Abe Aderyn!'

Abe extends the hand of friendship to this Crafter specifically.

At this gesture, all five Crafters laugh with glee, their collective noise turning the whole sky above the site a shade brighter.

'I'm here with a strange request,' says Abe.

Another change occurs here, the Girl Child with the Hidden Name being ousted from her position within Stevens.

'We know why you're here. We've been expecting you.'

Abe – along with the three unseen sisters watching from the side-lines – is dumbfounded.

'Expecting me?'

The spirit giggles, 'Man cannot be trusted to use magic without serving his own desires. For that reason, we have brought you here, boy with the silver hair!'

Abe feels his temper flare, asking, 'Why forge the pentacle in the first place, if you knew one day its magic might be abused by the very people it was meant to protect?'

The Girl Child with the Hidden Name now sails forward, taking possession of Stevens.

'I'm the only child of the Mother Goddess. She's done her best to nurture me, provide for me, love me as one might a human child, but my father is less reliable.'

Abe shakes his head, knowing what's coming next.

'Mankind is the masculine,' she continues, 'the father I long to know! But alas, a father who shuns me when I need him.'

Another spirit speaks now.

'We made the sacred pentacle as a symbol of hope, boy. It represents humankind's willingness to create and evolve. But now it could fall into the hands of selfish men, whose only thought is to destroy. In the hands of the feminine, the sacred pentacle will make new all that has fallen into disrepair: rejuvenation over decay. For this reason we shall unmake the pentacle until such a time when it can be reassembled and its power wielded by women.'

Abe notes Stevens is suddenly present but the older man's mind seems still very much clouded with abstract images.

'What happened to me?'

Abe says, 'The Crafters have agreed to my request. The pentacle will be unmade.'

'Good timing,' Stevens says, 'for I hear horses in the distance: a small army, no doubt belonging to the judge!'

'Something evil this way comes,' the spirits sing, their voices heard as howling winds leaping over the upright stones of the henge.

The Crafters soon set to work on unmaking the sacred pentacle. The four elemental spirits, joined now by the Girl Child with the Hidden Name, form a tight circle about the plinth on which the object currently rests. Abe and Stevens step away from the scene, the older of the two taking charge and drawing the boy to his side.

Watching from a distance, the pair see the Crafters dance about the plinth, moving counter-clockwise and bringing to Mary's mind the fairy lights she'd seen out on Harrowing Point the evening of her disappearance – and the last time she'd seen Stevens, her grandmother and Abe.

The Crafters recite an ancient song:

'Birth to come magic the let
Grail the ensoul Lance the let
Earth the touch lightning the let
Anvil the strike hammer the let
Aradia, oh Aradia
Trust Perfect and Love Perfect
Passwords two have I
Ama thee to call we

Mother sterile dark
Return must life
manifested all whom to thou
Tremble men whom before
Return, return, helper lovely O
Return, Light the of God
Sun the of God
Return, oh return!'

From the very ground beneath them, Abe and Stevens identify a second great rumbling, but this one is travelling along the topsoil to reach their position.

'Those horses are getting close,' Stevens says. 'We must take cover!'

But the great shaking earth feels not the galloping charge of Lord Rees-Repton's riders. It moves instead with a great stirring from the Mother Goddess as she rises from Her slumber to meet with the Crafters.

'Look!' shouts Abe.

High above them hangs a volley of arrows, suspended on the very air itself, as if frozen in time.

Stevens looks off into the distance, pointing out a small outfit of riders and horses, and there: a clutch of archers with their faces upturned to the morning sky, all frozen mid-gallop and creating a tableau of one single moment in time.

Abe cries out, 'We're safe so long as the Crafters hold their magic!' He moves, with Stevens, to the far side of the henge, where they are able to witness the continuing spectacle.

Each of the elemental spirits and the Girl Child with the Hidden Name now turn inwards to face the centre of the spinning circle, the stems of their ghostly fingers hooking onto separate portions of the pentacle and drawing a great moan from somewhere deep beneath the ground. Then comes a perfect moment of uninterrupted silence, in which the sacred pentacle is pulled apart by the very seams that have held it together for so long.

And so it comes to pass that the sacred pentacle is unmade, signalling the start of its adventure as five separate fragments, each one as powerful as the next but containing very different properties.

'Where are you going?' Abe yells to Stevens, who now appears to be wandering off towards one of the stone portals. All about the area a fierce, blinding light leaks out between great cracks in the ground, as if the molten earth beneath them is being deconstructed. *Perhaps to mirror the destruction of the sacred pentacle*, thinks Indigo, watching on in silence.

The Crafters repeat their song, a poem of sorts spoken in reverse, for time itself is, instead, being re-shaped by a mortal occupying space within their sacred boundary. Stevens stands before one doorway, which presents him with a series of moving images, as if being instructed to move in the opposite direction to that in which time normally operates.

'Come away!' begs Abe, his eyes fixed on the unusual doorway.

Stevens says, 'The pentacle looks into a man's heart, son. It allows him to see what he wants to see, not always what's right or good for him.'

'So true,' Mary whispers, hoping the farmer is able to hear her.

The Crafters complete their ritual, flying to various positions around the circumference of the circle, where a spectral doorway waits for each of them to make their exit when the time is right.

Stevens watches on as the Girl with the Hidden Name enters Abe's body, preparing to speak. As happened with Stevens, the young witch's eyes turn white.

'Owen Stevens, stand aside and let me pass!'

'I want to go with you, child.'

'I cannot just let anyone enter the doorway, sir. None shall pass except the Last of the Knowing Ones!'

Stevens grabs hold of Abe, shaking him by the shoulders.

'Since my wife passed, I've waited for an opportunity to see her again. Will you not grant me this one wish, spirit?'

The child says nothing, its white eyes quite characterless.

Stevens presses on with a final question.

'If I'm to be denied, then at least tell me: what is the time and manner of my death?'

The Girl Child with the Hidden Name knows the answer to the farmer's question and says, without deliberation or sentiment, 'Why, this very moment, Owen Stevens, with an arrow in your back!'

In the blink of an eye, time returns to its normal direction and beat, the spirit children retreating to the interiors of their doorways. Each one holds a fragment of the sacred pentacle locked between their teeth and they quickly disperse to their own realms, wildly different to the henge. The arrows, now freed from their stasis, continue on their deadly arcs towards the stone circle – one from Lord Rees-Repton's bow finding Stevens and bringing the farmer to his knees. And true to the Girl Child's word, Stevens dies on the very spot he expected his new life to commence, drawing a soul-shattering scream from Mary, her hands almost slipping from the glass disc in front of her. Indigo and Harriet exchange a pitiful look with one another, wondering if they should terminate the experiment. Instead, they drag their eyes back to the portal.

'No!' cries Abe, rushing to his companion's side.

Stevens knows exactly what he's going to say, his voice croaking at its edges.

'It's been an honour, boy, to have helped you get this far. Now, go home. Fly like the wind and save yourself …'

… In the final scene, the three sisters watch a lone eagle rise into the morning air, a glorious sun dappling its wings with spectral light. Mary's tears travel through time and become a deluge of rain on the other side of the portal, finding the inert body of her one-time friend amongst the stones, a simple doorway marking out the borders of Stevens' grave …

… Mary is unable to take any more. She faints, curling away from the glass disc and onto the cold floor of the laboratory, the engine's lasers losing their momentum and quickly grinding to a halt.

'Mary!' calls Indigo, rushing to her sister. Harriet, quickly following at her heels, says soothingly, 'We're here. Everything's going to be fine. We're right here, Mary.'

But everything is going to be far from *fine* for the sisters of the broken pentacle, as a number of Rees-Repton's security guards now burst into the laboratory, rifles at the ready and with orders to take the girls into custody – whether they go willingly, or otherwise.

A Midnight Darkness

Sir Oliver Rees-Repton has acted on a hunch, based on an intuition about how the minds of mischievous children operate. After all, he has been one himself, albeit long ago. At the age of seven, the orphaned Oliver found mild amusement in casting spells at the closed door of his uncle's study. But despite the multitude of opportunities to build bridges between the two, this never occurred. The relationship remained a purely functional one, in which the nephew met with his benefactor only ever intermittently - perhaps three or four times a year - and only ever to discuss key matters. For example, Oliver is thirteen before he first hears mention of the broken pentacle.

Vitus looks across the desk at his nephew.

'You're my brother's sole surviving heir and destined to inherit a sizable fortune, should my quest to gain a son or daughter continue to prove … unfruitful.'

Oliver says nothing. *Best not to engage*, he thinks.

'I've sent for you today, boy, as I think it's time you were told about your family's keen interest in matters pertaining to the occult.'

Vitus smooths the dark band of hair against his scalp, before continuing, 'In short, you're descended from a line of powerful witches that dates right back to the dawn of witchcraft itself.'

The news comes as no surprise to Oliver for he had, at the tender age of eight, been sent away to boarding school, only to be sent home mid-point through the first term for forming an, *'unhealthy attachment to that period of time between lights out and morning,'* as his house master had stated in a letter. He'd been found creeping among a midnight darkness of shadows, and duly reprimanded for this unusual crime.

'Have you heard of the Aradian Crafters?'

Oliver shakes his head.

'They were a small coven of witches who practised an ancient form of the Craft here in Britain many thousands of years ago, long before the Romans or Vikings took it upon themselves to invade these shores.'

Oliver's attention wanes here, for the narrative has about it the pungent odour of myth and he prefers to deal in facts.

'Interestingly,' Vitus adds, 'one of the original Crafters happened to be a member of the Rees-Repton clan. He was of Aradian descent and took his place alongside other notable witches who conceived the idea to draw together the disparate elements of our Mother Goddess in a single expression of energy.'

Oliver's mouth gapes open slightly, revealing a lower bar of crooked, ivory-white teeth.

His uncle presses on with his story.

'The Crafters drew on powerful magic to construct the sacred pentacle, an object that contains within its circumference all five aspects of nature itself and is able to imbue its keeper with unrivalled magical powers.'

'I suspect this item is somehow connected to the demise of my parents,' Oliver says, his first words since entering the study.

'Very good, boy. It is true your parents fought a deadly battle with one another – the whereabouts of the object's various pieces at the heart of their conflict.'

'I see.'

'Anyway, many millennia later the pentacle came to be unmade, the elemental spirits intentionally separated from one another. I suspect this was done to ensure the object would never fall into the *wrong hands,* as it were. The fragments ended up in different parts of the world and, over time, this fracturing of the Mother Goddess allowed man the freedom to harness all manner of destructive technologies and profit from this great rift in the natural order; where once the sacred pentacle symbolised balance and equilibrium it now carried with it the negative connotations of chaos and misrule.'

Oliver's mind begins to quietly hum with the new information.

Vitus adds, 'Men like us have gained a great deal from the pentacle's destruction. Capitalists, industrialists and entrepreneurs have happily plundered the planet's natural resources and constructed empires built to stand the test of time. Indeed, the quest to re-assemble the pentacle might well restore order to a world in disarray but would also signal certain doom for our family and future generations of Rees-Reptons, you understand ...'

Here, the lizard-like Vitus pauses for dramatic effect, before arriving at a final thought.

'That is, unless we take it upon ourselves to acquire the fragments before other parties, thereby securing an advantage over our competitors.'

○

As it stands, many of the complex's inhabitants are comfortably in the pay of Sentinel Technologies. So much so that the arrival of Rees-Repton's henchmen plays out as a mere rumbling at the edges of Carmichael's consciousness. Suddenly concerned for Indigo, but without really knowing why, he slides out of bed and calls to the wall panels to provide him with enough light to see by. The strained bulbs slowly emerge from blackout, bringing into focus a familiar face.

'Good evening, Professor.'

Carmichael loses his footing and tumbles backwards onto the bed. Searching, he finds the metal frames of his spectacles, able then to confront Oliver Rees-Repton, who towers high above him.

'These are my private quarters, sir!'

Rees-Repton sighs, 'There's no such thing as *private* in this corporation, Professor.'

Carmichael is able to discern the shadows of Maxwell and Anton lurking in the doorway and wearing identical expressions of blank indifference.

'What do you want?'

From behind the group a young girl emerges, teary-eyed and pale. Her hands are bound behind her back. It's Indigo.

'Father!' she cries.

Rees-Repton smiles and merely hands the professor a lab coat.

'Get dressed. You and your daughter have work to do.'

'What have you done with Indigo?' Harriet shouts as she's thrown forward into the little cell.

Moved to support the young witch, Helen calls after the guard who has deposited not one but two young girls into her cell, although he doesn't respond, closing the door behind him with speed. Behind her, Mary lands face down on the cell's bed, her body limp.

A long, drawn-out minute passes before Mary manages to regain her composure, in which time Helen and Harriet have become re-acquainted with one another.

Harriet's voice is a salve for the ears.

'Mary, are you recovered?'

'I'm fine,' she says. 'I tried a spell on one of them, but it didn't work; in fact, it backfired and knocked me out. The guards are protected by a number of powerful deflector spells.'

'Who's this, then?' Helen asks, her eyes looking kindly on Mary.

Well-disposed to performing acts of courtesy, Harriet takes it upon herself to make introductions between the woman and her sister of the broken pentacle.

'Another of the professor's prisoners, then?'

The two girls look at their fellow inmate in confusion, until eventually Harriet offers, 'It wasn't the professor who summoned us, kind lady, but his daughter, Indigo. We're *sisters* of a kind, destined to reunite pieces of a magical artefact that promises to bring peace and order to the planet.'

Helen falls silent, thinking to herself that a difficult night lay in store for her in light of these new facts.

Mary and Harriet sit down next to the woman, the bed's feeble springs straining beneath the combined weight of their bodies.

'What do you think they're going to do to Indigo?' asks Harriet.

Helen says, 'Who exactly are *they*?'

Mary looks up.

'Actually, you look like us – *like Indigo*, I mean.'

Helen suddenly finds her every movement being closely observed by the two sisters.

'And that is important, because?'

Mary reaches across and captures a lock of Helen's hair between two fingers.

'There's a spell, a rather gruesome one, that requires a little of this and a special incantation.'

Helen panics, certain she's in the company of devils, leaping to her feet and backing into one corner of the cell.

Undeterred, Mary steps towards her, the opening strains of an incantation heard bubbling away in her throat.

'Catch the bracken between ye finger and thumb,
For thrice his spirit will haunt your face.
Aberon of Manderon,
Much-loved spirit of frivolity and fun,
We call upon thee
Thrice times beneath the sun,
Thrice times beneath the moon,
Thrice times beneath the stars,
To come unto us, thrice times your girls.'

Far below the seabed, the accelerator engine blinks into life, its long banks of coloured lights appearing like an elegant rainbow cutting through cloud. In silence, Rees-

Repton watches on as the broadcast portal emits an eerie, otherworldly glow and – like the unsheathed eye of a great sleeping dragon – it observes him, too.

Indigo and her father exchange one or two uneasy glances, but the young witch is certain her father shoulders a deeper hurt than any she currently feels. She thinks she hears him whisper, 'Stay strong,' to her but she can't be certain.

'Your friends are safe,' says Rees-Repton, as if able to read the young girl's mind.

'My sisters can take care of themselves, sir. Keeping company with such despicable characters, I fear for my own safety before theirs.'

Carmichael turns to his daughter, saying sharply, 'Indigo, mind your tongue. These people are dangerous.'

'You should listen to your father,' warns one of the twins from somewhere to Indigo's left.

As instructed, Carmichael inputs a chain of commands into one of the mainframe's keyboards, fully aware Rees-Repton is marking his every action.

'It's ready,' he says after some time.

'Ready for *what*, exactly?' asks Indigo.

'Well, *there's the rub*,' Rees-Repton smiles, sliding over the tiled floor until he's standing between father and daughter. 'You're to demonstrate the power of the pentacle fragment you have about your pretty little throat,' he continues. 'I'll get to see exactly how you managed to use one of our own machines against us, Miss Carmichael.'

The professor seems adrift on a body of water, truth itself swirling beyond the reach of his fingers.

'What?' he says. 'You know how to operate the engine?'

Indigo remains silent. Rees-Repton speaks for her.

'Your daughter's *a witch*, Professor, possessing considerable intelligence and a steely determination rarely witnessed in one so young.'

'I'm a lot older than you think,' Indigo smiles. 'I've lived many lives before this one.'

Rees-Repton's dark humour bubbles to the surface.

'Well, they must have been bad lives for you to end up so ... *deficient*.'

Indigo inwardly reels from the insult but refuses to show his remark has hurt. Folding her skinny arms across her chest, she tilts her chin defiantly.

'And what makes you think I'll co-operate?'

Right on cue, Maxwell and Anton transform from human to canine form and manage to draw a little shriek of surprise from the sister.

'It was them all along! The ones who chased us through town and tried to kill me!'

The dogs now lope across the floor, teeth bared, the pelts of their coats shining jet black, which accentuates their every move.

'The professor is your target,' Rees-Repton instructs them, 'not the girl.'

The dogs respond, leaping at the flailing arms of Carmichael and sinking their teeth into the sleeves of his lab coat. In a moment, they have him pinned against the wall.

'Father!' cries Indigo.

'The engine requires your attention,' Rees-Repton reminds her, coldly. 'Please, go ahead, Miss Carmichael.'

Indigo rubs at thin trails of tears marking her cheeks but manages to focus on the task ahead, hands stretched out before her in search of a single glass plate.

○

The young man standing guard outside Helen's cell is snapped back to wakefulness by a sudden flash of blinding lights that fill the whole of the corridor and briefly rob him of his sight. He stands to attention with an uneasy stumble, his radio controller's panel now blacked out as if its battery has been burnt out.

'Hello?' he calls through the cell's little window.

On the far side of the room stands a line of identical-looking girls, rather than the three individuals he left just a short time ago. They presently have their backs to him, heads lowered as if meditating, but with silver hair hanging forward across their faces like the fronds of some exotic flower.

'Stay where you are, I'm coming in,' he shouts. 'And I don't expect any funny business!'

After some thought, he grips the door handle and moves it from horizontal to diagonal, seconds easing by until the first of his steel-capped boots lands within the perimeter of the room. He cocks his head to speak into his lapel. 'Anderson calling in … Anderson requesting back up – over.' But the little device shows no signs of life.

The guard creeps forward until he's just a few feet from the line of witches. He has his gun raised but its muzzle, catching a little of his nervousness, is dipping earthwards. He's been told only to use force if absolutely necessary.

'Turn around, so I can see your faces,' he demands, his tone stiff and unconvincing. 'I order you to turn around!'

The three girls wait another few seconds, until they're sure the guard will use force against one, or all, of them. And only then do they begin to quietly hoot like owls of the forest. The haunting sound is quickly followed by the gruesome image of three heads twisting through a half-circle to face the guard, their bodies remaining parallel with the wall.

'What the …'

Most distressing of all is that the three faces appear to be faithful replicas of the guard's own, except for the eyes. In the space where they should be, each face is showing a picture of manhood at different intervals along Anderson's lifeline: young boy, fully-grown adult and an old man.

'I must be asleep! That's what this is: a nightmare!'

The boy-guard speaks first, its voice light and airy to match the pallor of its skin.

'Jacob was a lonely boy.'

Adult-guard goes next.

'Jacob is a lonely man.'

Followed by aged guard, withered and grey, with white hair to match its eyes, concluding the incantation.

'Jacob is to die alone.'

This final curse proves too much for Anderson, who collapses in a heap on the floor.

'Unbelievable,' Helen says, returning to her usual form.

Harriet steps over the motionless body of the guard. There is a little of the man's colouring still in the young witch's features, but she knows they're now free to explore the corridor, unlike the guard who's about to become a prisoner of his own making.

○

The image which fills the broadcast portal is that of an elderly gentleman seated on a bench. He's dressed almost entirely in cream-coloured linen, a perfect match for the straw hat perched on his head. He has the look of an academic, stressed by the presence of a rather dense volume of poetry balanced on his left knee, where it crosses over his right. Large bronze-coloured toes poke out of the ends of sandals that seem unable to contain his two great feet. The light is dazzlingly pure and clear, suggesting a hot, sunny climate. On the gentleman's nose squats a pair of sunglasses whose tinted lenses mask the colour of his eyes ...

… Indigo guesses the man is waiting for a train, for all around him people stand still or pace up and down a narrow platform, many of them dressed differently to the gentleman, choosing instead colourful outfits for themselves and loved ones. Men and women congregate in large and small groups. Children run between the legs of more senior figures, all babbling a language Indigo doesn't immediately recognise; even the voice slinking through the speaker system at the station belongs to a foreign, alien world and altogether different to her own.

'He has a pentacle fragment. Look!' says Rees-Repton, pointing a finger at the screen and marking the outline of a triangular-shaped fragment of metal hanging loosely from a silver chain.

Carmichael glances first at his daughter and then at the screen. The whole of Indigo's face is bathed in light, prompting him to tell Rees-Repton, 'She appears to be drawing energy from an unknown source – severing the plate's connection with the locator and bypassing it to reach the engine and, beyond it, the portal.'

Rees-Repton whispers his response in hushed, ghostly tones, '*Light holes*, one suspects – using the divine power of the Mother Goddess to locate the separate elements of the sacred pentacle and reveal the identity and whereabouts of each keeper.'

Indigo looks up from the glass plate for a moment.

'What are *light holes*?'

Carmichael says, 'An incredibly rare phenomenon, child, and therefore we still know very little about them. We think perhaps they're made up of the most powerful particles known to science and – if their power can be harnessed correctly – could be used to help us travel vast distances across space and time. Needless to say, there are very few who've been privileged to witness one in its genesis form.'

Indigo is confused.

'Genesis, as in the Bible?'

Carmichael places a fatherly hand on her shoulder, as if preparing his daughter for bad news.

'As in the origins of all life.'

Indigo's hands finally slip free of the glass plate, taking with them the image of the gentleman as he begins to board his train.

Rees-Repton growls, 'You've scared the girl and we've lost sight of the keeper!'

Indigo recovers enough to ask one last question of her father.

'If a light-hole appears at the birth of a new universe, is it possible one created the system of stars we find ourselves living in today?'

With reluctance, Carmichael nods, evidently reeling from the news his own daughter appears to be imbued with an extraordinary brand of magic to rival that of a god or goddess.

With the two sisters and Helen now set free from the confines of the cell, a great hullabaloo erupts up and down the corridor. Prisoners of every description bang at their little windows, wielding objects such as plastic cups and plates to register their presence.

With the guard's security pass, the small group work quickly to unlock each cage, dozens of prisoners pouring into the narrow channel of grey concrete as though a reservoir's floodgates have suddenly been opened. Some are openly grateful, one shaking Harriet's hand and another hugging Mary until she's sure her backbone comes close to snapping. Some openly weep against Helen's shoulder and – having a great deal in common with those she's freeing from captivity – she sheds a few tears of her own.

It doesn't take a great deal of time before the alarm is raised, but the force of pent-up aggression proves too great a force for any guard in Rees-Repton's employment; none dare bar the way of these maligned souls.

Helen draws the girls aside, shielding their eyes, when one guard is trampled underfoot.

'How ghastly!' shudders Harriet, looking away in horror.

The group progresses through yet more networks of corridors, attempting to ignore the emergency sirens blaring out. In the distance, gunfire can be heard, with its deadly crack of powder and lead.

Helen says, 'It sounds like people could be losing their lives, and I feel responsible. If only I'd allowed myself to be seduced by the professor's dream that I was good enough to be passed off as his dead wife! He would have freed them then, I'm sure of it. My sacrifice might have allowed them to return to their old lives.'

'Wait!' interrupts Mary, snapping free of the group, 'I can smell smoke!'

Harriet's face blanches.

'You're right, Mary, I can smell it too … Oh no! The zoo, on the floor below us – where Indigo kept you when you were a hare – if there's a fire, the animals will all be trapped in their cages!'

But as they attempt to alter their direction to allow an unscheduled visit to the zoo, the group find they're unable to move against the flow of prisoners – scores of them – yelling and pushing past one another to escape the effects of dark, billowing smoke climbing up from the floor below.

Far beneath the scenes of mutiny and mayhem, the broadcast portal fizzes out until it's a mere speck of light on a dark background. In its place, a loud siren pierces the air. Indigo watches on as Rees-Repton's twin sons, still in canine form, follow their father out of the room, as he makes his escape.

Indigo turns to her father.

'Where do you think he's going?'

Carmichael says nothing, pre-occupied as he is with trying to plan a way out of the lab for them without attracting the attention of the marauding masses.

Wondering if his daughter is in danger of falling to the might of prisoners now filling the room, the professor executes the most tender of actions. He loops Indigo's two arms about his neck and inspires her to draw her legs up and about the trunk of his body. 'Never too old for a piggyback!' he laughs, breaking the tension in a moment.

'If a little too heavy these days,' laughs Indigo, hearing then the raucous shouts of escaped prisoners breaching the sealed doors and entering the facility.

'We must get you a broom, daughter witch, and together we'll fly away from our present troubles!'

'Ride on!' Indigo shouts, enjoying the brief moment of jollity.

And off they go, father and daughter, negotiating a series of inter-connected rooms until finally they're able to disappear into one of the many air vents that connect different parts of the complex.

Elsewhere, Agatha Grimswold remains locked in a cage. Nearly an hour ago, Kilpenny had convinced her it was the safest place to be while he went to 'assess the situation'. Via a monitor linked to the closed-circuit television, they'd watched prisoners surge through the corridors directly above them, as if on a rampage. At that point, neither Agatha nor Kilpenny had any knowledge that a fire that would travel down to the zoo and put so many lives in danger.

That same fire is now moving swiftly through the zoo's stores; much of the animal feed already consumed by the raging flames.

'Michael!' she shouts, as powerless to save herself as the other animals around her.

She tries again, desperately now as the thickening, acrid smoke billows across the ceiling, dragging intense heat in its wake.

'Please! Can anybody hear me?'

Her pitiable cries rise like the flames on all sides of her. Louder still, the yelps of other distressed creatures to her left and right, who now sense the end drawing near. As Agatha sinks to the floor of the cage she thinks she hears a familiar voice.

'How could you let yourself be taken in by that devil of a boy, Agatha?'

It's her mother! Agatha can see her kindly face amongst the palls of smoke. And then she sees her father, his twinkling eyes and wry smile flickering like a spark.

'How exactly did you manage to end up inside a cage, our Agatha?'

The voices and images fade as Agatha closes her eyes, almost overcome with the toxic smoke. But then she hears another voice – and this time it's real.

'We're going to get you out!'

Agatha, with renewed vigour, opens her eyes in an instant. 'Who are you?' she whispers.

Harriet curtsies before reaching a hand through the vertical bars. 'Miss Harriet Gordon. Pleased to make your acquaintance!'

Responding, Agatha attempts a formal handshake, prepared, as she is, to be rescued.

'My name's Agatha, I help out here and around the complex.'

Mary steps forward, placing a hand on Harriet's arm. 'She's not to be trusted.'

'What can you mean?' asks Harriet.

'She and her boyfriend take delight in torturing the poor animals housed here. They even tried to do the same to me!'

Helen is off somewhere, searching rooms that branch off from the central area, so isn't available to settle the emerging quarrel between the two girls.

'That's not true, miss,' Agatha protests, 'Michael doesn't have the patience for working with animals … not like me.'

Harriet says, 'Who is this *Michael* you speak of, and where is he now?'

Mary looks about her in panic, realising he might be watching the whole scene from the side-lines.

'He said he'd come back for me,' Agatha continues. 'He even convinced me it'd be safer to be locked in one of these cages!'

Mary narrows her eyes. 'How did the fire start exactly?'

'I don't know, miss, maybe one of the rioters started it on another floor and it spread.'

The girls wonder if they'll fall prey to the dense blanket of smoke that is now enveloping much of the zoo; Agatha's eyes are already becoming irritated, turning from pink to red.

Helen now joins the group, breathless from her search.

'What I guess to be the control room has a manual locking system. I could try flipping that to get the cage doors open?'

Agatha grips the bars nearest to her.

'That lever won't just free me though, it'll open all the cages!'

Harriet looks about her at the nearest containers and the specimens currently housed within each of them: a bear, a tiger, three horses, five deer, a wolf, a goat, a lion, a pair of orangutans and an over-sized pig!

Mary's still not quite done baiting poor Agatha.

'So, we free her and risk losing our lives?'

Harriet responds with authority, 'It's not like we have a moral choice to make, sister. Human life is human life, after all, and should be preserved at all costs.'

Agatha grips the hand of the young witch to show her gratitude, emotion brimming the edges of her voice.

'I'm indebted to you, Miss Gordon, truly I am. I won't forget this act of charity.'

'We'll hold you to that,' says Mary.

'Are we ready then, girls? We haven't much time!'

Helen heads for the far side of the zoo and the room that contains the master lever. Harriet and Mary step away from the door of the cage that currently houses Agatha Grimswold and shout as one, 'Ready!'

In a single moment, the door cages swing open and the sprinkler system is activated. As if a cloud had burst, a heavy rain falls, slowly extinguishing the flames and giving all living creatures a good soaking.

'Sorry. That was me as well,' says Helen, appearing next to Mary, Harriet and Agatha. 'Two birds with one stone, I thought.'

Father and daughter emerge from the dark mouth of the air vent like a pair of animals waking after a spell of hibernation. Indigo wonders how her sisters are faring without her, clutching the pentacle fragment to her throat as if it had the power to connect them across space, if not time. She knows nothing of their adventures in the prison sector – their plucky and successful bid to escape – nor their present predicament in the zoo. She searches her feelings for signs any of them had come to harm and discovers none.

'What is this place?' she asks, turning to her father.

The room is a square of concrete walls, each one filled with amateurish sketches and designs, some crafted by the hand of an infant, others by a more mature sensibility. In one corner of the room there stands an upright filing cabinet, its skin as grey as the walls about it.

'Welcome to my secret place,' the professor says.

'You drew all of these pictures?'

'Yes.'

'What are they?'

'The outpourings of a boy who fell for the charms of an altogether different mistress to Madame Craft, but one no less seductive.'

'Science?' guesses Indigo.

'Yes!'

'But I still don't understand why you've brought us here.'

Carmichael approaches the filing cabinet and pulls at the handle of the top drawer. Peering in, he retrieves an ornate wooden box. He quickly sets it down on the ground between them, indicating for Indigo to sit on the floor next to him.

'Go ahead – open it,' he says, turning the item on its base until it faces his daughter. 'There's a Greek myth that goes by the name of 'Pandora's Box' – actually thought to be a vase, but that's irrelevant, really. The story features a young woman who is instructed not to open the box; of course, her curiosity eventually gets the better of her.'

Indigo is a little swayed by the mood of the room, claustrophobia part-tightening her throat.

'What did Pandora discover, within the box?'

Carmichael rises to his feet, eyes turning cold and distracted by the multitude of pictures.

'The usual vices: vanity, greed, envy, deception …'

Indigo wastes no time and lifts the lid in one smooth movement, curious as the youth of the Greek myth. Her excitement is soon evident, as she says, 'Letters, photographs, journals, spells and incantations! These stretch back many hundreds of years. Your inheritance, Father, as a witch of the … Carmichael Coven, I'm guessing?'

The professor blushes and says nothing, allowing Indigo to continue, 'You were the first of the Carmichaels to dream of a world beyond Craft philosophy, tradition and lore. A scientist.'

He says to Indigo, 'Ungrateful wretch, they called me, whose stubborn refusal to take up the Craft led to endless quarrels with your grandparents.'

'And yet …' Indigo smiles, her voice trailing off into the distance, only then to be taken up by her father.

'And yet, I still went and built a machine of pure magic and produced a daughter whose powers place her at the very top of the Carmichael Coven! It seems we can't always escape our destinies.'

'But what exactly *is* my destiny, Father?' asks Indigo, placing each of the heirlooms back within the ornate box and drawing the lid down on its many secrets.

'You'll know what to do when the time comes,' he replies. 'You always know what to do.'

'At least tell me what lies beyond that door,' Indigo asks, rising to her feet and handing the box to her father.

'An angry mob, who will no doubt put me on trial for the abduction and unlawful imprisonment of hundreds of innocent people.'

'Then let's face them together,' Indigo says, the proudest she's ever been of her father. 'And offer to help them, for charity is equally part of your nature.'

Carmichael kisses his daughter, just once, on the crown of her head and the warmth of his love spreads quickly through her body like a spell of astounding beauty and power.

○

Harriet leads the way, recalling with graceful ease the route from the zoo back to the main hall of the complex. Helen falls in directly behind her, her whole frame weighed down by the various trials she's endured in order to secure freedom for herself and the girls. Mary comes last of all in the human chain, caster of a spell that has successfully bewitched the twenty or so wild animals that now follow the group.

The three of them say nothing as they enter the auditorium, its domed roof catching the conversations of freed prisoners who've gathered in a large group to deliberate on the fate of Carmichael and his daughter, both of whom now stand at the centre of the crowd.

'Harriet!' Indigo calls to her sister, only then spotting another of her friends among the assortment of animals. 'And Mary, too! And Helen, of course. All of you are quite safe?'

Helen steps forward and gives Indigo's hand a gentle squeeze. Indigo smiles before turning to her sisters, her hands outstretched to receive them. Where the group of witches connect, a great light illuminates the hall, making the prisoners feel an abundance of warmth to one another, if not the Carmichaels.

Indigo says, 'You're very wet. What happened?'

'Sprinklers,' smiles Helen.

Mary begins by saying, 'I smelled it first. A burning of the air, Indigo!'

'I merely followed Mary as she tracked down the scent to the zoo,' says a breathless Harriet.

Indigo's brows knit together as she says, 'I'm sure you were equally useful, Miss Gordon!'

'Well,' says Harriet, 'At one point, she did lead us to a dead end.'

Mary's eyes widen at the fib, 'I did nothing of the sort!'

And so further stories unreel, spun out between bewildered parties like yards of splendid silk. The professor's spirits lift when he sees Helen, but he's kept in his place by an armed prisoner. With reluctance, the professor steps back within the confines of his allotted patch of ground.

Humans and animals form a tight circle of protection about the witches, keeping even the most curious of children at a safe distance.

Indigo asks, 'What became of Agatha, then, after you set her free?'

'I've not the faintest idea,' Harriet explains. 'Although one wonders if she went in search of her unpleasant boyfriend.'

'Ugh! That man Kilpenny,' Indigo growls.

The girls look about them in awe at the spectacle they've helped make a reality.

'And what became of Rees-Repton?' asks Mary.

Indigo shrugs her shoulders.

'He disappeared at the first whiff of trouble – like the coward he is. It turns out those sons of his were the very same dogs that chased us through Tenby.'

It's Harriet who thinks to ask, 'What of the pentacle fragment? Is it safe?'

'Don't worry, I have it right here,' says Indigo, an air of playfulness to her tone. 'The athame, too.'

Indigo then relays for her sisters what it is the fragment revealed to her, describing the elderly gentleman and the pendant in his possession. 'Interestingly,' she says, 'I noticed it was marked with two triangles.'

'Then it's in Egypt,' says Harriet with surety, 'making him the keeper of the Fire element. Africa is renowned for its searing temperatures.'

'Or the Water element,' adds Indigo. 'Remember, Egypt also has the Nile.'

Beside the two witches, Mary is busy shaking the hand of the larger of two orangutans. The image fills her sisters with awe.

Harriet turns to Indigo and asks, 'What are we going to do with these animals now the zoo is destroyed?'

'We're going to set them free,' says Mary, answering for her sister. 'I promised them I would do so – if they behaved themselves and overcame the desire to eat any of their fellow creatures, or humans.'

'And when are *we* going to be set free?' pipes up a prisoner, a young man whose outward beauty is quite striking. His question stirs the crowd, setting off a ripple of reactions – threats and accusations soon reaching the centre of the room where Lance Carmichael stares in disbelief at those around him.

'It was never my intention,' he attempts to shout above the rising voices, 'to detain any of you against your will! And not *all of you* hate me, surely? I've made some good friends of you these last few years. And you must believe me when I say that if I possessed the skill to reverse the mechanics of the engine that brought you to me in the first place, I would.'

The crowd respond with cries for the professor to tell the truth, one or two even asking for him to be put on trial. Reacting, the animals pace the circle, picking up on the negative vibrations sent out by each freed prisoner.

'Shh, my lovely ones,' says Mary, 'they mean you no harm.'

The professor is soon joined by Indigo, who grips her father's hand, the perfect picture of unity.

'My father may not possess the skill to get each of you back home, but I know someone who is more than capable of carrying out the task.'

Harriet closes her eyes in genuine horror, refusing to believe her own sister would place her in the line of such deadly fire.

'Indigo?' she says, spurred into action and pushing through the crowd of people to reach her sister in time.

'Here she comes, now!' shouts Indigo, stoking the crowd into a frenzy. 'Harriet Gordon: scholar, inventor and all-round genius!'

This final show of flattery from Indigo cools Harriet's temper enough so that, as she arrives at her sister's side, she's all smiles for her and the legions of believers that look to her now to perform a miracle of the highest order.

Closing Rituals

Indigo awakes with a start. She's alone, except for the hum of the air filtration fans. Further off, the complex rings with the sounds of laughter and goodwill, a world markedly different to the one she'd grown accustomed to during her short life in the keep of her father. It's been two days since the small band of renegades managed to overthrow those in the pay of Sentinel Technologies, and there's still no sign of Rees-Repton, his sons, or the company's expected retaliation.

When she's not being called upon to help Mrs D and the kitchen staff, Indigo spends her time with Mary, the two sisters working together to oversee the removal of all animals from the complex. They'd initially worried about the air quality of the atmosphere surrounding Tenby, but meter readings now deem the region to be safe. Both sisters suspect the pentacle fragment has administered its magic to make such possible but keep this knowledge between themselves, for now.

'I saw Harriet this morning,' says Mary, 'But only briefly. She said she was close to making an important discovery.'

Indigo doesn't smile as she makes her reply, 'She's sounding more and more like Father with each passing day.'

Mary doesn't press for more information, choosing instead to stroke the flank of her most prized of friends: a Bengal tiger.

'His name's Rupert,' smiles Indigo, joining her friend and the large cat, its ears little mounds of soot-coloured fur.

Mary says, 'Whereas his *secret name* he's revealed only to me.'

The pair are soon on their feet and begin the slow march past a group of prisoners, each set of eyes scrutinising the large cat trailing behind the two girls. Indigo feels a little guilty that, although they are no longer confined to cells, she has not yet made good her promise of securing freedom for each of the humans in her care. Although able to walk at will around the complex and on the island, they are still trapped in this universe and time. Indigo knew a mood of buoyancy could quickly turn sour; the even ambience of comradeship quickly becoming strained because of inaction on her part.

The sky above Forgotten Point is a pulsing, radiant blue, with not a cloud in sight. The sisters ramble over hawthorn-heavy brush to reach the edge of the cliff and, just beyond it, the narrow steps that lead down to the stretch of beach some hundred feet below. Indigo is relieved to discover that her father's estimation of tide times was correct on this occasion. The sea is far out, revealing a long strip of beach, with a flock of gulls riding updrafts of warm air.

The tiger's nostrils expand and contract to allow quantities of fresh air to enter its lungs, its coat seeming to glisten following each measured inhalation.

There are even a few freed men and women scattered across the beach, one nearby group watching the girls issue their farewells to the tiger.

'Goodbye, dear Rupert,' says Indigo, kissing the cat on the expanse of its broad muzzle, 'I'm no longer your turnkey.'

The tiger, disinterested in all this fussing, wanders from the pair and, after a short period of deliberation, leaps for its freedom, disappearing over the edge of the cliff, down the man-made steps and onto the open expanse of sand.

'Look, there he is!' Mary cries after a minute of silent observation.

Indigo squints, trying her best to focus, until she spots the tiger astride a large boulder at the far end of South Beach.

'One for the memory book,' says Indigo, placing two hands on Mary's shoulders.

Mary says, 'You're unusually cheerful today, sister.'

'There you are!' sounds a voice from behind the pair. It's Harriet, newly arrived.

Turning, Indigo and Mary are confronted with a very different picture to that of the tiger mastering its rocky terrain, though no less revelatory: Harriet Gordon with a hand stretched out before her, the pentacle fragment dangling from her palm.

'I've done it,' she says. 'I've discovered a way to return the prisoners to their worlds. The pentacle fragment showed me how.'

Harriet only explains all to her sisters once they're safely stationed in the Carmichael living quarters, where they are joined by Helen, eager to know when she might be able to see her daughter again. An ever-patient Mrs D takes round a tray of cold drinks, which allows her to listen in as the most intelligent of the sisters takes centre stage.

'Last night, the solution came to me in the form of a dream,' says Harriet, pausing to partake of the liquid she thinks tastes like sour lemonade. 'Thank you, Mrs D. By the way, your father is an incredibly intelligent man, Indigo.'

Indigo says, 'Of course. But what happened in your dream?'

Blinking, Harriet returns to her story.

'Yes, agreed, I must retain my focus. There's much to do before the day is out.'

Harriet gulps her drink down – it might be said rather indelicately, as some of the liquid caught on her chin.

'These last two days I've learnt more about black holes. Each fact I've learnt, I've kept safe in the storeroom of my brain, waiting for the right cue to begin solving the mystery of the pentacle.'

'And last night your dream began that process?' asks Helen.

'Absolutely!' Harriet replies. 'My dream detailed a narrative of how black holes are really just the products of mankind's foolish disregard for life and for the value of matter itself. In my dream, I saw the sacred pentacle being torn apart by a black hole of epic proportions, the entire universe sucked into a region of space the size of our galaxy, and with it the lives of each and every mortal soul on this planet. A rather terrifying prospect, I must say! But also, I came to see the sacred pentacle was crafted from light – life-giving, soul-enriching *light*. It was unmade many hundreds of years ago, we know that much, but what the handbook hasn't yet revealed to us is how black holes began to appear only once the article was dismantled –'

Indigo interrupts, 'But the black holes of my father's experiments are not random phenomena, Harriet. They've been assigned their own, individual co-ordinates. You saw that with your own eyes when you visited the locator facility.'

'True,' Harriet says, 'but the longer the pentacle remains in pieces, the more blackholes – man-made or otherwise – will continue to appear, and the closer our universe will creep towards total, irreversible collapse.'

'How exactly did the professor find so many of them?' asks Mary.

Harriet nods, acknowledging the validity of the question, and saying, 'Yesterday, he confessed all to me. He's been creating tiny micro-holes for many years by colliding minute particles together, sent at enormous speeds within his accelerator engine. He was able to track each black hole to its source in an alternate dimension, shortly before it evaporated.'

'Home,' says Helen, her eyes flashing with hope for the briefest of moments.

'Exactly – *home*,' Harriet agrees. 'The problem we've faced is how to match each of the prisoners to the myriad co-ordinates stored within the locator. After all, we don't want any of our guests returning to lives that in no way resemble their old ones. They're done with that sort of folly!'

Indigo cuts in with, 'Outside, you mentioned the pentacle fragment showed you *how* to solve the problem?'

Harriet thinks for a second before resuming her monologue. 'Yes, of course! In my dream, the spirit of Air itself spoke directly to me. She told me we could harness magic locked deep within the pentacle fragment to locate the shadow left by each particular black hole. We would then be able to open up an avenue that connects two parallel universes.'

'Wormholes!' Indigo surmises, standing from the sofa and making for the door. 'Come, sisters! We've much to do before the last of my father's prisoners can travel home.'

Helen remains seated for a moment, mulling over the idea she might be the *last* of the prisoners Indigo mentioned on her way out of the door. But inside her chest, a tiny flame has been fanned, which now burns brightly in her irises and can be seen in the rouge-tinted pallor of her skin.

'You look quite different, ma'am,' says Mrs Dalrymple at last, clearing away the clutter of empty glasses.

'Yes,' Helen answers, 'I'm sure I do.'

Just two hours later, the time-napped form a serpentine queue that wends its way from the engine room to the threshold of the old prison quarters. One hundred and ninety-nine men, women and children lean against walls or toy with the hems of their clothes, stony silent and oddly incommunicative. The two hundredth member of the group, Helen Carmichael, has been assigned the role of gatekeeper. She stands at the entranceway to the engine room, focused and determined to prove herself capable in the role.

Carmichael says to her, 'You can admit the first of them, Helen.'

The woman's heart fills with relief that the professor, who has thus far mistaken her for his dead wife, should call her by her actual name.

'Yes, Professor,' she answers, finally able to smile.

As planned, Mary, Harriet and Indigo are positioned at the three glass plates farthest away from the broadcast portal and in order of size from past time to present – the fourth plate next to them remaining empty, save for the pentacle fragment sitting at the centre of the circle. Its two crescent moons glint beneath the sterile, florescent lights.

Carmichael inputs a series of commands into the terminal, his fingers like little flashes of lightning. Meanwhile, Mrs D stands in one corner of the room, observing the action with a vested interest in the outcome of the experiment. She knows the sisters are now working together and capable of producing astounding magic.

'The first of our subjects is Geraldine Gardner,' announces Helen from her station. 'A mother of three from 2010.'

Here, the professor turns from his terminal to study the prisoner who has entered the portal room and, as instructed by Indigo, takes her place at the fourth glass plate.

'It's okay,' Harriet assures the woman. 'Do as we ask, and we'll soon have you home.'

The professor takes a moment to personally apologise to the prisoner for the inconvenience caused by her prolonged detention, before turning back to his terminal.

The accelerator engine is soon heard moving up a gear and on the other side of the glass partition the little corridor of lasers begins to hum.

'That noise!' exclaims Geraldine Gardner. 'I heard it in my garden as I pegged out the last of my washing.'

Here, little tears of upset flash in her eyes; Lance Carmichael is moved to almost the same degree.

'Right! After three,' begins Harriet. 'We have to place our hands on the plates, sisters. Including you, Mrs Gardner!'

The prisoner nods and, copying the younger girls, spreads her fingers until the tips of them frame the large glass plate in front of her, asking, 'What's that?'

'It's a fragment of metal,' Indigo explains. 'We believe it possesses the power to send you home.'

'One …' begins Harriet. 'Two … Three! Now, everyone – connect with your plates!'

Almost as a single entity, four sets of palms connect with glass and, responding, the wires that connect the plates to the ceiling high above them emit the purest white light.

'What's happening?' calls Mrs Gardner.

The witches remain silent, locked as they are in a meditative state from which they cannot not be stirred by words alone.

'Are they okay? Should I remove my hands from the plate?'

Carmichael turns and faces his one-time captive.

'Do nothing of the sort! Focus on the little screen, next to me on the wall here. It's called a broadcast portal. If the wormhole establishes a connection with a parallel universe, images will be projected onto the screen.'

Mrs Gardner nods and takes one last look at the three girls stationed at their glass plates – still not a flicker of life between them. Beyond the partition, the corridor's lasers are now spinning at a tremendous speed and the first etchings of a light ring begin appearing in this dimension. She concentrates on the broadcast portal, its fuzzy screen showing a signal that seems to be faulty.

After a short time, a frustrated Carmichael looks back over his shoulder at the arrangement of glass plates. The Gardner woman is starting to suspect the experiment is a failure, after all.

'Professor, *you're the missing element*,' says Mrs D from her station at the far wall.

'What?'

'You brought her here and you're required to guide her home.'

The professor stares into the kindly face of his old childhood mentor and friend. In that moment, he's five years old again, peering over the rim of Cook's mixing bowl and marvelling at her ability to transform its strange-looking contents into a delicious cake.

'Go on – take the fifth plate,' she urges. 'As I understand it, some hidden part of you located these people with a purpose in mind – and a force powerful enough to rob them of their freedom.'

Carmichael shakes his head in confusion, his temples creased with anxiety.

'Something *in me*?'

Mrs D offers a smile for the man who now stands before her.

'You're a powerful witch, Lance. Who knows what you're capable of once you put your mind to it?'

Carmichael is soon standing directly in front of the last of the glass plates. It's the same one he'd stood at when he commanded the accelerator engine to create each of the black holes that made inter-dimensional travel a reality. Before long, he connects with the final glass plate and the whole of the room begins to rattle.

Beyond the glass barrier, the corridor of blinding lights slows down. The whirring noise of the machine's internal mechanisms become less pronounced until, finally, it grinds to a halt. At the very point when it begins to spin in the opposite direction, each of the sisters is drawn back to full consciousness, Mrs Gardner suddenly springing to life when she sees her own children in the eye of the broadcast portal.

'Look! Your father is at the last of the plates,' Harriet says under her breath to Indigo. 'I understand it at last! He must be the sacred source, capable of powering each of the black holes!'

And there, beyond the wall, the corridor of lasers bleeds a dark, ominous light that threatens to become a full blackout.

'What do we do now?' asks Mary.

Indigo breaks free of her plate and runs to the portal screen.

Harriet calls after her. 'Indigo! What are you doing?'

'Look,' replies Indigo. 'The denser the black hole becomes, the more defined the image in the portal.'

'I want this to stop!' cries Mrs Gardner.

'That's it!' says Indigo after a few seconds. 'We have to use the fragment to conjure a white circle just as each black hole threatens to evaporate.'

Harriet adds, 'From here it looks set to explode!'

Mary is first to place her palms against the edge of the plate that contains a terrified prisoner and the pentacle fragment, saying to her, 'You can let go.'

The woman's whole body is shaking.

'But, I might never see them again.'

'My sister's right,' agrees Harriet, also pressing two palms against a fresh section of the glass plate. 'Letting go is your best chance.'

Cautiously, the woman allows Indigo to release each of the digits of her fingers that grip the sliver of glass.

'Mrs D,' begins Indigo, 'would you be so kind as to escort Mrs Gardner through to the accelerator engine?'

'Of course, Miss Carmichael.'

When the sisters are in position, they speak as one, reciting an invocation that is sure to countermand the effects of any black hole.

'I conjure thee, O Circle of Power,

That thou beest a meeting-place of

love and joy and truth;

A shield against all wickedness and evil;

A boundary between the

world of men and

the realms of the Mighty Ones;

A rampart of protection that shall preserve and contain the power that we shall raise within thee.'

The moment arrives when the magic of three sisters proves more than a match for any spectacle of science. In fact, as the professor's black hole reaches saturation point and *'pops'* into inexistence, a light-hole forged by three determined friends retains the connection between their universe and the one belonging to the first of the prisoners. It's a sight to behold for the many dozens of inquisitive onlookers who now pour into the portal room: one of their own stepping into a corridor of light, a circle crafted from pure love - an attempt to put right the wrongs of a rogue scientist.

It takes the rest of the day to transport each of the prisoners back to their universes. While they have been absent, many of them have lost loved ones, some to accidents, some to cancer or heart disease, some to alcohol or substance abuse, or even old age. Harriet concludes the professor's own grief at losing his wife during childbirth showed itself as an ability to connect two regions of dark matter, across space and time. These two separate expressions of mournful loss made possible the opening of interconnecting doorways between universes.

Carmichael says very little as he watches his prisoners return to their own worlds. The realisation is suddenly with him that his tireless pursuit to recreate a dead wife had deprived hundreds of others of the opportunity to love and be loved by those closest to them.

Of course, not all the prisoners are eager to re-join relations back in their original universes. Some have moved on, both emotionally and physically from their old lives, become quite different people to those characters they'd left behind on the other side of the light ring. Not even images of loved ones appearing in the broadcast portal are enough to persuade them they should not remain within the confines of the complex.

The moment eventually comes for the last of the prisoners to leave the universe she has, until recently, despised with every fibre of her being. However now, with friendships forged between her and the three girls, Mrs Dalrymple and even Professor Carmichael, Helen takes up her position at the glass plate with more than a little apprehension.

'Are you okay?' asks Indigo.

Helen shrugs before smiling at Indigo, her lips pressed together for just a second.

'It's strange,' she says, 'That I should feel so sad to be leaving here.'

The sisters form a tight huddle of protection around the woman, allowing their grief to test the limits of the circle's edges.

'Your daughter is waiting for you,' says Harriet.

'That's true,' Helen says, tears landing on the tips of Indigo's fingers as the young witch attempts to soothe the woman's grief. 'It really is remarkable, the adventures you've taken me on. No one is going to believe a word of it.'

'What will you tell them?' asks Carmichael, looking up for a moment.

'I'm not sure yet.'

These are the woman's final words to the professor and her company of friends, before she takes her place at the glass plate, eyes dipping downwards and alighting upon the pentacle fragment. The object's two crescent moons become the curved lashes of her daughter spotted in the broadcast portal.

Goodbye, Mother, Indigo thinks, as Helen Carmichael disappears through the door and towards the spinning circle of white light where a black hole had recently been. She does look back, just once, raising a hand to the three girls who gaze intently at her through the glass partition. And there ... yes, a fragile smile for the man who snatched her from her universe many weeks ago.

Led by the professor, the three sisters and Mrs D quietly descend the three hundred or so steps that lead to the locator; their shadows fall against the dank walls and merge with one another, as if sliding down into a grim underworld. They've done their job and the time has come for the professor to temporarily shut down the machine that has caused so much heartache and distress.

At the viewing platform edging the hollow crater of rock, the three sisters and Mrs D huddle close together as Carmichael powers up his terminal. As Harriet had discovered for herself, the last time she had ventured down here with the professor, the space above the crater quickly fills with an assortment of black stars, light moving like a treacly substance between them and framing their dark splendour.

'A terrible beauty,' sighs the cook.

'How do we get rid of them?' asks Mary.

Indigo looks across to her father for the solution. He appears pensive as he taps away at his little keyboard. She has the handbook under one arm and gives it a gentle squeeze using her elbow.

'Maybe Father will help us get to Stonehenge now we've helped ease his conscience?' she says.

'What makes you think he's heard of such a place – or even that such a place still exists?' asks Harriet.

The professor approaches the group.

'We've only scratched the surface of the problem. There are still thousands of these drifting about the universe.'

'Whole, the pentacle offered us protection,' Mrs D says firmly, the witches and professor soon in the thrall of her words. 'With the pentacle fragmented, the universe is vulnerable to all sorts of attacks – and not just from black holes.'

The professor asks, 'How old is the sacred pentacle, do you think?'

Cook purses two cracked lips together, then states, 'The Mother Goddess is as old as the universe itself. No one can be certain why, or how, she emerged from the very first light ring, but she set about crafting the third dimension – a process lasting many billions of years –'

'I see,' Harriet interrupts. 'Earth is the physical representation of magic located deep within the heart of the Mother Goddess herself. We sisters are an expression of her spiritual consciousness. If we fail her, we fail ourselves and she'll have to –'

'– begin anew,' Mrs D interjects, with a sense of finality.

'*Genesis*,' Lance Carmichael adds, his attention drawn to the leather-bound text Indigo has in her hands. 'What's that?'

'It's a guide,' says Indigo. 'One we've been using to locate the missing fragments.'

The professor's mind reels from such news before flicking through the tome's pages, quickly scanning the reams of information for signs and codes that might help him in his life as scientist, first; witch, second.

'We wondered whether you'd come with us to a location highlighted on one of the maps,' says Harriet.

'Here,' Indigo adds, pointing it out for her father once he's on the correct page.

'Stonehenge?'

'You know it, Father?'

'*Know it?*' he laughs, hysteria edging his voice. 'I've often seen it during my trips to Sentinel Technologies.'

The three witches exchange a number of uneasy looks between them.

Carmichael continues, 'The stone circle is housed in a vast hangar at the very centre of their headquarters. Many decades have been spent trying to decipher the stones' meaning and unlock the ancient power said to be contained within them. Worse still, they're Rees-Repton's pride and joy.'

'There is one further clue about the stones in the handbook,' says Harriet, taking the tome from Indigo and flicking through its pages until she finds the one she is after. 'Here – it mentions a central stone that is both birth and resting place of life itself.'

'Interesting,' smiles the professor. 'I think I know the exact stone the book is referring to. I have always wondered about its purpose. It could be an altar of some sort. A door – or a portal, perhaps – that connects this world with the spirit realm.'

'Of course,' declares Harriet. 'And our fragment is one part of a key that will open that door!'

Across the Hallowed Turf

As the helicopter eases onto the landing pad its four long blades whisk the dark, polluted air into a frenzy, making the dozen or so attendants on the ground hold onto their hats. In a matter of moments, a side-entry door slides noisily along its runners to reveal a single human passenger and three cages occupying the remaining seats.

'Professor, good to see you again!'

Carmichael nods in response to the most senior of the staff that constitute his welcoming committee.

'Likewise, Commander.'

'Just the three specimens?'

Carmichael keeps his cool, affording the cages a casual glance. Beyond the mesh of each container, he's able to make out the three distinct shapes of his daughter and her two friends, but in their animal forms.

'A fox, hare and mouse,' another guard says, as he checks them off against his electronic device.

'That's correct,' the professor says. 'But I'll take them over to the labs in the morning, if that's okay with you? It's late and I could do with getting some sleep.'

The guard stamps his left foot and raises a hand to one eyebrow.

'Of course, Professor. I'll have my men transfer them to your room.'

Carmichael then realises he's forgotten to wear the oxymask that is standard issue for all Sentinel Technologies transport. The air around the Carmichael complex has been fresh and wholesome for a while now and he's got out of the habit. In addition the pentacle fragment, which he now has around his neck, allows him to breathe comfortably even where the air is still polluted. Not wishing to arouse suspicion, Carmichael reaches back into the helicopter and grabs the mask dangling from a hook by the door.

'Nearly forgot,' he says to no one in particular, strapping it onto his face. He makes for the lift he knows will take him down into the lower levels of the facility.

The professor is not aware of it yet, but the magic imbued in the pentacle fragment has extended beyond the limits of his personal space. As the helicopter flew low over Wales and England, it quietly roused the forgotten spirit of the Mother Goddess. Now, long-dormant plants are springing to life from beneath the soil and thrusting up green shoots of hope here and there.

A short time later, the professor is pacing back and forth across the room he's been assigned as a member of the corporation, drink in one hand and all three girls – now transformed back to human form – staring at him.

'I simply don't understand why we've been allowed entry. *Where is he?* What's become of Rees-Repton?'

'Maybe,' Indigo says, 'Rees-Repton wants us here?'

Carmichael, still pacing and sipping at his drink, mumbles, 'Every now and then I get this odd feeling, like he's nearby. Do any of you feel it?'

The three younger witches shake their heads.

Carmichael finishes what's left of his drink and turns away from the group.

Mary speaks next.

'Are we not to sleep then, this evening?'

'Yes,' replies the professor, 'but I have one more thing to show you first.' He removes the pentacle fragment and hands it to his daughter, continuing, 'Unless you don't want to see the henge, now you've made it this far?'

There's a degree of madness in his eyes, thinks Indigo, the likes of which I've not seen since I was a child, in the early days of his experiments.

'No matter what comes of our adventure,' she says, a little concerned for him now, 'I want you to know I love you, Father.'

Carmichael takes Indigo by the hand and leads her to the door, mindful of the fact that her vision means she's not too comfortable out of her home environment.

'Come, follow me,' he says. 'Tread across the hallowed turf to the henge, where the children sing and play for the light of day to keep their spirits aloft! For all too soon the light will fade, taking with it the sweet song of youth and leaving us with night.'

'Wherever did you hear such a refrain, Professor?' asks Harriet.

Carmichael pauses for a moment, bringing the group to a standstill before answering, 'I suddenly remembered snatches of a poem Mother used to recite to me when I couldn't sleep.'

Sentinel Technologies surrenders few of its secrets as they make their way through its maze of corridors. Each witch steals the occasional look at ghostly shadows moving back and forth behind verticals of frosted glass. Indigo suspects that the world's best scientists are gathered here, where they have the resources to experiment with the latest technology.

'Quantum mechanics,' her father had once explained to her, 'is the future. It will allow man to travel to the ends of the universe in search of life. It will fuel his home, his car, his computer and much more besides.' And Indigo remembers thinking at the time, *male scientists seem to have all the fun*.

'We're here,' the professor announces at last, pressing his key card to a panel. The door disappears into a recess in the wall.

'Quickly!' he says, the three girls flashing past him and into a chamber that houses the brooding monoliths of Stonehenge.

As they'd once appeared before Abraham Aderyn, on the morning of the sacred pentacle's destruction, the huge, grey stones of the henge loom high above the small group in the containment hangar. However, the room no longer buzzes with activity, as it had done in Carmichael's youth. In fact, it lies deserted, a fine powder lingering in the air as if the room were an Egyptian tomb still to be discovered.

Many decades ago, Sentinel Technologies extended its reach into the county of Wiltshire, claiming the mythical site as its own. They poured vast amounts of money into a venture codenamed *Chorea Gigantum*. A team of handpicked researchers were personally appointed by Rees-Repton to observe the unusual arrangement of rocks from sunrise to sunset. Their machines buzzed and crackled but the stones remained upright and silent, as if waiting for the right moment to be beckoned to life. Rees-Repton had been hoping that technology would help him unravel the mystery of the sacred pentacle, as well as reveal the locations of all five fragments. The ongoing lack of activity within the hangar did nothing to appease the old witch's frustration at being denied both.

'Ma and Pa wanted to visit the stones,' Mary says after a period of silence. 'They were going to take me one day.'

Harriet falls immediately to capturing the scene in the witches' handbook, her artistry both fluent and convincing, saying to the others after a few minutes, 'Did you know it once sported an outer circle, a line of stones connected without a single break?'

'Like a light ring,' Indigo smiles, moving through one of three doorways that now comprises the structure's inner courtyard.

'Theorists believe there were actually five doorways that made up the centre ring,' says Harriet, very much in a world of her own.

Carmichael approaches a stone plinth near the centre of the edifice, suspecting it might be the sacred altar, as mentioned in the handbook.

It is Indigo who says, 'How come you know so much about it, Harriet?'

The sister completes her sketch and presents it to each member of her little group, saying, 'The Gordon family library contained many photographs of these stones, Professor, again making me wonder if my parents nurtured an interest in matters relating to Craft practice.'

Mary asks, surprised, 'Were they witches do you think?'

'Not openly, no, sister. I don't think they would ever have declared themselves as belonging to any cult other than one which endorsed material gains!'

'Here,' Carmichael says, breaking the mood of good humour.

Only when all three of the girls arrive at the stone positioned near Carmichael does Harriet say, 'Ha! Look! Just as the handbook describes it,' pointing out a shallow impression in the granite. 'The pentacle's resting place.'

As the sisters had witnessed Abe and Stevens via the broadcast portal, they now bend down until they are at eye-level with the boulder's apparently flat horizontal top.

'You can just make out a circle, when you run your fingers over the surface,' says Mary, the others awed into silence. 'Have a go yourselves.'

Harriet and Indigo do so, running their slender fingers along the cold surface as if it were fine silk.

'Maybe we shouldn't have come after all,' says Carmichael.

Indigo looks at her father. 'What's wrong?'

'I'm not entirely sure. A series of images came to mind, that's all.'

Harriet joins in, asking, 'What did you see?'

Carmichael's voice is a fragile as porcelain when he speaks. 'I ... I saw Indigo fall. I held her in my arms, held her to my chest, that is ...'

Now upright, Mary and Harriet reach out and each place a hand on Indigo, as if prepared in that moment to counter or break such a fall. Indigo shows no sign of fear in her voice as she says, 'It might well be *you're* the Last of the Knowing Ones, Father.'

Carmichael edges away from the plinth, like a possessed spirit on the move, saying, 'What do you mean?'

Indigo reveals the pentacle fragment for all to see.

'All along, we've thought it was my duty to unlock the power within the sacred pentacle – with the help of my sisters, of course.'

Mary and Harriet look on as Indigo places the fragment in one corner of the resting place, as if intuition alone had helped her find the right section of the circle.

'Should I fall, Father, it will rest with you to restore the world to its former glory.'

Harriet sees where her friend is heading and says, 'And what candidate is better suited to the task than he who helped push it to the edge of extinction in the first place?'

Carmichael looks on in disbelief.

'I think you're quite mad, all of you,' he says.

Mary is first to spot a glimmer of starlight appear above the tallest of the stone doorways, interrupting the flow of conversation.

'Look! Something stirs within the earth, within the sky, within the light, within the waters and the spirit realm!'

At this stage, I enter the witches' narrative via one of five elemental spirits; the time has come to reveal my true identity to those who've waited all this time to hear the truth. In my current Carrier, the body of an archaeologist named Howard Carter, I pass through a doorway of light and find myself amongst a circle of stones.

'Who's that?' asks one of young girls.

I answer, 'I'm a single aspect of the Mother Goddess, child.'

Now a gentleman, who seems in charge of the three girls, takes a measured step towards me. He's thrown a little by the unusual manner of clothes the archaeologist chose to wear that morning.

'But you're a man,' he says.

'So, it would seem,' I laugh. 'As are you!'

I encourage 'Carter' to bridge the distance between the stone doorway and the plinth that currently houses the first of my elemental spirits.

'What are you doing, sir?'

Another of the girls is speaking now, so I address her directly, for I know her well enough to consider her a sister.

'I'm summoning the third of my spirits, Miss Gordon.'

'How do you know my name?'

My reply is rather curt but does the job of silencing the girl.

'I'm *everywhere* and *everything*, dear child.'

Here, 'Carter' tugs at the chain about his throat and releases a second pentacle fragment from the links of pure silver. He's nurtured Fire deep within his soul, which he now deposits alongside Air in the resting place.

'I saw you in the broadcast portal,' says another of the children.

'And I saw *you* looking at me, Indigo Carmichael,' I say. 'You possess great power and a determination to succeed.'

Next, I draw each of my elemental spirits from their hiding places. In fact, as 'Carter' places his fragment within the holy plinth, I emerge through the doorway in another Carrier, a young woman of Icelandic descent named Aðalstienn Tomasson. With her elemental fragment – the symbols of a horned bull emblazoned in its metal – in place, I move to yet another of my Carriers, this time a small boy, of Mexican origin, called Erubiel Medina. His fragment holds the symbol of two snakes and he places it alongside the other three elemental spirits.

Air, Fire, Water and Earth are in position. Only the fifth and final fragment is needed now, so I emerge from the last Carrier and call out for the most elusive of my children to reveal herself.

'I'm the Girl with the Hidden Name.'

The three sisters and the man look to one another. Carter, Tomasson and young Erubiel all bow their heads, as if awaiting their next instructions.

One of the girls then looks directly at me, beyond my translucent skin, as if able to see into my heart.

'It's you! The one I painted!' she says, her face and hands having turned white. 'It wasn't Indigo, after all!'

'Yes, it's you I saw at the centre of the light ring that night out on Harrowing Point!' cries another girl.

I float across the ground towards the third girl and survey her lank, brown hair. 'I'm keeper of the last of the pentacle fragments,' I say. The young witch backs away from me, despite my outstretched hand reaching towards her in an act of goodwill.

'What element does it represent?' she asks, keeping her distance.

I merely stare at the girl as I hand her the final fragment. 'I cannot be measured, indexed, catalogued or surmised. I'm the stuff of dreams and of the wildest, most fervent outpourings of the greatest imaginations. You could say I'm the spirit of creativity encapsulated in a single expression of energy!'

I'm then interrupted by the man who begins scratching at the nape of his neck as if plagued by some unseen fever. And there, for all to see, a simple flea that has played stowaway among the tight curls of the man's hair, leaps for its life and lands a short distance from its host. The man stares at the ground in disbelief, before raising his eyes to watch as, at the centre of the stone circle, emerges a six-foot-tall, razor-shouldered witch.

'Rees-Repton!' cries one girl.

'His animagus is a flea!' shouts another.

Another girl folds her arms across her chest as she says, 'Of course. He was with us all this time!'

The great witch's sudden appearance sours the atmosphere of the whole site. The three sisters are lost for words as he issues instructions to the edges of the hangar, drawing from the shadows a quantity of guards, each one armed to the teeth with guns, grenades and ammunition. Anton and Maxwell, in canine form, drag Michael Kilpenny and a distraught-looking Agatha out into the sullied light of the room.

'Well, well, Professor,' begins Rees-Repton. 'My thanks to you for making my task a less onerous one.'

Here, Rees-Repton slinks across the ground as a predator might when out on open ground.

'Give it to me, child. And the athame, too.'

Indigo is caught directly within the confines of the old witch's shadow and her eyes glisten as she looks up at him.

'And if I refuse?'

'I'll have one of your precious sisters killed. I care not one which dies first. That decision will be yours alone.'

Harriet and Mary both shake their heads, sending a signal to their friend she shouldn't bend to Rees-Repton's will.

Rees-Repton looks directly at Indigo. 'Hand them over. Now.'

Indigo obeys, her actions slow and done half-heartedly.

'There,' smiles Rees-Repton, accepting the articles into his care, 'that wasn't so difficult, was it?'

In spirit form, I follow at the heels of Rees-Repton as he completes the short walk to the centre of the circle and to the holy plinth. He regards each of the other Carriers as if they were constructed from altogether different matter, before setting the final piece of metal in the altar's resting place.

'With the making of this sacred pentacle,' he says, 'I command the elements of Earth do my bidding!'

All about the hangar a strange moan of complaint is heard, as if the source of unrest lay in the steel and mortar of the building itself. I beckon my sibling spirits, calling them forth from within the metal of the sacred pentacle. All five of us rise from the holy plinth, like souls ascending through the ether, drawing little yelps of surprise from the humans far below us. The hangar's metal sides begin to buckle and warp as if made from paper or fabric, not some of the most resistant materials known to man.

The girls far below us huddle together as one, using the man as a kind of shield against falling masonry. Sirens ring out their eerie tune, while red and amber lights take it in turns to offset the darkness. Guards who've managed to hold their ground against the gathering tempest of destruction scatter, in fear of their lives.

Harriet shouts, 'It's like a pop-up picture book!'

Rees-Repton holds his nerve, as do Kilpenny, Agatha and the two dogs. *Quite the little family they make*, I think, as I hammer once more against the hangar's skeleton of concrete and steel, fashioning mayhem as I move.

All about the space, my fellow spirits hover in the air, joining me in song as we work.

'Return, oh, return!
God of the Sun!
God of the Light, return,

O lovely helper, return, return,
Before whom men tremble,
Thou to whom all manifested
Life must return,
Dark sterile Mother,
We call to thee, Ama,
I have two passwords,
Perfect Love and Perfect Trust,
Aradia, Oh Aradia,
Let the hammer strike the anvil,
Let the lightning touch the Earth,
Let the Lance ensoul the Grail,
Let the magic come to birth.'

Of course, the company gathered below hear not our gentle song of joy but, rather, the sounds of destruction. They are cowering, hunched double and remain low to the ground.

'Look there!' cries Mary. 'The night sky!'

'Incredible!' says Indigo, utterly entranced.

'Astounding!' remarks Harriet.

In a moment we Crafters reach the apex of our assault on the building, taking a corner each of the vast hangar's domed roof and peeling it back as one might the outer skin from citrus fruit. Moonlight drenches the space; it's an unfiltered, spectral wash that connects with the five fragments of the sacred pentacle and melds them together along fractured seams. In this way, beneath the canopy of a twinkling constellation, the henge is restored to its former glory, as is the sacred pentacle, now in Rees-Repton's hands.

My work complete, I sink through vacant space until I connect with the sacred pentacle, all four elemental spirits falling in behind me, as if we're refractions of a single shard of light.

○

'Look,' whispers Carmichael to his daughter and her two friends. 'It's like the stones that make up the inner circle have returned!'

Harriet, Indigo and Mary strain their eyes to catch sight of the phenomenon.

'They're only projections,' Harriet corrects the professor, 'a mirage of sorts, fooling the eye into believing the circle is complete.'

'Actually, you're right,' Carmichael concedes. 'You can see through them to the other side!'

'As one might a ghost,' Mary adds, gripping Indigo's hand a little too tightly.

The five elemental spirits await the command of their new keeper, Oliver Rees-Repton. They quietly swim around the circumference of the sacred pentacle – ice cold against his skin – as they had once pressed against the palm of Abe Aderyn, the last keeper of the intact pentacle.

'The time has come,' says Rees-Repton. 'To truly test the magic of the pentacle!'

He moves across open ground until he's standing just a few metres from the largest of the stone doorways, along one edge of the inner circle. He seems to fill the space, so menacing are his figure and mood. And then, as if he'd been rehearsing for this role the best part of a lifetime, he raises the sacred pentacle until it lies parallel with his heart.

Through the doorway, the disc of a full moon greets him. Where the sacred pentacle and the moon appear to be reflections of one another, an otherworldly cloud of rising mist begins to fill the oblong of the doorway nearest to Rees-Repton.

'What's it showing him?' asks Indigo.

Harriet recalls the words uttered by Stevens on the day of his demise. 'The pentacle shows a man what's in his heart.'

'You've failed, man!' Carmichael suddenly shouts across the circle, his words sounding like cracking icicles in the bracing night air.

Rees-Repton looks on as the doorway before him bristles with an unidentified menace. Indeed, the world beyond the threshold of the doorway seems a nightmarish place where phantoms of dense smog linger in the air and putrid, howling winds sweep across a bleak territory of waste and decomposing matter.

'I disagree, Professor. In fact, I would consider my experiment a resounding success.'

The three sisters and Carmichael take a collective step towards Rees-Repton but are forced to keep their distance by Kilpenny and two salivating dogs.

'Notice, Professor,' Rees-Repton continues. 'The sacred pentacle shows each one of us a world of his or her own making. Should it be you standing here, your daughter or one of those infernal *sisters* of hers, I'm sure the doorway would present a more agreeable vision.'

Indigo scratches at her scalp.

'But that world through the doorway is in a worse state than our current one.'

'You're quite right there, child. Which is why I've decided to donate it to you, your father and your annoying friends.'

'You're mad!' says Carmichael.

'Oh no, Professor, I think you'll find I'm the most rational of us all. You see, with you dispatched to another universe – and one entirely cut off from this one – Sentinel Technologies can proceed with harnessing the magic within the sacred pentacle to generate a huge profit for its shareholders.'

Harriet steps forward, convinced she's fathomed the riddle of the man's words.

'You're going to sell universes?'

'To begin with,' says Rees-Repton. 'Imagine, being able to escape your life and this world for a better one, to start again. And then, when I've grown bored of that, I'll leave mortalkind to this dead world, creating a new one for me and those I've chosen to save.'

Mary is furious.

'You can't use my family's pentacle in that way! I won't let you!'

The young witch leaps towards Kilpenny, Agatha and the snarling dogs, who quickly form a wide semi-circle of protection around Rees-Repton.

Harriet and Indigo scream, 'Mary, no!'

But before they can reach her, the brave sister has already reached into her jacket pocket and produced a pendant: the very item of jewellery that contains her Genius, a 15-foot-long viper. Raising it until it is level with her right eye, Mary grips the pendant's chain and invokes the spirit from deep within the stone.

'O thou blessed Genius,

My angel guardian,

Vouchsafe to descend with thy holy influence

And presence into this spotless crystal,

That I may behold thy glory.'

The dogs whimper and retreat when a flash of green light erupts and is followed by the hissing of a deadly serpent, the scaly creature soon towering above everyone.

'Kill it!' Rees-Repton shouts.

Kilpenny releases the dogs and, side-by-side, they sprint across the circle until within range of the creature.

Agatha screams, but is kept in check by Kilpenny, who presses the muzzle of a small handgun into her ribs.

The sisters and the professor step to one side of the circle, near to Tomasson, young Erubiel and Carter.

Assembled, the company of witches and mortals look on as the snake sinks its fangs into the hind legs of one of the dogs, bringing it to the ground in an instant.

Rees-Repton can do little more than say, 'Think of a strategy! Attack it from behind, boys!'

But the serpent seems to hear the words and understand them, opening its great jaws and catching the more vicious of the two dogs within its fangs. The poison from a single bite surges through the dog's veins, making it falter on its paws. The creature that is now half-man, half-dog crawls, shaking, towards its father.

'Get up!' orders Rees-Repton.

'Father, I … I'm sorry. I've failed you.'

Anton shudders one final time before the deadly poison reaches his heart and stops it from beating.

'Good for nothing, hound,' Rees-Repton snaps, even using his foot to prod the body of his son away from him.

A few feet away, the second of the dogs has managed to pin the snake to the ground by clenching its teeth, pincer-fashion, around the reptile's head. And in a moment, Kilpenny is standing above the dog, nudging its head out of the way with the edge of one foot so he can empty a round of bullets into the snake's skull. Mary turns away in disgust.

'He was your son,' sobs Maxwell, now back in human form, dumbfounded and upset at his dead brother's treatment.

As he faces his remaining son, Rees-Repton clings to the sacred pentacle as if it has the power to protect him from his own kin.

'I tried not to show my disappointment in your brother, Maxwell, but it's always been the case you were the stronger of the two. We both know Anton's death comes as no surprise. Indeed, his departure means there'll be more inheritance for you.'

But Maxwell will not be consoled, not this time.

'You watched your own son die at your feet with no last words of comfort, and you offer me money?'

'Now, Maxwell, you mustn't let your heart rule your head.'

Maxwell transforms one final time into his animagus and leaps for his father's throat, sending the pair of them into the doorway of dark, swirling mist and casting the sacred pentacle to the ground, where it lands near the centre of the stone circle.

Rees-Repton's final scream of terror quickly recedes, giving way to a howling wind that whistles through and over the henge.

'It cannot be! Rees-Repton took the athame with him. It's gone!' cries Harriet.

Kilpenny, sensing his game is up, places his gun on the ground and raises both hands in the air in surrender.

'I don't know what came over me, do you?'

But his nervous giggle does little to conceal his anxiety at being exposed.

'You're an idiot, Kilpenny!' says Agatha, claiming the gun for herself. 'An idiot, a liar and a heartbreaker!'

Kilpenny's voice begins to crack.

'Now, Agatha, do calm down, will you?'

But before he can get to her, Agatha points the gun directly at Kilpenny.

'There's only one bullet left, my girl,' he whines. 'And that's not for me, is it?'

Nudging him with the weapon, Agatha manoeuvres the pair of them across the space to a stone doorway that still echoes with the last strains of Rees-Repton's agonising shriek.

'Go on, in you go, after your master, Michael.'

Agatha waves the gun, her confidence growing by the second.

'You'll not be joining me then, my girl?'

Agatha shakes her head, her lower lip trembling.

'Turn around and walk towards your future,' she says, flicking the gun's safety catch. 'It will be one without me.'

The sisters, Carmichael and each of the pentacle's Carriers look on as Kilpenny is forced to step through the stone doorway and into the realm of industrial wasteland.

Agatha closes her eyes, just for a second or two, before turning to face the three girls – in particular, Indigo.

'I'm sorry for any upset I may have caused you, miss. I've been a fool too long, and that part of my life is over. I hope my actions today have proven I'm on your side.'

Indigo smiles.

'Of course, Agatha, what you've just done –'

Indigo is standing directly above the sacred pentacle and just a few yards from Agatha, when a pair of monstrous hands lunge back through the stone doorway and drag poor Agatha backwards into the alternate universe.

'No!' screams Indigo, stepping towards the portal, her hands reaching out before her to grab Agatha.

The sound of a single gunshot can be heard reverberating around the henge, coming to rest in the ears of those standing inside the stone circle.

Harriet is first to note a small but pronounced stain of crimson blood in Indigo's tunic. A bullet fired from Kilpenny's gun has slipped though the ever-diminishing hole that connects this universe with another and has lodged in her sister's body.

'Indigo!' cries Carmichael, rushing to his daughter's side as she staggers back. She looks down at the spreading red stain, confusion in her eyes.

'Indigo, you're injured,' says her father. 'Let me help you!'

Just as he'd foreseen in a vision that very night, it comes to pass that the professor catches his daughter as she falls to the ground, the young witch mortally wounded and already gasping for air.

Mary says, 'The athame, I need the athame to save her!'

Indigo, whose skin has already turned a deathly white, says to the nearest of her sisters, 'Harriet, do stop Mary wailing like a banshee; she'll wake the dead if she carries on.'

Harriet smooths away a cluster of sweat-matted, dark curls from her friend's left cheek.

'There, there. Be quiet, sister, you mustn't say anything. Conserve your energy.'

Indigo's eyes close for a second – revealing glistening sweat in the creases of their lids – before they snap open again.

Harriet is soon standing over the group.

'Is there anything we can do, Professor?'

Carmichael holds his daughter to his chest, protective of her – as he now realises he should have been right from the start of her life.

'Request the help of the Mother Goddess,' Mary says.

'How do we contact her?' asks Harriet.

Mary strides over to the spot where the sacred pentacle came to rest. She snatches it up, saying, 'I think I know how. I'll try.'

The young witch raises the little disc of silver as Rees-Repton had done before her, the light of the moon caught in its intricate design.

'Do be careful,' says Harriet.

'She's gone,' announces Carmichael, the two simple words not quite registering with those around him. 'My beautiful, brave little girl. She didn't make it.'

'You're wrong,' says Harriet. 'It can't be so! I won't believe it. Indigo cannot die! She has to help us save the world. She called to us! She made this happen; the whole plot to bring us together was her doing!'

Mary stares into the swirling mists of the stone doorway as it reveals the image of a heart-shaped face, eyes of crimson and a mouth of roaring flames, the pores in its skin seeming to contain whole galaxies of suns, stars and planets.

'Mother Goddess,' the young witch whispers with great reverence. 'My heart called out to you and you came to my aid. Peace be your friend.'

The heavenly vision draws the attention of one and all.

'I applaud your daring, children, for the journey to reach me has proven a tiring endeavour and – as you can see from the casualty that rests at my feet – a costly one for my daughters of the sacred pentacle.'

Harriet joins Mary at the doorway and says, 'We've done as you requested, Mother Goddess. The pentacle is restored – although it has cost us the life of a dear friend.'

The face twitches its nose and the clutch of stars high above the henge shift back and forth across the shimmering night sky. When the Mother Goddess speaks, it is with the deepest and most heartfelt compassion.

'Before I can begin my work repairing this tired world, I require each of my daughters to return to the lives they left behind.'

'What's that?' asks Harriet, her tears drying in an instant.

'Your work as Knowing Ones is complete. You must use the sacred pentacle to return to your old lives, especially if you are to stand any chance of reviving your fallen sister.'

Carmichael looks up from his position on the ground, an inert Indigo enfolded in his arms.

'Revive Indigo?' he asks, not quite daring to believe that this might be possible.

'Ancient lore states that all witches, except the Last of the Knowing Ones, will have to sever their ties with me. Only then will the most powerful magic be unleashed from the sacred pentacle.'

Mary holds Harriet's hand and whispers, 'She is saying we won't be witches, Harriet. But such a sacrifice will mean we might be able to save our sister.'

'Then it is very clear,' Harriet nods. 'We have no choice, Mary. Indigo would do the same for you or I.'

'Agreed, then,' says Mary, turning her attention one final time to the stars. 'Mother Goddess, we've reached a decision. As hard as it will be for us, we wish to sever all ties with you. We bring mortality upon ourselves and wish for our sister to be brought back to life.'

'Very well,' says the Mother Goddess. 'Now hold the sacred pentacle to your heart, child, so I may open up a pathway between the realms of present and past.'

Caldey Island rises out of the morning fog to take its place among the curve of coastline. A deathly hush occupies the tranquil air and serves to amplify the smallest of sounds. The wash of tide strides forward, depositing seaweed and shells along the strip of golden sand, before retreating back to its fathomless den. High above, an eagle cocks its head to and fro, examining a settlement of wooden huts and farm buildings before commencing its descent.

On landing, Abraham Aderyn emerges from the plumage of the bird. He's flown directly from Stonehenge, having unmade the sacred pentacle, traversing land, water, hill and dale to get home. But surveying the carnage of burnt-out buildings – many of them containing the charred bodies of coven-folk – the young witch senses his swift flight was not quite fast enough. In fact, it takes him only a short time to discover the lifeless bodies of his mother and three younger siblings among the various rooms of the family cottage.

'It's all your fault.'

Abe turns on one heel to face his dark-eyed brother, Eron – a little taller and broader than he remembers.

'*My* fault?'

'You should never have meddled in business beyond your understanding.'

Abe feels the set of deadly talons flicker at the edges of his trembling hands, unsure if he will be able to contain his temper much longer. 'What do *you* know about the pentacle?'

Eron issues a throaty laugh, casting him in the image of a mad thing. 'Only what someone told me: that it will restore order between us and the mortals.'

Abe shakes his head in disbelief. 'You thought it had the power to put witch above all others?'

Eron nods to his brother.

'Look around you, Eron. See what your faith in a stranger's words has done to our family.'

'Necessary sacrifices, that's all.'

Abe grabs his brother by the upturned collars of his shirt. 'You fool! The pentacle was unmade for that very reason: to prevent it from being used as a destructive force. It was crafted to sustain life, not take it away.'

Abe's shock changes to become the bitterest of angers, tail feathers appearing behind him and eyes moving from hazel brown to midnight blue, his nose quickly extending and becoming the sharpest of beaks.

'That's not fair!' Eron screams, stumbling backwards into a patch of bramble and transforming into his animagus: a sly weasel.

Abe gives chase, rising from the ground in one fluid motion. From an elevated position, he uses the bird's talent for tracking prey. The weasel does his best to evade detection, sprinting through hedgerows and crawling through marshland in the hope of losing his pursuer. Abe suspects he's lost sight of his target but sees Eron emerge again some fifty metres ahead, scampering up and over sand dunes that separate the beach from the village.

Positioned at the summit of a dune, the weasel looks towards the horizon he has left behind, realising too late the eagle is directly above him. In fact, it plummets through one hundred feet of air to sink its claws directly into the creature's pelt, lifting it deftly from the ground. The weasel shrieks and complains, digging his teeth into the eagle's talons to break free of its influence, but to no avail. In his impotency, the older witch wonders what fate awaits him as his captor pitches high above the causeway of water separating Caldey Island from the mainland.

Abe is soon directly above Harrowing Point. The blue sky knows nothing of the conflict between the two brothers this fine morning. It's a battle destined to reach no satisfactory conclusion. The swirl of rock and grass beneath them becomes a whirlpool of riotous colour. *Quite beautiful*, thinks Abe.

Just at that moment Abe fails to contain his brother within the compass of his talons, the weasel soon becoming a mere dot of chestnut fur amongst the flora of the Point.

Turning, Abe drops through space until he reaches Eron, now in human form and lying crumpled in a heap of muscle and bone. Abe's wings become all-encompassing, as he says, 'Look what you made me do, brother.'

The young witch draws his dead sibling to him, whispering a short prayer to accompany his soul on the next part of its journey.

'O, Circle of life, you close about me once again.
I give to you my skin and bone, so you might know
Of deeds both wholesome and divine.
I am your son; I give myself to you.
Oh Goddess, make me new again.
Where the Circle ends, so begins my life.'

Suddenly, all about the Point, a great rumble and shaking of the ground can be felt. Responding, Abe clings to his brother's lifeless body, closing his eyes to numb the pain of his loss. Only at the gravest, bleakest reaches of his darkest thoughts, does his mind register a light so fierce it refuses to be ignored, making him ask, 'What magic is this?'

And on opening his eyes, Abe notes the appearance of a pillar of light, an entity resembling the fairy orbs that once took Mary Harries out of his life. Intrigued, he steps forward. Standing at the very edge of the bright column, he can see that it bristles with a quantity of tiny stars; it makes his mind race with questions.

Eventually, he calls out, 'Who's there?'

After a short time, he identifies the edges of a shadowy form that whispers to him, '*Abe …*'

Here, the shadow breaks down into a million particles of ash, only to re-form again just a few feet in front of him as Mary Harries.

'For the love of the Mother Goddess!' says Abe, truly astounded such magic should come full circle and deposit a fellow witch safely on the spot of grass where he had last seen her. 'It's you, Mary!'

Exhausted, she falls forward across the circle's circumference and disconnects herself from the magic's source. The whole Point grows dark for a moment until a normal level of light returns, allowing the pair to see for themselves they're quite alone.

Mary looks about her, noting the corpse at her feet and stepping back.

'It's my brother,' offers Abe.

'Dead?'

'Quite dead, I'm afraid.'

'I've a memory of stepping into a light ring,' Mary says dreamily, 'but it's not yet clear to me why I've stepped back through it to come back ... home.'

Abe looks into her eyes. *Two emerald jewels,* he thinks. Then, noticing a strange object in her hands, he asks, 'What's that?'

'I'm not sure how it got there,' she replies, 'but it's a book of some kind.'

'I can't read,' Abe says, the fingers on his right hand marking out a run of letters along the book's leather-bound cover.

Mary reads aloud for them both, 'It says *Handbook for Witches of the Broken Pentacle.*'

Abe asks, 'What's going on?'

Mary places the book on the grass next to them and looks down at Abe's hands. She reaches for each of his fingers in turn. 'You're bleeding. You must get these wounds cleaned and wrapped.'

Where they connect, blood moves from Abe to Mary just as a sudden gust of wind sweeps across the Point. As if it were an unseen hand, it ruffles the pages of the handbook until it locates the final page. As quickly as it appeared, the wind disappears.

Instinctively, Mary breaks free of Abe and kneels down until she is level with the ground. As if in a world of her own, she reaches across to the handbook and places a flat hand against the square of cream-coloured paper. She keeps it there for a few seconds until she pulls it away. And there, for her and Abe to see, is a red handprint.

Abe grows impatient. 'Mary, you have to tell me. What happened to you?'

Mary draws level with his gaze. 'A circle of stone doorways …'

'You went to Stonehenge?'

'Yes – I think,' Mary nods. 'But I had no choice, Abe. They made me leave my sisters, to make the magic work.'

'Sisters?'

'*Sisters*,' Mary repeats, her voice cracking, 'of the broken pentacle.'

Responding, Abe retrieves the handbook from the grass. He then takes Mary by the hand and leads her away from Harrowing Point. Part of him wants to know more, but he also realises she's in need of rest and food before he asks any more questions.

Almost as a whisper, Mary asks, 'So, this is what's in my heart?'

'It's okay,' he smiles. 'I'll take you to Rowan Cottage and you can tell me and Nancy all about your adventures.'

'She's full of the plague,' says Mary, suddenly recalling what she saw one night in the broadcast portal.

Abe frowns and says: 'How could you know that?'

'I'm not sure … I just do.'

Mary takes a moment to glance over her shoulder at Harrowing Point as it recedes from view. She notes a pair of seagulls circling the air high above the headland – as if the two of them, her and Abe, were to embark on an entirely different adventure.

There comes a gentle tapping at the large oak door that separates Harriet's quarters from the rest of the fort. The young witch looks up from her easel, as if being drawn from a type of light sleep her mother often referred to as 'daydreaming'. Her canvas bears a study, in watercolour, of Tenby's North Beach. She can clearly see the setting now, from her bedroom's oval window. In her mind, other images linger, too – more powerful than her painting, but dissolving all too quickly, as if mere shadows of the past: a circle of stone doorways … a painful farewell.

'Harriet, are you in there?'

Her mother's warm voice seems comforting today, so she decides on a suitable response.

'You may enter, Mother.'

The door opens noiselessly, just enough for Mrs Gordon to slip through it, clearly mindful of her daughter's need for solitary repose.

Suddenly, Harriet experiences a flash of déjà vu. She's lived this moment before, she knows that much. But the painting presently displayed on her easel is somehow different; the quality of daylight in her room is much improved and there's a serenity in the air that is unusual, to say the least.

'I've come to speak with you,' says Mrs Gordon.

'I've been painting.'

The young girl turns her easel a full ninety degrees towards her mother.

'Your finest, darling,' says Mrs Gordon. 'You must curate a little exhibition once your final work is completed. Be sure to invite your father; I'm confident your efforts will meet with his approval!'

Harriet pauses for a moment, allowing a string of words to enter her mind.

The pentacle only shows you what's in your heart.

'This evening, your father and I are entertaining from seven o'clock onwards,' her mother says, drawing Harriet from her trance. 'We're requesting you to be prompt to welcome a number of distinguished guests.'

Harriet says, somewhat involuntarily, 'Mr Churchill and Bert Wells.'

Mrs Gordon smiles and kisses her daughter on the crown of her head. 'Someone's been talking, I see – but let's leave the name Bert for Mr Wells' close friends, shall we?'

'Yes, of course, Mother.'

'Seven o'clock, sharp,' Mrs Gordon repeats and trips lightly out of the room.

Alone, Harriet stares out at the swell of water that separates Tenby from St Catherine's Point. A thousand moving images drift through the ether of her thoughts, some settling for a moment or two before taking flight again. Each time she attempts to put a name to a face – or a face to a name – she finds she's left wanting. Her adventures into the light ring now seem like the fabric of her imagination, as if her escapades alongside her sisters of the broken pentacle had merely unfolded in the glorious confines of her mind.

As Harriet contemplates an afternoon spent in the company of her brothers – whom she hopes are no longer quite so dastardly – she fights back the precious tears she'll no longer be required to shed on hearing of their passing. Indeed, the pentacle has made possible all she'd thought was lost to her: restoring a family she now has chance to love and who will hopefully love her in return; the wonderful fort and its easy splendour; the long curve of golden beach and its creeping tidal flow; the air itself, to be consumed without fear of it shortening her life. Yes, Harriet Gordon has everything to live for and suspects that the pentacle has offered her the chance to live her life again, re-fashioned and renewed.

The ending of this particular story fast approaches. See how the sisters sacrifice the privilege of being together, in order to save the life of one of their own. Mary was first to step through the highest of the henge's doorways, walking out onto Harrowing Point and back into the life of one Abraham Aderyn. Before she left, she planted a warm kiss on Indigo's cheek. She said nothing to Harriet or the professor, as if the pressure to form words might find expression in tears alone.

Similarly, Harriet kissed Indigo with great tenderness, before turning to issue a farewell to the man who'd taught her a great deal about the power of black holes and much more besides. She didn't look back as she placed the sacred pentacle on the ground before her, stepping through the circle's stone doorway and into her old room back in St Catherine's Fort: the year still very much 1900.

The professor, cradling his daughter's cold body, stands alone at the centre of the stone circle, the deathly hush of night giving way to first light and the strains of birdsong. He calls to the sky, 'What should I do now?'

Carter slowly prises Indigo from Carmichael's embrace and nudges the professor towards the pentacle, saying, 'Maybe it is your turn to take the sacred pentacle and hold it to your heart?'

Carmichael stares out, beyond the debris created by the fallen roof, to appreciate the splendour of the stone circle. As far as the eye can see, the amber glow of dawn bleeds over distant sloping hills. Holding the disc of metal to his chest, he closes his eyes for a moment ... And he's a child again, no more than seven years of age, his whole life ahead of him, and incredibly happy.

He holds onto this feeling of contentment until he opens his eyes and surveys the image cast within the perimeter of the stone doorway. A world seemingly identical to the professor's own hangs there – complete with a landscape of dandelions and grass.

'My heart reveals nothing but weeds,' remarks the professor.

'You're quite mistaken,' says Carter. 'Look closely at the seeds returning to the heads of the dandelions!'

Carmichael squints. 'Actually, you're right. It's a world in reverse!'

Swapping the sacred pentacle for his daughter, the professor thanks Carter for his help. Carmichael then passes through the stone doorway to take up residence in a universe that travels in the opposite direction to the one he's grown accustomed to during the first forty years of his life. It's a world where dandelions snatch back their feathery progeny and grow back into the ground; where grass becomes shorter; where decaying matter becomes wholesome again as it travels towards the spark of inception; where even dead things come back to life at the moment of genesis.

It is in this world that the professor – as the Last of the Knowing Ones – sets his dead daughter down amongst a bed of wilting flowers, only then to observe life return to each petal, just as the flow of blood makes ruddy the plains of Indigo's cheeks. For such a world does exist, through the long and twisting avenues that connect one universe with another.